BITTER WINE

"I've never quite understood people like you," Ross said.

"Oh? What kind of people is that?"

"You know. You're always drinkin' that lizard wine, gripin' about the taste, then sittin' on your butts, waiting for the good things to happen to you."

Elise struck what she hoped was a thoughtful pose.

"Lizard wine?"

"Yeah. Russians drink it. They think it makes them live longer."

"Does it?"

He shrugged. "They think it does. And they live a long time. So that's the question. You know that wine made out of lizards can't be very tasty, right? So does the lizard wine really make them live longer or do they live longer because they drink this nasty shit believing that it's good for them?"

"I don't get it."

"Don't get what?" Ross asked through a mouthful of sandwich.

"Why do you say I'm drinking lizard wine?"

"Come on, Elise. You're too old for the rebellion-against-the-rich-parents thing. That's what you're doing, you know. You've got some resentment stuck in your head, and you're going to act it out if it kills you. And it might, you turning tricks in the parking lot like that. Lizard wine, that's all it is. It tastes terrible, but you keep right on doing it because you think it's good for you, but you know what?"

She didn't answer.

"Those Russians, they die anyway."

BOOKS BY ELIZABETH ENGSTROM

When Darkness Loves Us

Black Ambrosia

Lizzie Borden

Nightmare Flower

Lizard Wine

LIZARD WINE

ELIZABETH ENGSTROM

Delta
Trade Paperbacks

A Delta Book
Published by
Dell Publishing
a division of
Bantam Doubleday Dell Publishing Group, Inc.
1540 Broadway
New York, New York 10036

Library of Congress Cataloging in Publication Data

Engstrom, Elizabeth.
    Lizard wine / by Elizabeth Engstrom.
        p.   cm.
    ISBN 0-385-31249-0
    I. Title.
    PS3555.N48L48   1995
813'.54—dc20   94-32665
                                                              CIP

Manufactured in the United States of America

Published simultaneously in Canada

Book design by Susan Maksuta

January 1996

10 9 8 7 6 5 4 3 2 1

BVG

LIZARD WINE

ONE OCTOBER

BUCK PULLED THE BATTERED GREEN PONTIAC WAGON UP to the gas pump and ordered $1.50 of super. He fished around in the pocket of his paint-spattered pants and came up with $2.47, all in change. He counted out $1.50 in quarters and held it out ready for the kid.

Niles started to cough and hack in the backseat and kept it up until the Songster took off his white painter's hat and slapped Niles on the side of the head with it.

Finally, Niles gave up the coughing and opened the back door of the old wagon, put his feet out on the ground, and put his elbows on his knees and his chin on his hands. Then he took the crumpled cigarette from behind his ear and stuck it between his lips and put his hand back underneath his chin.

"Hey, no smoking at the pumps," the acned service station attendant said.

"Yeah, yeah," Niles replied.

It only took a few seconds for the kid to spurt gas into the tank and collect his money.

"Get yourself inside, Niles," Buck said, then started the car.

Niles brought his feet in and slammed the door shut. He took a match from the breast pocket of his overalls and struck it on the floor of the car where the carpet had rotted away. He lit his cigarette and suppressed the cough. "Hey, Buck, how come I always gotta sit in the back?"

"Cuz you smoke, you derelict. We've been through this a hundred times."

"I'm gonna quit," Niles said, and settled back. Being in the back with the paint fumes always got him carsick. He wanted to ride up front with Buck and the Songster, but they would never let him. He rolled down the window, and the rush of wind blew ashes into his eye.

"Son of a bitch," he said under his breath, and rolled the window back up. His eye was watering, and that made him want to cough.

"Friday night," Buck said. He pulled off onto the side of the road barely a hundred yards from the gas station and turned off the engine. Buck never bought more gas than he needed, and he never wasted any either. "What would you gents like to do this fine evening?"

"Shit," Niles said, wiping the tears from his cheek. "Don't have no money, don't get paid till next Wednesday."

"I got ninety-seven cents," Buck said, then dug around in his other pocket. "Here's another twelve dollars. What about you, Songster?"

"Fourteen."

"Niles?"

"Nothin'."

"You fess up, Niles, or we'll take those pants right off you and look for our ownselves. You ride in this car, right? We let you smoke your stinking butts, right? Then you share. Call it gas money."

"I gotta buy some smokes."

"Okay. Smoke money. Then what?"

"Twenty-two dollars."

Buck whooped. "We're rich, boys. Let's go get us a little beer."

He chugged the Pontiac to life and made a U-turn in the middle of the road. He cut the engine in the grocery store parking lot and let it glide into a parking space. "Gimme," he said, holding out his hand.

Niles fished out his money and handed it over in a wad. "Don't forget my smokes," he said. "I'm down to my last one." He took the crumpled pack out of his back pocket and tore open the top. One last Camel, squashed flat. He took it out and rolled it between his fingers, then stuck it behind his ear, wadded up the empty pack, and threw it on the floor, where it settled, along with dozens of others just like it.

"We'll be back," Buck said. He and the Songster jumped out of the car, and Niles watched them go into the store. He felt like the little kid, left in the car while the adults went in to do adult things. He always had to remind himself that he preferred to wait in the car. Didn't he? Or did he prefer to wait in the car because that's what they always told him whenever he wanted to go with them?

He watched them walk away. Buck walked like an executive, standing tall, flat stomach, well-kept blondish hair that was starting to gray, hands swinging easily by his side. He wore his threadbare clothes well, too, his shirts always neatly tucked in, his socks always turned right side out and matching. The Songster slouched along, hands in pockets, collar turned up against the chill breeze of late afternoon. The Songster's brown hair was long and shaggy, which somehow fitted him, too. He'd have looked weird with hair as short as Buck's. Sometimes the Songster didn't even wear socks.

Niles ran a hand through his own dark, curly, greasy hair. He liked it slicked back. At thirty-seven he thought he might be only a couple of years younger than the others, but there wasn't a gray hair on his head. Not yet. He pulled his knees up to his chest, put his feet up on the seat, and looked at his own socks. They were full of holes. He picked at one, making it bigger, while he waited for them to come back. One of these days they wouldn't come back for him, he was sure. Sometimes they didn't seem to like him very much.

In the store Buck got a cold pack of Bud, a roasted chicken hot from the warming oven and shrink-wrapped to keep in those great-tasting spices that really set him off, a frozen cherry pie, and three packs of Camels for Niles.

"Want anything?" he asked the Songster.

"Gin."

"Good idea." A state liquor store was in the next building.

Buck paid for the food and beer, then carried the bagged groceries into the liquor store to stand next to the Songster while he looked for the best buy in gin. He chose two cheap fifths.

Buck tried to flirt with the checkout girl, but she only had eyes for the Songster. All the women had eyes for the Songster. He was striking-looking, that was true, but he was as sick as they come, soul-wise. If only the women knew that. But they didn't. They didn't know what a pure heart and lovely intentions Buck had. They just saw the hard-line good looks of the Songster, and they fell for him.

But he was dirty.

Buck wondered for the zillionth time if it was the Songster's attitude that gave him that grim line that women loved or if that harsh bleakness to his face was what had given him his attitude. Women love men with an attitude.

Buck ran his hand over the top of his head. His hairline had receded so far it left a strip of blond hair down the center of his head like a Mohawk. The Songster had lots of hair, thick, casually long, graying in all the right places. Why do the evil ones get all the breaks?

He handed the grocery bag to the Songster, hid the bottles of gin inside his coat, and led the way from the store. It was understood that Niles needn't know about the gin. Not yet.

Buck lifted the hood and put the cherry pie on top of the engine block to thaw. In the car he stowed the gin under the seat, then tore the plastic off the chicken, and they all pulled parts off it and slid them, finger-greasy, into their mouths. They each popped a Bud to wash the chicken down with, and when the last bone had been sucked clean, they opened the cherry pie and scooped out its rich red innards with their fingers.

"A meal fit for kings," Buck said, passing the last of the pie back to Niles, who didn't get quite as much. Then Buck wiped his face and hands on a paint rag and handed it around.

Niles lit a smoke.

The Songster belched.

Buck leaned back against the door, picking his teeth with the corner of a matchbook. "We've got enough change to do laundry." He nodded to himself. "We ought to go take showers."

"Then what?" the Songster asked, too quickly.

Buck looked over at the Songster. Every time the Songster got clean, he wanted to find himself some company, something that made Buck and Niles very uncomfortable. Buck thought the Songster probably had some kind of a *history* with women, the way he treated them.

"Dunno. Niles?"

Niles hacked and spit out the window.

Buck fired up the Pontiac and made for the closed-down mill. The night watchman there let them into the echoing, hollow building for the price of a beer, and they took long, hot showers. On the way out, Niles, feeling clean and in a party mood, always had to shout a few things just to hear himself inside the cavernous building with its gigantic, silent machinery. Then they took their wet towels and week's worth of dirty clothes and drove to the Laundromat and washed it all in one big load.

"There's something nice about travelin' light, isn't there?" Buck asked nobody in particular as he watched the clothes go around in the dryer.

Nobody answered. Niles was picking at a burn hole in his T-shirt, making it bigger. They'd all need a trip to the Salvation Army soon for some new clothes. Some winter clothes. October was becoming right chilly. The Songster stared out the window at the women coming out of the minimart next door.

Clean, fed, and with next week's clean clothes tidily packed away in a plastic bag next to the spare in the back end of the Pontiac, the guys piled into their customary seats, and before firing up the engine, Buck tried to come up with a plan, an idea for the rest of the night, something they could do that would be fun, something they all would enjoy. But his mind was blank. He couldn't think of a thing. So he asked, "What now?" He dreaded the answer. He was afraid that the Songster was going to want to find some company, the way he always did. That meant going to a bar. That meant that Niles would get drunk and stupid, and Buck would end up baby-sitting him, taking him back to the boxcars before he insulted somebody or threw up, and then Buck would lie awake all night waiting to hear the Songster come home.

He didn't like listening to the Songster come home. He was rarely alone, and the boxcars amplified each echoing noise the Songster or his guest made. They weren't always good noises to listen to.

Buck tried covering his ears, but he was fascinated, in a terrible way, by the sounds coming from the Songster's lair. He hated it. He didn't want to have to deal with it.

Then Niles said, "Let's go camping."

A slow smile spread over Buck's face. He hadn't been camping in years. Well, the way they all lived was kind of like camping, but it was also like *life*, and to go *camping* would be different and fun.

It would keep the Songster out of the bars and away from the women, and it would keep Niles under their thumb. They could control his liquor intake, they wouldn't spend all their money, and not only that, it would be damned good to get out of town.

The Songster seemed to like the idea, too.

"Genius, Niles," Buck said. "Saddle Lake?"

"Good," Niles said, then flopped back into the backseat and put his feet up on the door, a self-satisfied look on his face.

Buck clicked through a mental list of things he had to do, an old habit from former days. Then he realized that if he didn't have to go to work, there was nothing he had to do. No lawn to mow, no "honey do" list on the fridge, no leaking faucets, no broken gutters.

He was free, and it felt great. He ground the starter on the Pontiac until she caught, tried to figure out how far they'd get before they needed more gas, put 'er in gear, and they were on the road.

Camping. A little wilderness experience would do them all some good. Scenes from his former life flashed through his mind. Catching salamanders in an icy creek with Ron. Fishing in a little-known trout hole with Kaiser. Making love to Cara in the woods under a full moon while coyotes howled.

Camping. Yes.

Life was good.

* * *

Buck's chewed-up Pontiac wagon was hard pressed to make it up that mountain road. They stopped at the Last Chance for more gasoline, expensive gasoline. That made Buck mad because their money was going fast and they wouldn't get paid again until next Wednesday.

Niles sat in the back and bitched about the cold wind that blew through the car's various rust holes. Buck began to wonder at the wisdom of this idea.

The night was swooping down fast. *There's never twilight in the mountains,* Buck thought. Soon it would be dark as dark, and if there were a moon, they'd never see it with all the clouds overhead. There was no traffic on the road, either, as most sensible people were probably home in their cozy houses with their central heating and their hand-knit afghans in front of their color TVs, kids arguing and moms cooking. It seemed as if it ought to be a very attractive scene.

But it wasn't. It was poison. It was a killer.

He loved the drive along the river and up through the trees. He liked the well-tended campgrounds and the national forests that made up a big part of Oregon. There was nothing like this in California. There was nothing like this in Chicago.

He wished he were young again, living in Oregon. He and Ronnie would take their fishing poles to any one of a zillion lakes or rivers every day after school and all weekend. They'd sit in the sun, barefoot, and catch grasshoppers and poke fishhooks through their brains and let the fish bite on them. Ronnie would have loved Oregon.

"Saddle Lake," the Songster said, and it surprised Buck out of his daze. The one headlight that cocked off to the left illuminated the campground sign. He slowed and pulled in. A chain crossed the entrance.

The Songster jumped out of the car and walked up to the

chain. He looked at one end, then walked in front of the headlights to the other end. He unfastened it and let it drop to the ground.

"Wasn't even locked," he said with a snort as he got back into the car.

"Jesus, it's cold," Niles said.

Buck drove slowly through the deserted campground and pulled into a camping spot overlooking the lake. At least there wouldn't be any mosquitoes. Or yellow jackets.

"Think it'll snow?" Niles asked.

"You got shit for brains, Niles," Buck said.

Niles hung his head.

Buck got out of the car and hugged his arms to himself. "Hey," he said to the two guys still in the car, "it is precious cold out here." He walked down to the lake's edge, skimmed a rock off the glass surface of the lake, then flapped his arms against his torso and ran back for the car.

"Jesus," he said, "it's freezing."

"We ain't got no sleeping bags, Buck," Niles said, "or food or jackets or fishing poles or nothing. What are we doing here?"

"It was your idea, Niles," Buck said.

"My idea? I never had no idea to come all the way up to Saddle Lake."

"Shut up," the Songster said, and everyone fell silent.

A low orange glow spread out behind the tall pines on the far side of the lake, and darkness descended. Ripples popped up as fish fed. There was no one else at the campground.

TULIE SAT ON THE END OF ELISE'S BED AND WATCHED her pull hot curlers out of her short red hair and dump them into a drawer. "I hate that it gets dark so early," Elise said. "Makes me feel like I'm late for everything."

"We have a biology midterm Monday," Rebecca said, still sprawled on her bed. She took off her glasses and rubbed the bridge of her nose. "Did you study?"

"A little, yesterday," Elise said. "I took good notes."

"That professor is hard to keep up with," Tulie said. "But that's really all it takes. Keeping up."

"I just don't get it," Rebecca said. "I mean, it's really hard for me even to pass these classes, Elise, and you breeze through. How do you do it?"

Elise shrugged, fluffed up the curls with her fingers, frowned, and spritzed some evil liquid on them, fluffed them again, then began the deliberate arranging. "Are you ready to go?"

"I don't think I better." Rebecca picked at her bedspread. "I'm not doing very well. My folks'll kill me if I don't bring my grades up."

"Fuck 'em," Elise said. "You're only young once."

"Yeah, well, I could party out for six months, flunk out, and end up going home to work at the Seven-Eleven, or I could party every now and then for four years and end up with a degree, you know?"

"It's Friday night," Elise said. "Nobody studies."

"Same with Saturday night," Rebecca said. "And on Sunday we're so wiped out we sleep. I can't study Sunday."

"What about you, Tulie? You ready to go?" Elise gave her the once-over with that smirk she had.

"No, not yet," Tulie said, still undecided about going at all. She looked back at Rebecca. If Rebecca wasn't going, then for sure she wouldn't go. She wouldn't go anywhere alone with Elise. "What are you guys wearing?"

"The green machine," Elise said, and nodded toward her unmade bed. A latex tank dress lay across her pillow in its shrunken state. It wasn't any bigger than a swimsuit. Stretched over Elise, it covered her nipples and her crotch and not much more.

"Oh, man," Rebecca said, "nobody can compete with that. I've got nothing to wear."

"Wear my red dress," Elise said.

Rebecca's eyes got big; she put on her glasses and looked at her. "Really?"

"Sure." Elise stroked on eye shadow. "What about you, Tulie?"

"This is a cowboy bar, right?"

"Yeah."

"I was thinking of boots and jeans."

"Well, *some* guys like that look," Elise said with obvious distaste.

"Cowboys do."

"Whatever. But let's get a wiggle on, girls. It's dark already."

"It's only six o'clock."

"Two and a half hours from Eugene to Bend. Minimum. C'mon, Rebecca. Stow that book."

11

Rebecca closed her heavy biology text and got off the bed. "The red dress? Really?"

Tulie got up. "I'll go change," she said, then walked out of Elise and Rebecca's trashed-out dorm room, down the hall, and into her own.

It was blissfully quiet. Her roommate had gone away with her boyfriend for the weekend, and Tulie was tempted just to lie on the bed and eat popcorn or something all by herself.

But then . . .

She looked at her rumpled bed, and she thought of the nights and days she lay there crying, her heart smashed, and she thought that perhaps that old feeling would come back again if she didn't keep busy. And she remembered that nothing made a person forget a broken heart as fast as a new broken heart. Tommy wasn't likely to break her heart, he didn't have enough passion to infect her properly, but maybe some slick-talkin' cowboy would.

She heated up the iron and went to the closet. Boots and jeans might be a little too butch, especially if Rebecca and Elise were wearing those rubber dresses.

She pulled out a long-sleeved white blouse with embroidery on the front and ironed it. She slipped into a fresh pair of cotton panties, then put on her denim skirt and her cowboy boots and tied a turquoise scarf around her neck. She added turquoise earrings and bracelet. Her Arizona clothes felt out of place in an Oregon October, but she knew cowboys, she knew how they dressed, she knew what they liked. They liked cowgirls. They didn't necessarily like whores. Then she brushed her long hair, pleased by the blond highlights she had weaved into it, streaked on a little blusher, a little eye shadow, a little lipstick, grabbed her purse and she was ready. It didn't take her hours of fussing the way it did the others. She hoped they were ready.

They weren't. They were still arguing.

Elise was helping Rebecca put on makeup, Elise's makeup, Elise's way. Rebecca looked as much a tart as Elise, especially in that red dress that was just a tiny bit less revealing than Elise's green one. They looked like Christmas harlots.

"Why are we going all the way to Bend anyway?" Tulie asked as she poked around in Elise's makeup case. "There's lots of fun places here in Eugene."

"Yeah, full of students. I have to see those immature yahoos all day long. I want to party with some real men."

"There's real men in Bend?"

Elise gave Tulie a withering look, and Tulie had that feeling again that Elise was sorry Rebecca had opened her mouth and invited her along.

"I've heard about this place," Elise said. "I heard it jams." She smoothed that green dress over her waist and her hips. She picked at the indentation her panty hose waistband made. "This will not do," she said. She pulled the waistband up, then pulled it down, viewing herself in all ways. "Shit," she said, and stood looking at her reflection in the mirror. "Oh well." She pulled up the dress and pulled down the panty hose, took them right off, and threw them onto the bed in a wad. Then she pulled the dress down again and smoothed it over her nice curves. "Better."

"You're not going to wear any hose?" Rebecca said.

"I don't like the elastic lines."

Tulie rolled her eyes. Elise was going to go out into the October cold in Bend with nothing on her legs.

"No panties?" Rebecca couldn't believe it.

"What for?" Elise stared her down.

Rebecca shrugged and looked at her own waistline in the mirror.

"Come on," Tulie said. She wanted to get them out of there before Rebecca took off her stockings, too.

Tulie felt up to a good time. She liked Rebecca; there was a wholesome innocence about her that Tulie found appealing. Tulie had a joint that Tommy had given her, and she was ready. Not even Elise could ruin it for her. Besides, anything was better than feeling sorry for herself on a Friday night.

Elise fluffed Rebecca's hair and pronounced her done. Rebecca put her glasses on and stared at her reflection in the mirror.

"When are you going to let me pluck those god-awful eyebrows of yours?"

"Never," Rebecca said. "I tried that once. It hurt."

"Well, take those glasses off," Elise said. "It ruins the effect. Where are your contacts?"

"I lost one."

"Wear the other one. C'mon, let's go."

Tulie leaned up against the doorjamb and watched the final activity as the two girls got themselves together. She couldn't figure out how anybody could find anything in that mass of tangled clothes that covered the floor. The walls were covered with posters of screaming rock stars in black leather and wild hair with red lights behind them. The mirror was spotted with toothpaste spatters and hair spray goo and probably stuff spit out of zits and God knows what else. There was a clean circle rubbed in the middle where they both looked to check themselves. She could never live in a place like this.

Tulie thought they both looked stupid in those tiny dresses and those little high heels and down parkas. It was October, and it was cold outside, and they'd be driving through the Cascade Mountains into Bend, and it would be a lot colder up there. Snow on the ground, probably.

They walked fast and shivered out of the dorm and down to

the parking lot to Elise's car, a dark blue Camaro. Tulie held the passenger door open, and Rebecca, dutiful little Rebecca, climbed into the backseat.

Elise started the car, turned up the radio, and put it in gear. "Okay," she said. "Let's party."

As soon as they were off campus, Tulie pulled the joint from her purse. She lit it and took two heavy hits, then passed it to Elise. She toked, then handed it to Rebecca, who sat forward with her face between the bucket seats. Rebecca took two little hits and then coughed. "Let's get some beer," she said.

"Good idea." Elise turned into the 7-Eleven parking lot and, leaving the engine running, went inside and bought a six-pack of Lite. She came back, handed the sack to Tulie, put it in gear, and burned rubber out of the parking lot. She got on highway 126 and headed straight east.

Tulie opened the bag and took out three beers. She stashed the other three behind her seat where it was out of the heater's reach. All three popped their beers and swallowed away the harshness of the marijuana smoke.

Tulie settled back in the comfortable seat, pressed into it by Elise's heavy accelerator foot. She liked the Camaro. She wished she had one. She wondered why the jerks of the world always had the cool stuff. Elise was a true jerk, but then she'd had a kind of difficult life. Perhaps a Camaro was scant comfort. Tulie pulled a roach clip from her purse and passed the joint around one more time. The world was mellowing nicely.

She looked over at Elise, who was tapping her long red fingernails on the steering wheel and mouthing the words to the song on the radio. She was a beautiful girl, no question about that. She had rich, artificially colored auburn hair, which she kept short, a nice face with a small button nose and nice reddish brown eyes that very closely matched the color of her hair. She wore a brownish red lipstick that was very dramatic on her, her teeth were braces-perfect, and all the way around, she had the well-tended look of a rich college senior, majoring in psychology.

"Tulie, did you take biology?" Rebecca asked from the backseat.

"Yeah," Tulie said.

Elise said, "Would you quit it with the biology, please?"

"I should be studying," Rebecca whined.

Tulie thought Rebecca was a sweet kid, but she was a firstterm freshman and, being from a fairly small Mormon town in Idaho, was wide-eyed at college life in general and at Elise in particular. Rebecca seemed to idolize Elise, and Elise lapped it up. She took Rebecca with her wherever she went, kind of like a puppy, Tulie thought.

Rebecca had rich, long brown hair that she usually wore in a ponytail with bangs, a style straight out of the fifties that was somehow, for some reason, coming back into fashion. She was tall and thin, a knockout in Elise's minimalist clothes. Inch by inch Elise was making Rebecca over into a more sophisticated girl, although Tulie thought Rebecca could have a little better role model. Elise was all right, but she was spoiled and bitchy.

Rebecca reveled in her new look. She said in high school she had always been skinny and gangly, but suddenly her slim figure looked smashing. Tulie and Elise agreed that the Mormons must not know how to dress, or shop, or something. Then again, not many people had the kind of money Elise had to spend on clothes.

Tulie and Rebecca had met in a comparative literature class. They hit it off right away. They had coffee together after the first class, which became a routine every Tuesday and Thursday. Tulie enjoyed watching Rebecca's discovery of herself in university life. She watched Rebecca's Elise-inspired transformation and hoped that the pendulum would swing back a little for Rebecca. The dowdy Mormon look she had at first wasn't right, but neither was this slut look. Given the chance, Tulie would dress Rebecca far differently, with denim and tweeds, and Tulie liked Rebecca's glasses . . . But then, Tulie liked studious, conservative women with a little mystery.

Tulie wasn't skinny like Rebecca, but she had nice long legs that looked great in a pair of jeans. Like Elise, she was a senior at the University of Oregon, but Tulie was a liberal arts major, unable to decide on anything interesting enough to major in. She got average grades with an average amount of studying, and her parents had other things to worry about, so as long as she didn't flunk out, she was on safe ground.

Going to Bend through the mountains in a fast car on a dark October night sounded like her idea of a good time, especially if it ended in a few shots of tequila and some slow, sweaty dances with a cowboy humming in her ear. Yes, ma'am. A Friday night to die for.

Life was good. Damn good.

"I'm hungry," Rebecca said.

"Road food," Tulie said to Elise, and they kept an eye out for the next minimart.

This time Tulie went in. Rebecca wanted chocolate, so Tulie bought her a Chunky. She grabbed a bag of pretzels for Elise, who didn't want any fat, and a bag of corn chips for herself.

The woman at the little country one-stop gave her long legs a real look before she rang up the goods. "Gonna snow," she said.

"Uh-huh." Tulie wondered if her eyes were too red. She wondered, suddenly seriously paranoid, if everybody knew she was loaded. She wondered if they could smell it on her clothes. She was stupid not to pat herself down a little after she left the car. Jesus, the marijuana smoke was probably steaming right off her.

She handed the woman a five-dollar bill and took her change.

"You a student?" All polite questions deserved answers, Tulie had been brought up to know.

"Yes."

"Headed for Bend?"

"Yes." Tulie leaned against the door and pushed her way through. Why did they always want to fuck with her mind when she was stoned? They knew, that's why. They knew she was loaded, and they just wanted to play with her. Human beings had a cruel streak.

She slammed the door and hugged the groceries to her chest.

"What's the matter with you?" Elise said.

"Just drive."

Elise turned the key, and nothing happened.

"Come *on*," Elise said. She turned off the radio, turned the lights on and then off again, pumped the gas and tried the key again. Nothing.

"What? What's the matter?" This was a bad omen. Tulie felt as if she should never have come on this stupid trip. There were shots of tequila and sweaty cowboys to dance with in Eugene.

"It's nothing," Elise said. "Sometimes it just does this . . . thing. It'll start." She pumped the gas again, then turned the key and the Camaro roared to life. "See?" She revved the engine far too high for far too long, and then they headed out onto the road again.

"You ought to get that looked at," Tulie said.

"I need to find me a mechanic," Elise said. "One with *all* the right tools."

Rebecca snickered.

Tulie relaxed. It wasn't her car. She'd take better care of her car, especially if she had a Camaro. She handed around the goodies and then sipped her beer.

Good dope, good beer, good munchies. Road trip. Life didn't get much better.

Gradually they left civilization behind as the road bordered the McKenzie River. They passed through little whistle-stops, and then there was nothing but the darkness of forest on both sides of the road. Now and then a big logging truck would come roaring down the road toward them, headed to the Springfield mills, but other than that, they were alone.

Tulie loved Oregon. In the three years she'd been at the university, she'd seen a lot of the countryside, from the gorgeous mist-cloaked rocky coastline populated with thousands of barking sea lions to the high desert plains of eastern Oregon, the snow-peaked Cascades to the lush Rogue River valley. She'd gone on lots of excursions with friends, with other students, with Anna Marie, mostly, until Oregon felt like home. Felt much more like home than Arizona ever had.

She'd probably settle in Oregon. If she settled anywhere.

She listened to the music and watched the miles fly by beneath the Camaro. They didn't talk much, they were too loaded. Tulie kept munching chips, feeling the womb of the car around her. She looked into the backseat. Rebecca's eyes were closed as she lip-synched the song on the radio. Elise held the Camaro to the road in enviable fashion.

Tulie wondered if they had snow chains. She wondered if they would be needed.

As if the universe had heard her muse and were reminded that October in the Cascades was cause for ice, the Camaro hit a patch of black ice and slid out sideways. The engine revved as the wheels spun. Elise took her foot off the gas, and a little cry came out of her mouth as she worked the wheel.

Tulie felt her chips and beer rise to the back of her throat.

The car swung its rear end around to the front and then did it again, making a complete 360. Tulie was pressed against the car door, and her hand grabbed the handle. She was ready to jump, but the car slowed and slid off the side of the road. It stopped with a lurch on the gravel, lined up as if it had been parked there, its engine dead.

"Fuck," Elise said, and pulled a bottle of José Cuervo Gold tequila from her bag.

"Hey, good job," Tulie said.

"Yeah," Rebecca said.

"Scared the shit out of me," Elise said.

"Black ice," Tulie said.

"Fuck," Elise said, unscrewed the top, and took a big swig. She rolled down the window, and a lick of frozen air swooped in.

"Brrr," Rebecca said.

"Do you have chains?" Tulie asked.

"No. Didn't even think about it."

"We'll make it," Rebecca said.

"Damned right we will," Elise said. "I'm looking for to put a little of that Bent cowboy money in my pocket."

"Bend," Tulie said, and then laughed. Bent cowboy.

Rebecca laughed, too. "Well," she said through her giggles, "isn't that what they go to Bend for? To get bent?"

Even Elise laughed at that. She took a second long pull on the bottle, screwed on the top, and stashed it back in the bag. "What time is it?"

Tulie looked at her watch. "Seven-forty."

"No problem. We'll just drive slower, that's all. The action doesn't start there until ten or so anyway." She turned the key. Nothing happened.

"Oh, no," Rebecca said.

Elise turned off the radio and the heater, checked to make sure the lights were off; then she tried it again. No answer. She pumped the accelerator and tried again. Nothing.

"The oil light is on," Rebecca said. "Maybe it needs oil."

"Shut up," Elise said. She pumped the gas like crazy and turned the key again. Nothing.

"Maybe there's a phone somewhere," Rebecca said.

"Yeah, we'll all look real cute after tramping around in the woods in these high heels for an hour looking for a telephone. Looking frozen and frazzled isn't going to make us any money."

"Money?" Tulie asked. That was the second time Elise had mentioned money.

"Yeah, money." Elise was getting an attitude.

"You're kidding, right, Elise?" Rebecca asked.

Tulie was lost.

"Kidding? Do I look like I'm kidding? No, I'm not kidding," Elise said. "Of course I'm not kidding."

"I don't understand . . ." Tulie said.

"Elise mentioned making a lot of money in this cowboy bar," Rebecca said, her voice low. "But I thought she was just kidding, you know, just . . . kidding."

Tulie hoped she didn't understand. "Make money? How?"

Elise turned and fixed Tulie with a cold look. "Turning tricks," she said. "How else?"

"You're going to this bar to *book*?" Tulie was flabbergasted.

"Beats waiting tables at the pizza place."

"You weren't in on this, were you?" Tulie looked over the seat back at little Rebecca.

"No, of course not," she said.

"You're an idiot," Tulie said to Elise.

"Hey," Elise said, "don't be calling me names."

"You are," Tulie said. "You're going to get into trouble, and it won't be long before Rebecca follows you into something bad. You'll probably get Rebecca here infected with AIDS, and both of you are going to die ugly deaths. Either that or get beaten up or killed or something. Turning tricks is stupid. You're stupid. You're stupid." She grabbed her purse. "God, I can't believe I came along."

"Me neither," Elise said. "I thought you'd be hanging with your *girl*friends."

Tulie looked at Elise, barely able to see the outline of her face in the mountain darkness. "What is that supposed to mean?"

"You know."

"Tell me."

"You're a *dyke*," Elise said. "A lesbian. A bull. I don't know why you want to hang with us at all, unless you're trying to seduce Rebecca."

Tulie's face flooded with hot blood. She punched the door open with her shoulder and caught a glimpse of Rebecca's wounded face when the interior lights went on.

The gravel felt frozen as it crunched underneath her boot.

"Wait, Tulie," Rebecca said. "Where are you going?"

"We passed a park entrance a ways back. There's probably a phone there," Tulie said, slammed the door, and began to walk.

A moment later she heard the ignition click a few more times, a muffled curse, then the car door open, close, and quick high-heeled footsteps as the other two hurried to catch up to her.

"ANYBODY KNOW ANY GHOST STORIES?" NILES ASKED,
then tittered.

"How old are you?" the Songster asked.

Niles didn't think that question needed an answer.

"Jeez, Niles, I don't know how old you are either. You know
we've lived together for what, six, eight months, and we've
never known that about each other?" Buck was dumbfounded
by the revelation.

"Don't know much at all," Niles said. "I'm thirty-seven."

"Forty," Buck said. "You guys got family?"

"Not me," Niles said.

The Songster was silent.

"I got a sister," Buck said. "She lives in Chicago. Has two
boys, but me and her husband don't get along a-tall."

"Say," Niles said, leaning up and putting his elbows on the
back of the front seat, "why do we all call you the Songster?"

"Don't know," the Songster said.

"Well, who started it?"

"That's how Bill introduced us, remember, Songster?" Buck
said.

Songster nodded.

"Why, do you sing?" Niles asked.

"No." The Songster's voice was flat. Buck could tell that this
was a line of questioning the Songster didn't want pursued.

"Who's Bill?" Niles asked.

"A guy on the paint crew," Buck said. "You know. Bill."

"How long you guys been painting?" Niles was on a roll.

"This is my first painting job," Buck said, happy to have the spotlight off the Songster. "We've all been there about the same, what is it now, about eight months?"

"You were there first," Niles said. "Then me, then Songster came after I was there about three months. Where'd you come from?" Niles asked. "I came from Montana. I lived in Montana all my life." Niles lit a cigarette, and the Songster pushed him back into the backseat with his elbow. "Hey, it's cold back here. Can I come sit up front with you guys?"

"I came here from California," Buck said. "I drove this here green Pontiac all the way from San Diego."

"How'd you find those railroad cars, Songster?" Niles was back up against the front seat again. I mean, it's a great place to live. We each have our own place and all that." Niles was wired, and his chatter was beginning to wear on Buck.

"It's free," the Songster said.

"Yeah, that's what I mean. What do you suppose those railroad cars are doing out there like that anyway?"

"Waitin'," the Songster said.

"Waitin'," Niles said. "Yeah, that's right. They're just waitin'."

They each opened another beer, watching the final colors fade from the clouded sky.

"How'd you guys get hitched up with that paint crew anyway?" Niles asked.

"State sent me over," Buck said.

The Songster said nothing.

"It's been a good job," Buck said.

Niles opened the back door. "Gotta piss," he said.

"Well, close the door," Buck said. "It's freezing."

The door slammed.

"Gin," the Songster said.

Buck looked over at Niles's silhouette, heard the stream of beer urine splashing on the dirt. He pulled a bottle from under the seat, unscrewed the cap, took a long pull, and handed it over. He didn't like keeping the gin from Niles. He thought they all ought to contribute the same amount and be entitled to take the same amount, democraticlike. But then he had learned: There was no dividing things up fairly. Niles always gave more, and the Songster always took more, and that was life. There was nothing that Buck could do about it.

The Songster took a little sip of the gin, licked his lips, then took two deep swallows. He screwed the cap back on and set the bottle on the seat.

Niles got back in, puffing, coughing, and bringing in cold air. "Gonna freeze tonight. Probably snow. Hey, what if we get snowed in? We don't got any food."

"Then we'll eat you," the Songster said with a perfectly straight face. Buck shivered.

The Songster pulled a little plastic bag and some rolling papers from his pants pocket.

"A joint!" Niles said. "The Songster's got some dope! Where'd you get it?"

The Songster elbowed Niles back into the backseat. "Gimme light."

Buck turned on the dim yellow interior light, hating to waste the battery, but the thought of a good smoke was too tempting. The Songster rolled three in a row; then Buck killed the light, and Niles lit a match. The Songster took a long toke, held it, then added to it twice before he passed the hot joint to Buck. By the time it got to Niles, it was barely long enough to hold and so hot it hurt his lips.

All three lapsed into comfortable, contemplative silence.

The cold seemed to diminish. If Buck didn't move at all, he stayed nice and warm.

"Hey," Niles said. "Songster. I wanna know. We're your friends, right?"

"So?"

"So how come you never tell us nothin' about yourself? You never tell us nothin'. Buck and me, we'd tell you anything you want to know, right, Buck?"

"Don't want to know nothin'," the Songster said.

Niles leaned up against the seat. "That ain't the point. The point is . . ." But he seemed to have forgotten it.

"The point is," Buck said, "that friends know things about each other." The Songster turned and looked at him squarely in the face, and Buck felt that weird chill again. "But I don't care, Songster," he said, backing down and hating it, "I don't want to know much either."

Buck leaned against the car door. He was beginning to get kind of cold after all.

"I do," Niles said. "I want to know where you're from and why you don't want to talk about yourself. Jeez, I could never understand people who could just *not talk*. Know what I mean? So, Songster, I'm askin' you right out. Where are you from?"

"Connecticut," the Songster lied.

"Well, see there? That wasn't hard. Now the next question. How old are you?"

"Forty-one. Who gives a shit?" Niles was beginning to wear on the Songster, too.

"Last question," Niles said. "Where did you do time and why?"

The Songster whipped around and grabbed Niles by the front of his shirt so fast that Buck didn't even know what had happened until Niles had gotten a shake and the Songster was back in his seat, calmly lighting up another joint.

"What the fuck—" Buck said.

"He's been in prison, Buck, and I want to know why, that's all," Niles said.

"How do you know?"

"Because I've been there. And I can spot somebody else who's been there. So can he. Can't you, Songster?"

Buck had never seen Niles quite like this before. The beer and the dope made him bold. Or maybe it was the isolation. Or the cold.

"You knew I'd been in prison, didn't you, Songster?"

"Yeah," the Songster said, and Buck felt that something was happening in the car, something out of his control, something he wasn't sure he liked very much. He didn't know either of those guys had ever been in prison. He didn't know much of anything, he guessed.

"Where?" Niles probed.

"California."

"For what?" Buck wanted to know.

"None of your business."

"Listen, Songster," Niles said, "we all live together, sorta, and I think we ought to be able to know these kind of . . . basic . . . things about each other. Like, are you dangerous?"

"Only to little simpering assholes who ask too many questions." The Songster licked a fresh joint, stuck it in his mouth, and fished around in his pants for his lighter.

"Yeah, Niles, that's enough," Buck said, although he really wished Niles would ferret out all of Songster's secrets.

"Is that how you know Bill?" Niles kept it up. "Was he in with you? Songster sounds like a prison name, doesn't it? And you got that tattoo." Niles started to giggle.

Buck wasn't sure what to do, but he could feel danger brewing next to him. "Shut up, Niles," he said, then accepted the lit joint from the Songster and toked on it.

The Songster did have a peculiar tattoo. It was on his chest, just in from his right shoulder. It was a little square, kind of like a picture frame, and inside, it said, "Sharp is silent." Suddenly Buck really *didn't* want to know what it meant. He passed the joint to Niles, who took it and handed up a couple of beers.

The Songster opened his beer, drank half of it down, then opened the gin, took a hearty swig, and poured a hefty amount into his beer can. He passed the gin to Buck, who did the same. They had plenty, so he passed the bottle back to Niles.

"Gin!" Niles uncapped the bottle and drank deeply. "Gee, guys, nice of you to tell me, since I bought the friggin' stuff. You guys are assholes, know that?"

Buck thought that was probably true, but he was starting to feel kind of brotherly toward these two guys. It was probably the booze and the dope, because usually he kept his distance. Tonight might prove to be a real breakthrough in brotherly love here in his old Pontiac wagon. As long as Niles didn't puke.

"So what did you do, Songster?" Niles asked.

Buck was just about ready to yell at Niles when the Songster spoke, quiet and gentle, like he almost always spoke. Buck had heard one of the other painters call it a Clint Eastwood syndrome.

"I killed a woman," the Songster said.

There was silence in the car so deep Buck felt he'd fallen right through it. He didn't know what to say. He never knew anybody who'd ever killed anybody before. He wasn't too sure he wanted to now.

But even though he hadn't known that particular about the Songster, he'd known something was wrong with him.

Now and then the Songster would bring a woman home

with him. Buck would wake up when the headlights on her car flashed into his boxcar as she brought the Songster home. She'd be loud and laughing, like as not both of them drunk, as they stepped down into the weedy gully, then up the graveled side of the hill that supported the train tracks. Then the Songster would help her up into his boxcar. Buck could just see her trying to do all this with panty hose, high heels, a short, tight skirt, carrying her purse in one hand and a bottle in the other.

Then their voices would boom in the empty boxcar until suddenly it would get quiet for a while, and Buck could just see them on the raggedy sleeping bag in the corner.

Usually the women didn't stay long.

Sometimes they yelled and then they left.

Sometimes they screamed and then they left.

And one time one didn't leave at all.

Buck woke up when her car started in the morning, and he looked out and saw the Songster driving. Nobody else was in the car. He took off down the street, and when he came back late that afternoon, he was walking. Buck never asked, and the Songster never mentioned it. There were some things that were better left unknown about friends.

And now the Songster had put it right out in the open. He'd killed a woman once. And gone to jail for it. That meant that the woman whose car he drove off that morning . . . What the hell *did* that mean?

"Jesus," Niles finally said.

The Songster popped the top on another Bud.

Buck's bladder pushed on him. He opened the door, and fresh, frigid air poured in. "Gotta piss," he said, and stepped out. He closed the door behind him. He didn't want to see the Songster's face with the light on. He didn't want to see the Songster's face at all.

He took a deep breath. There was barely enough light to

see his breath plume out from his mouth. The woods were dark black in a starless night.

He wished the Songster hadn't said anything about this. Now Buck felt as though he couldn't trust him. He unzipped his pants, listening to the crackling of the forest as the thermometer plunged.

There was another sound. A rhythmic sound.

Somebody was walking up the road. Buck walked around the front of the car, took a leak, zipped up, then walked over to the Songster's window. He tapped. The Songster rolled his window down a crack.

"Someone's here. Walking toward us."

"Who?"

The back door opened, and Niles got out. "Hey," he said, "who's there?"

The footsteps stopped.

"Shut up, Niles," Buck whispered loudly.

Then a female voice called out, "Who are you?"

"It's a girl," Buck whispered to the Songster's open window. The Songster opened his door and got out.

"We're camping," Niles said.

"Oh." Footsteps came closer. "How many of you are there?"

"Three. What are you doin'? C'mon out."

"There are three of us, too. Our car quit. We thought there might be a phone here and some shelter so we wouldn't freeze to death."

"And food," said another voice, also female.

"And a toilet," another said.

"We got Budweiser," Niles said.

The three women came closer. Buck could make out their shapes in heavy winter coats, but it was too dark to see anything else. "Toilet's over there," Niles said. "Behind that there bush."

"It's pretty warm in the car," Buck said. "C'mon. Get warm. We aren't going to hurt you." He felt as if he'd said that to the Songster as much as he'd said it to the girls.

"Where's your tent and stuff?"

"This was kind of . . . whatcha call . . . spur of the moment."

"Oh," Elise said. "Pint of whiskey and six-pack camping, eh? Well, I'm not shy." She opened the car door.

Niles got in and scrambled about, picking up all the trash in the backseat and on the floor and throwing it into the back of the wagon. Then he got out and held the door open for the women.

"Phew," she said. "Stinks like cigarette smoke. You guys smoke?"

"Nah," Niles said. "Previous owner."

Elise and Rebecca got into the backseat. Niles got in next to them and closed the door.

Buck and the Songster stood looking at each other until the other one came back from behind the bush, and then Buck ran around again to the driver's seat as the Songster opened the door for her and invited her to sit between them.

Tulie stuck her head in and looked at the two girls shivering under the yellow dome light in the backseat.

"Get in," Elise said. "It's cold."

Tulie looked first at the Songster, then at Buck. They looked all right, and there was really no choice to be made. She got in, slid over to the middle, and the two men got in and closed the doors.

"What we need," Rebecca said, "is a telephone."

"There aren't any phones here," Tulie said, her breath still coming hard from her fast walk in the cold and her anger at Elise.

"Hey, maybe you guys could drive us to one," Elise said.

"Nope," said Niles. "We're camped for the night."

"Well, couldn't you just kind of like *un*camp?" Elise was persistent.

"Couldn't you camp with us?" Niles asked.

"I don't think so."

"Elise," Rebecca whined, "it's so *cold* out there."

Tulie could smell the man sitting to her right, the one on the passenger side. He smelled clean and fresh and masculine. He moved slightly so that his thigh matched hers, all along its length.

Niles emptied the cold pack of Bud and handed one up to the front seat. The Songster took it, opened it, and handed it to Tulie. She heard tops pop in the backseat, and could hear Elise as she drank at least half of hers, then burped. She sounded stupid. God, everything Elise did was stupid.

Tulie felt something behind her, something in her hair, and she jerked forward, brushing at it.

It was this guy's hand. He had his arm around her, and he was playing with her hair. Little warning signs began to flash in her mind, but she ignored them. Let Elise see her with a man. Let Elise see that she could be attractive to a guy. Show Elise that she could be attracted to a guy, too. Fucking Elise.

She drank her beer and let him toy with her hair and then her ear.

"Say," Elise said, "what are all your names?"

"I'm Niles, the driver is Buck, and the other one is the Songster."

"The Songster? That's a weird name."

"Yeah?" Niles said. "What're your names?"

"I'm Rebecca," the one next to him said. "This over here is Elise, and Tulie's in the front seat."

"Tulie?" the Songster said, quiet and low. Tulie felt his voice resonate in her lower belly. She looked over at him and could see his eyes shining. She could smell his breath—beery with some marijuana on it. Warm. His thumb brushed against her cheek.

"So what were you ladies doing out there anyway?" Niles asked.

"Headed to Bend," Elise said. "And my stupid car . . . I don't know what the hell is wrong with it. I need to call Triple A."

"If you'd take care of it . . ." Tulie said.

"Nobody's going to come by here tonight," Buck said. "It'll be safe until morning."

"Yeah, but *I'm* not going to sit here until morning. Maybe we can find somebody else. Somebody who's willing to drive us to a phone."

"I'm staying here," Tulie said, her throat tight, her voice firm. Songster squeezed her shoulder in approval.

"You're kidding," Elise said. "Rebecca?"

"I don't know," Rebecca said, and she sounded as if she were about to whine. "You can't go out there by yourself, but then I don't want Tulie to stay here by herself either. Don't you think we ought to stay together?"

"Yes. C'mon, guys, drive us to a phone," Elise said.

"I don't think so," Buck said. "Camping is much more fun. Stay with us. All of you."

"Please?" Rebecca said. "You guys can't send us out into that cold again."

"We're not sending you anyplace," Buck said. "Stay."

"No way," Elise said. "C'mon, Tulie, let's go."

"No. You guys go. I'll be all right."

"Tulie!"

"I'm not going with you, Elise. Period." The anger blazed again, burning hot spots in her face, making her see red globules in front of her eyes in the dark. "You go on, have your good time," she said sarcastically. "These guys will give me a ride home in the morning. Won't you, Songster?"

The Songster nodded slowly.

"Tulie." Elise leaned up against the back of the front seat. "I'm not about to leave you here with three strange guys full of beer in an old beater station wagon."

"I'll take my chances, Elise. I'm safer here than with you. You're a pain in the ass. Go on. You just . . . go on."

"Suit yourself, you silly bitch. Come on, Rebecca," Elise said, and the two got out of the car, slamming the door behind them.

"Fuck you," Tulie whispered. She felt herself begin to shake. She gripped her beer can so tight it dented. Heat steamed up to her face from under her bulky coat.

"Wow," Niles said. He lit a cigarette.

"Listen," Buck said, "why don't we pick up those girls and take them all home?"

"Now?" Niles said.

"Yeah."

"No," the Songster said.

"Songster, this isn't exactly what we all had in mind . . ." But Buck's voice faded into the darkness.

The Songster's lips brushed Tulie's cheek as he removed his arm from behind her, and he began to roll some more joints. Soon Tulie was toking and giggling a little bit and feeling better.

Tulie passed the joint to Buck, who toked and passed it on to Niles in the backseat.

"Hey," Niles said, "lookee what I found. Ta-keel-ya."

"It's Elise's," Tulie said.

"Not anymore." Niles unscrewed the top and took a drink.

"Where were you girls headed?" Buck asked.

"To a cowboy bar in Bend," Tulie said. "Elise had this idea

that a nice-looking coed could make some money at a cowboy bar. I wasn't in on the moneymaking part of it. I didn't even hear about that part, not until we were halfway here, that is. Then I discover she's going over there to turn tricks. She was probably going to get Rebecca drunk and recruit her. I don't know. I don't know how they could ever think I'd agree to such a thing. So I decided I'd just wait in the car until they were ready to go home." Tulie thought about Elise and Rebecca in their tiny dresses propositioning cowboys. "That Elise. What a bitch."

Niles handed the bottle of tequila to the front seat. The Songster took a long pull and then put his arm back around Tulie's shoulders. He held the bottle while she drank. The liquid warmed her, and she gulped greedily.

"Wait a minute," Niles said. "Those girls were hookers?"

"Catches on fast, doesn't he?" Tulie said. "Elise is, anyway. Rebecca isn't." *At least not yet.*

"Buck, let's go get them. We'll give them a ride all the way to Bend. Maybe they'll be grateful."

Tulie snorted. "Don't count on it."

"No gas, Niles," Buck said. "Forget it. You guys students at the university?"

"Yeah. I'm liberal arts, but leaning toward psych. Right now I'm studying abnormal psychology. It's grueling. I needed a break." Tulie shifted around in the seat. She was too warm inside her coat. The almost wreck, the brisk walk, the anger at Elise, the excitement of kissing Elise off to hang out with some new guys—it all contributed to her rise in temperature and made her perspire.

"We were just talking about abnormal psychology," Niles said. "Just before you showed up."

"Yeah?"

The Songster lit another joint and gave it to Tulie.

She inhaled, held it, then exhaled smoke in a rush. It made her a little dizzy. "It may be smoky in here, but it sure is warm. I hate getting cold. In fact, it's warm enough I can take off this bulky coat. Let me out, Songster, and I'll take this thing off."

"Niles, trade us places," the Songster said, and opened the door. It was freezing as they slipped out of the front seat and before she knew it, Tulie's coat was off and she was in the back, pushing Niles out the door. Niles ran around the front of the car and jumped into the front seat next to Buck.

"Gimme another slug of that José," Buck said.

REBECCA STUMBLED AND WHINED ALL THE WAY BACK TO the car. Elise kept her hands in her pockets, her head down, her collar up, and she just kept moving, even though it felt as if little ice crystals were building up on her shins. She let Rebecca whine; it probably kept her warm. Kept her alive at any rate. Elise's blood stayed hot just by listening to the little twit.

The Camaro would start as soon as they got back to it, she was certain. It had pulled this trick several times before, but it had never totally failed her. It would start. It had to start. She would *will* it to start.

But for the first time doubts began to crawl into her power play attitude. For the first time Elise allowed the possibility that she and Rebecca could freeze to death, right here on the highway.

No, she told herself, *that is not part of the plan.*

The organizational chart of Elise's life always had her at the top of the pyramid. She was the power, she had the power, and anybody who didn't like it wasn't allowed a fingerhold on her life's pyramid. This was one thing she took from the wisdom of her father and kept close. Be in charge. Paul was a feisty little guy and very powerful. Everybody danced to Paul's tune. Everybody danced to Elise's, too, or they danced at some other party.

But while Paul's iron fist contained money, Elise's held sex. Great sex. Or the promise of it anyway. Men were easy to control once she had them by their genitals, and their genitals worked best in their imaginations. Their genitals had no consciences. Elise had discovered the power of sex early in life, but she had just recently learned how to wield it. She'd practiced on the college boys, and they were a lot of fun, and it was easy to separate them from their allowances, but it was time for her to practice on some real men. Some older men. If she could go to Bend—way, way out of town—and wield the power of the classic little gizmo between her legs, then perhaps she was her daddy's daughter after all.

Once she had the idea, she was eager to try it. She'd had it with students and professors. She was ready for some cowboys.

And a recalcitrant Camaro didn't enter into the picture. Didn't enter into the picture at all.

Neither did freezing to death out here on a lonesome mountain road.

No, that's ridiculous, she told herself, giving a little extra hop for the heat. *There's lots of traffic.* She'd just flag someone down.

But not a single car or truck passed them the entire time they walked from the campground to the Camaro.

But they had resources. They had their coats, warm down coats, and if worse came to worst, they could trot back down to the campground and snuggle up to those smelly outlaws in that dirty car. Assuming, of course, they were still there.

Tulie would never let them leave the campground without first checking the Camaro, would she? Tulie. What a lame chick. No sense investing any more time in that friendship.

Elise hadn't realized they'd parked so far away. Finally the Camaro came into view, a dark hump on the side of the road. "C'mon," she urged Rebecca, who stumbled some more and was perhaps crying.

Elise ran the last fifty yards and fumbled with the keys. The door handle was frosted over, as were all the windows. She got the door open, opened the passenger side for Rebecca, who took forever to get there and even longer to get in.

"Okay, sweetheart," Elise purred, and she put the key in the ignition. She turned it. Nothing.

Fear flushed through her like anger, and she sat back, took a deep breath, let out an icy plume, and tried again. She was afraid she'd rip the upholstery apart if the car didn't start. She was afraid she'd cry. "Listen, my lovely," she told the car, "this is really important." She stroked the steering wheel and patted the dashboard. She turned the key. The big Chevy engine roared to life.

"Ya-hoo!" Elise shrieked, her power back full force, and Rebecca, teeth chattering, tried to grin. Elise turned the heater on full, which blew frigid air onto their naked knees. But soon it warmed, and they warmed, and the windshield defrosted.

Rebecca began munching on the chips that Tulie had left.

Elise put the car in gear and slowly headed up the mountain.

"Elise?"

"Hmm."

"We're not still going to Bend."

"You bet we are."

"But what if the car . . ."

"It won't."

"Aren't we going to go back and get Tulie?"

"No," Elise said.

"I think we should."

"She didn't want to come."

"We can't just leave her there."

"We can. We will. We are."

And that was the end of the discussion. Rebecca hunched down in the seat. All the fun of the Friday night road trip was gone. All the fun.

Elise drove conservatively, not wanting to spin out on any more black ice. Now she was damned determined to have a good time once they got up there. Damned determined. This was not only a good time; this was fleshing out her résumé. The chances of her finishing her degree were diminishing by the day, and she had to have some skill to fall back on.

She wished she had a beer. She rooted around in her bag for her bottle of tequila, and it wasn't there. Fuck. But they were more than halfway to Bend, and soon there'd be enough beer to swim in. Cowboys would be falling all over themselves trying to buy them drinks. She'd get drinks, all right, and she'd get thirty bucks for blow jobs out in the car and sixty for a quickie.

The idea of the cash in her hand—separating those fool men from their money—made her foot a little heavy, and soon they were clicking along as fast as they ever were.

Rebecca just munched.

Elise wondered why she let Rebecca hang around with her.

Next time maybe she'd bring Rebecca and maybe she wouldn't. She'd probably do better on her own.

A light sprinkling of snow covered the ground as they came out of the forest and began to see farms, then houses, then stores, and finally the lights of Bend. Elise slowed to just above the speed limit and reached over to touch Rebecca's hand. "It's a party Friday," she said, but she felt that Rebecca had lost the party mood, too. They needed to find some cowboys. A couple of tequila shooters would do a world of good for little Rebecca.

She turned left, and the cowboy bar she had been told about stood out, true to its "can't miss it" reputation. The parking lot was filled with pickup trucks, many of those with tool chests built right in or lumber racks on the back. Perfect.

Elise eased into the lot. It looked like frozen mud, complete with chuckholes and frozen tread marks. She rolled down her window, and fresh cold air blew in. She breathed deeply. Bass music of a live band pounded through the night.

"All right!" She felt the party mood returning with the beat and bounced up and down in the seat.

She slipped between two mud-caked trucks and turned off the engine. "If it won't start now," she told Rebecca, "I'm sure there will be a couple of guys here who can help us." Then she pulled the rearview mirror over and freshened her makeup. She touched the blush brush to Rebecca's cheeks, which did nothing to ease the scowl on Rebecca's face. Then she put on lipstick and passed it over to Rebecca, who pulled the mirror around to her side, dutifully applied lipstick, then automatically checked her mascara and fluffed her hair.

"Ready?"

Rebecca nodded.

They got out and picked their way over ice crystals and

frozen mud to the doorway, where body heat steamed out in a stream like right out of a pressure cooker.

Men in sheepskin coats and cowboy hats moved out of their way as they approached. Elise kept her head down and moved right through the crowd. She felt Rebecca close behind.

Inside, country music twanged from a stage in the far corner. The room was humid and smoky. Elise immediately noticed that they were not dressed appropriately—*all* the women wore jeans and plaid shirts, just like the men. Some wore vests. Some wore sweaters. Some even wore cowboy hats with colored feathers on the front and little beads dangling down off the back brim.

It's okay, Elise told herself, and pulled her down jacket tighter around her as she moved through the heated bodies toward the bar. She felt Rebecca's fingers clutching her arm as she followed. Elise pushed herself to the bar and ordered two beers. The bartender flipped tops off two brown bottles and set them on the bar amid the sea of spilled beer and sloppy ashtrays. Elise pulled cash out of her purse and paid him, handed a beer to Rebecca, then turned around and leaned against the bar, letting her coat fall open.

Appreciative eyes looked her up and down as the constant stream of men paraded past. Soon a barstool opened up, and Elise slid into it. Rebecca stood next to her. Elise crossed her legs and sipped her beer, scouting the crowd for her first target.

Suddenly there was a hand between her legs, and a young, bleary-eyed, beery-breathed man leaned into her face. "Hey, sweetie," he said, then his friend jerked him away from her.

"Sorry," the other man said. "C'mon, Dan, leave the lady alone."

Dan leered at her all the way to the door.

Elise pulled her skirt down another half inch. She tried to wipe the distaste off her face and regain her composure.

"Gross," Rebecca said.

Elise just sipped her beer, scanned the crowd, and moved a little bit to the music.

The barstool next to her opened up, and Elise muscled Rebecca onto it before somebody else got it. No sooner had she climbed up and sat down than an acne-faced boy asked her to dance. Rebecca looked to Elise with a one-eyed squint. Elise shrugged, sipped her beer, and continued scanning the crowd.

The boy helped Rebecca off with her coat, which she laid across the barstool. Elise watched men turn as Rebecca walked toward the dance floor. Those long legs were a knockout. And son of a gun if Rebecca didn't know how to two-step. Elise caught glimpses of them as he swirled her around the floor, circle dancing with the rest of the people, Rebecca grinning and laughing.

Elise finished her beer and ordered another.

A man in a blue down vest pushed in to the bar next to her and ordered a pitcher. While he waited, he turned, elbow on the bar, and looked her up and down. "You old enough to be in here?"

Elise turned and fixed him with an icy stare.

"Well," he said. "Guess you are." He paid for the pitcher. "You card this girl, Jake?" he asked the bartender.

Elise looked around at the bartender, then was ashamed she had risen to his bait. He could card her all he wanted. She was twenty-one. But Rebecca wasn't.

He smiled down at her. She hated him for putting her off balance. "From out of town?"

Elise sipped her beer and ignored him.

"Oooh, hard to get, eh? Got an attitude, eh?"

Elise looked over at him again, frantically looking for something to say that would make him go away but strangely unable to come up with a good dagger line. She wanted something that would wither him where he stood or pin him to the wall.

But nothing came to her. She was out of her element.

"Well, you *look* like you're from out of town," he said. "You look like one a them college girls from Eugene. I'm right, ain't I?"

Elise looked over at him and realized that he was nicely dressed and probably had a pretty fat wallet. He also probably had a pretty fat wife, and he just might cut loose with a few of those dollars if she was nice to him. *No sense in alienating the customers,* she thought to herself.

"Yep," she said. "You're right on the money." She smiled at him and sipped her beer.

He warmed right up to that smile. He slid Rebecca's coat onto his lap and cocked one cheek up onto the barstool. "I'm Farley," he said.

"Elise."

"Nice to meet you, Elise," and he held out his hand. She took it, and he gave her one of those half handshakes, the kind men give women. "Now what brings a pretty thing like you all the way to Bend in the middle of a cold snap?"

"Just looking for a little party action," Elise said.

"Are ya now?" He sat full up on the barstool and turned in toward her, locking her against the bar with his knee. "Now just what kind of action might that be?"

"Are you a partying man?"

"Been known to be, to the right party." He laughed at his own joke, then poured himself a glass of beer out of the pitcher he bought. He held the pitcher up. "You ready for another'n?"

Elise took the last swallow out of her bottle, wiped her mouth on her hand, then nodded. He got another glass from the bartender and poured her a full one.

He clicked her rim with his, his brown eyes looking into hers.

"So," he said after draining half his glass, "where do you like to party?"

"Most anywhere." She couldn't meet his look.

"And I'm sure you have a baby-sitter to pay?"

This line surprised her. She looked up at his smiling eyes, grinned, then lowered her head. She nodded.

"Do you suppose forty dollars could buy me a small share of this party of yours?"

She nodded again, looking out toward the dance floor. She could see Rebecca's red dress dazzling out there. A line dance was going on, and it seemed everybody in the place was moving in step.

The man beside her, Farley, was watching, too.

Elise downed her beer. If she was going to screw this cowboy, she'd better be getting on with it. She wanted this night to be worth her while, and his forty bucks alone wasn't going to do it.

"So, Farley," she said, remembering that this was a sport, "interested?"

"I'm thinking about it," he said, then looked back out over the crowd. Rebecca was still dancing with the same boy.

Farley filled their glasses again. Elise was feeling a little tipsy. "Time's awastin', big guy," she said.

He turned his face toward her, and his brown eyes turned icy cold. "Don't you be telling me what to do, you little slut," he said, and without blinking, lifted his beer and drank the whole thing while staring her down.

Elise lowered her eyes. Maybe this wasn't such a good idea after all.

Rebecca rushed up, perspiration running down the sides of her face, sticking her bangs to her forehead. "Whew! This cowboy's a dancing machine!"

He came up behind her, laughing, and put his hand protectively on her waist. They giggled together, their foreheads touching.

"Elise, this is Dennis."

"Hi," Dennis said, then got two beers from Jake and kept his arm around Rebecca. Within moments they were back on the dance floor, their beers left to sweat on the bar.

"C'mon," Farley said, then he grabbed Elise's arm with a harsh grip and pulled her off the barstool.

He pushed her through the crowd ahead of him, and out into the frigid air. He fished in his pocket for his keys as she followed him to his truck. He opened her side and she got in. He followed her, unzipped his pants, and pulled out his penis, stiff and ready.

"Suck this," he said. "Forty bucks."

Elise looked at the ugly man, at his ugly cock and wondered what she was doing there.

THE SONGSTER LEANED OVER AND KISSED TULIE'S NECK, putting his large, cool hands on her bare thighs. She didn't want to encourage him at all, but she didn't want to piss him off, either. She ducked out of his reach, then gently but firmly took his hands and put them back in his own lap.

"Tequila," she said, and blocked him with her shoulder. She leaned up against the back of the front seat, and when Buck handed her the bottle, she tipped it up and drank.

The warmth exploded in her stomach, and she could feel it erase Elise. She wiped her mouth with the back of her hand, handed the bottle back to Niles, then whooped as the Songster pulled her back to the seat. She giggled, knowing she shouldn't be doing this, shouldn't be drinking tequila right out of the bottle, shouldn't be with three strange guys in the middle of the woods, but here she was, and she might as well be making the best of it.

The Songster leaned over and rested his head on her shoulder. Cute. His shaggy hair smelled like baby shampoo. She reached up to touch it. It was silky and thick, and she scratched his scalp with her fingernails. He snuggled into her. *This is nice and romantic,* she thought, but then his hand was on her breast, and it pulled at her nipple through her shirt, and that was all the spark the alcohol in her body needed. Fire ignited between her legs, and within a few moments Tulie knew that if he didn't hurry and put his hand at her crotch, she was going to put it there herself.

For Tulie, anger was misdirected passion, and as soon as her passion had a focus and permission from José Cuervo, she was out of control.

Tulie could smell a bad boy from a mile away, and when she first got into this car, she knew he was bad. Real bad. Tulie wasn't sure she liked that part about herself, the part that was attracted to the bad ones, but she had come to accept it, for the most part. Tulie liked bad boys. The badder the better, and this one felt like a true work of art.

She grabbed two handfuls of his hair and brought his face up, then covered his mouth with hers. He kissed her so gently, so tenderly, so romantically that she wanted to strangle him. She wanted hot, urgent, passionate, now. She wanted now. She kissed him harder, sucking at his lips, at his tongue, and he rose to the occasion, and his cool, large hand slid between her thighs and under the elastic of her panties.

Tulie arched her back to help him, and his fingers were as expert as she knew they would be. This was the first time she'd been handled by an older man, and boy, oh, boy, it was just exactly what she needed. This was what she needed to forget Anna Marie. This was what she needed to forget Rebecca. This was what she needed to forget that bitch Elise. Lesbian. Ha. No lesbian would feel like this at the hands of an experienced man.

The thought of the two guys in the front seat even added a little fuel to her fire, and within a moment she had the Songster's jeans unzipped and held his warm, velvety penis in her hand.

With one orchestrated move the Songster slid a hand under her butt and moved her down on the backseat. Then he settled on top of her, and she felt her panties tear at the waist as he moved them aside.

"Love me," he whispered in her ear, and that tiny moment of tenderness in the midst of her raging heat melted her heart. She opened herself, and he slid smoothly into her, and with a shudder she was sober. She felt detached and stupid, sorry she'd gotten herself into this position, but it was too late now. She let him pound at her, hoping he would finish quickly.

Stupid, Tulie, she said to herself. *Stupid. No condom. What the hell were you thinking?*

And the other guys, what are they thinking? That I'll let them have a go at me, too?

She scrunched her eyes shut tight, the passion of the anger and the lust were now turning to despair, and tears squeezed out the corners of her eyes as the Songster breathed his beery breath into her face.

Then the Songster sucked in his breath, held it, and, beginning with a low growl, said "Maaaammmmmaaa," then collapsed on top of her.

She waited for a moment before rousing him, and as she waited, she realized she had become the Songster's property and was very likely safe from now on in this company. That was good. Beat being raped by the three of them.

But that didn't mean that what she had done was smart or in any way justified. It was stupid, *she* was stupid, and she knew it.

She rolled him off her, then sat up and pulled her skirt down. She pulled on the one boot that had come off. She felt dizzy and a little bit sick from the booze and the smoke and the emotion. She wanted to cry. Instead she got her purse from the front seat and took out a wad of tissues. "I'll be back," she said, then opened the car door and stepped out into a frozen wasteland.

* * *

Buck let his breath out in a long whistle. He was glad they were finished. His hands hurt from gripping the steering wheel while they were at their little activity in the backseat. He hadn't wanted to see what she and the Songster were doing in the backseat of his Pontiac wagon. *Kind of rude,* he thought. And he hoped to hell that the Songster would behave himself and be satisfied with a little coed ass and not have to dig deeper for his gratifications.

Well, at least the girl was safe. If she'd sounded as if she were in some sort of trouble, he and Niles would have helped her. They could deal with the Songster. *He* could deal with the Songster. In fact, he'd kind of like that, dealing with the Songster.

But Buck wished the Songster had gone to the cowboy bar with Elise and what's her name instead and left the girl there to give him and Niles some nice, young female company.

So he and Niles passed the bottle of tequila back and forth while they listened to the two of them making little noises in the backseat. Pretty soon there were clothing rustlings and then some major rearranging, and then they were doing it, doing it, doing it right in the backseat of the Pontiac.

It gave Buck a massive hard-on. He wondered if Tulie would be willing to go a mile or so with him in the backseat when the Songster was finished. Been a long time since he'd had any company that close. A long time.

The two in the backseat snorted and moaned and humped their way along, rocking the car, making Buck increasingly uncomfortable. He found his hand precariously close to his crotch and wondered if he was about to whack off right there in front of God and Niles and everybody.

He drank some more of that Cuervo Gold instead. Soon he could hear they were near some kind of climax. Then the Songster yelled for his mama, and then the car stopped rocking and everything fell silent in the backseat. Soon the breathing returned to normal.

The girl got her purse and stepped out into the cold to clean herself up.

"Never heard anybody call for their mama before," Niles said, then giggled. Buck knew there would be years of teasing in that.

He peeked over the backseat. The Songster held out his hand, and Buck passed back the bottle of tequila. The Songster drank from it, then held it loosely in his lap, staring out into space. "Hey, lucky break, eh, Songster?"

"She knows," he said flatly, then tipped the bottle to his lips.

"What do you mean?" Niles asked, but the Songster said nothing.

Tulie squatted, relieved herself, wiped away the Songster's evidence and dashed back to the car, her panties in tatters. She climbed back in and was surprised at how warm it was. Still, she pulled her down coat over her lap and shivered for a moment, scouting around for her place in this car. These three guys were some kind of closed unit, and she was an intruder. The more they drank, the tighter they would get, the more of an outsider she would become. She tried to clear her head of the drugs and think of her options. Her best option, it seemed at this point, was to keep them distracted, so they didn't get to thinking any dangerous thoughts about her. No way did she want them thinking any dangerous thoughts about her. Maybe if they got drunk, they'd go to sleep. Maybe if she kept them entertained, they could just mark time until morning. That's what she wanted, just to get through this god-awful night and get home to her quiet dorm room.

"Hey, guys," she said, warming up and trying to inject a

little levity into the mood, "let's play a tequila game. Want to?" There was no response. "Hey, what kind of camping trip is this anyway? You want to have a little fun, or do you just want to sit around and get morose?"

"Okay," Niles said. "In just a minute." He got out of the car door and lit a cigarette. The first big flakes of snow began to fall. They landed on his hand, then melted away. He could see flakes as big as a quarter falling softly. And it was cold enough that the snow would stick. It was cold as hell. He smoked fast, flicked his butt into the weeds and got back into the car. "Hey," he said, "it's snowing."

"Great," Buck said. "We'll probably get snowed in."

"Okay, listen," Tulie said. "This is a good game. Okay. What's yer name, Niles, right? You get to go first."

"Why me?"

"Somebody has to. Be a sport. Okay. You tell us something that none of us knows about you."

"Like what?"

"I don't know. Just something. *Anything*. It's not important. Just something."

"My first girlfriend's name was Lisa Stevenson."

"Good," Tulie said. "Pass him some tequila." She reached up and poked Buck in the shoulder. "You're next."

"This is dumb."

"C'mon. Niles was a sport."

"Yeah, but what he said was stupid."

"So? Give us something better."

"I don't know anything better." Buck sounded very uncomfortable. Buck sounded as if he had secrets. This could actually become a fun game if someone had secrets.

"Come on," she said. "These guys can't know *everything* there is to know about you."

"I almost blinded a kid once with a rubber band and a paper clip. I shot it in class, and it broke his contact lens."

"Wow, Buck," Niles said.

"Good," Tulie said. "Your turn, Songster."

"No."

"C'mon," all three said.

"I ain't got nothin' to say."

"Sure you do," Tulie said.

"I got laid first when I was thirteen," the Songster said.

"Good," Tulie said. "My turn. I lost my virginity in an attic."

"An attic!" Niles said. "What were you doing up in an attic?"

"Screwing," Tulie said, then laughed, wanting them to laugh with her. They did. She desperately wanted to be included as one of the guys. That way lay safety. She pretended to swig on the bottle of tequila and passed it around. The last thing she needed was more booze. "Okay, Niles, you again."

"How old were you?" Niles asked.

"I'm done. It's your turn."

"Okay. Um . . . I was married once, but it only lasted a month."

Everybody laughed.

"And somewhere I've got a twenty-year-old daughter. I could even be a grandfather by now," Niles said.

Nobody laughed.

"Buck?"

"I've got three kids. No, two kids."

"Well, which is it, Buck? Jeez," Niles said.

"Two."

"Songster?"

"I've got no kids." The Songster was bored with this game, Tulie could hear it in his voice.

"I made love to a woman once," Tulie said, hoping to rekindle his interest in the game.

"Really?" Niles said, turning around to look at her. He settled back with his back against the door. The car interior became kind of like a living room, with Buck leaning against the driver's door, one wrist hanging on the top of the steering wheel, the other arm over the top of the seat. The Songster was leaning against the door behind Buck, his long legs stretched out into Tulie's territory.

It might have been her imagination, but it seemed as though the interest level in the car did climb a notch.

"Really," she said, always and forever amazed at men's reaction to that statement. But it was the wrong thing to say if she wanted to be included as one of them. "Niles?"

Niles reached for the tequila bottle and took a swig. "You guys are the only friends I've got."

"We know that, Niles," Buck said. "Tell us something new."

"No, really."

"*Really*," Buck said. "Tell us something we don't know."

Niles looked down at the bottle in his lap. "I'd kill for you guys," he said softly.

"Oooh, good," Tulie said, sounding encouraging but feeling sick. She didn't want to talk about sex, and she didn't want to talk about killing either. "Buck."

"I couldn't ever kill anything. Life is too . . . I don't know. I watched my kids grow inside my wife, and . . . well, it affected me, I guess."

"Tell us something new, Buck," Niles said.

"I have a twin brother."

"No!" Niles was impressed. "Really?"

"Yes, really, for Christ's sake."

"Does he look like you?"

"Identical."

"Where is he?"

Buck didn't say.

Tulie listened to this with growing interest. This was a good game. It brought out the best and worst in people. Leastwise it always brought out some good juicy secrets that would be good for either ridicule or bribes, depending upon how drunk the confessor was. "Hey, you guys are getting pretty good," Tulie said, but she was beginning to feel rather poorly. She was starting to feel sick to her stomach.

"Seen him recently?" Niles asked. "Your brother."

"No." Buck slumped in his seat.

"Your turn, Songster," Tulie said.

"I hate this game."

"Why? What are you hiding?" Niles asked.

"Nothing. I ain't hiding nothing. I just don't like this, is all."

Buck felt emboldened by his confession. "Tell us about that woman, Songster."

Tulie felt the Songster tense up beside her. She felt adrenaline rush through her and make her heart hammer in her chest. She didn't like the sound of this, no matter the explanation. *The ultimate bad boy, Tulie,* she thought. *What the fuck have you gotten yourself into?*

"What woman?" the Songster said. Only he didn't say it like a question; he said it like a threat.

"You know the one. The woman you brought out to the boxcars."

"Don't know what you mean, Buck," the Songster said, but he said it slow and meanlike. Buck backed off.

"Okay," Tulie said, relieved to be cut out of an explosive topic. "So then tell us something else."

"I grew up on the streets of Denver," the Songster said.

"What do you mean? You didn't have no family?" Niles asked.

"That's what I mean."

Niles was astounded. "What about your mom?"

"My mother was a whore, and she died when I was four-teen."

"No father? No brothers and sisters?"

"No."

"Jeez. What about Connecticut? Didn't you say you was from Connecticut?"

"I lied."

"Your turn, Niles," Buck said.

"I stole a big compressor from a job I used to work at once and sold it to another company and spent all the money on whores and booze."

"And cigarettes," Buck said.

"Yeah, thanks for reminding me." Niles pulled one out of his shirt pocket and stuck it into his mouth unlit.

"Niles." It was the Songster.

"What?"

"Would you kill for me?"

"You bet, Songster. Buck, too. I'd kill for Buck, cuz I knew him first. But I'd probably kill for you, too. Yep, I probably would."

Silence jelled in the car. Tulie had to swallow to clear her ears from the sudden pressure. She had to stay alert. She wanted to stay alert, but she wasn't feeling good at all. The booze was taking over, and just when she thought she was doing all right, too. Did someone just mention killing again?

Then she felt her alcohol-filled body take control of her, jerk control right out from under her mind. She slumped. She wanted to say something, but she couldn't decide what—help? . . . uh-oh? . . . look out below!—and that was all too funny, but before she could laugh, she fell over toward the Songster, and felt his elbow push her over toward the car door. When her body was completely limp, she had a last thought about José Cuervo and what a traitor he was, and then her mind went limp, too.

"Your turn, Buck," Niles said.

"What happened to the girl?"

"She kind of fell asleep back here. Suddenly," the Songster said.

Just as well, Buck thought, she was getting pretty drunk. "I got a degree in engineering from Northwestern University," Buck said.

"No." Niles was impressed.

"Really."

"Well what the hell are you doing living in boxcars with us?"

"Don't know, Niles. Really don't know." Buck put the bottle to his lips and drank the golden liquid. He *did* know. "I like the freedom."

"Jeez."

"Songster?" Buck asked softly.

"What?"

"Tell me about that woman."

"What woman?"

"The one who never left your boxcar. You drove her car away."

"She left during the night."

Buck turned around and looked at the Songster, barely visible in the darkness. "That ain't true, Songster. C'mon. Tell us." The car was as quiet as a snowfall. Buck heard Tulie's nasal breathing, but that was all.

"I don't tell nobody nothing what ain't their direct business, Buck," the Songster said just as quietly.

"You c'n truss us, Songster," Niles said.

"I can't trust shit. I can't even trust this whore here. I mean, she already has to go, because she knows."

"Go? Go where? Knows what?" Buck's mouth went dry.

"Shut up, Buck," the Songster said. "You talk too much. Ask too many questions. Gimme the tequila."

Niles passed the tequila to the backseat. "Wha's going on here, Buck?"

Buck ignored him. He was busy thinking. He was thinking if he were half a man, he'd boot the Songster right out of the car right now and head back to town, drop the bimbo at the university, and everybody would be safe and sound, except maybe the Songster, but that would be okay, too. He'd survive. Or maybe he wouldn't.

But Buck knew he wouldn't do that. For one thing, he was afraid of the Songster. He was afraid of what the Songster might do if he were to get left behind, get mad and then show up at the boxcars, and Buck didn't have it in him to move and change jobs and all that. But he didn't have to have the Songster for a friend anymore either. And if anything happened to that girl . . .

If anything happened to that girl, it was going to happen in Buck's car, on Buck's camping trip.

There was *no* way Buck was going to prison. He had to have his freedom. He *had* to have his freedom. If he didn't want any freedom, he'd still be married with his wife and three —well, two—kids and working as a civil engineer for the stupid damned highway division.

So how much do you want your freedom, Buck? he asked himself. *Enough to ditch the Songster and take the girl home?*

Apparently not. The Songster could take away a lot more than Buck's freedom.

Wait it out, Buck, he told himself. *Wait it out, and see what happens.*

"I got a game now," the Songster said.

"Good," said Niles. "What?"

We're all too drunk, Buck thought. Niles was beginning to slur his words.

"How to dispose of this body."

"Wha' body?" Niles asked.

"The girl, idiot."

"She's just sleeping, you said." Buck felt hysteria rising. He looked over the back of the seat, but it was too dark to see life.

"She *is* just sleeping. It's a game, I said."

Buck reached over the back of the seat and touched her. She was warm.

"So," the Songster said. "How would you do it, Niles?"

"Prob'ly don't want it found till spring, right?"

"C'mon, Songster," Buck said. The Songster seemed horribly sober. "That's enough."

The Songster took a long pull from the tequila bottle, swallowed, then blew a low note across its rim. He opened the window and heaved the empty bottle out. "Niles. Let's say you had to kill this bitch. How would you get away with it?"

"After I fucked her to death?" Niles snorted, laughed and then had a coughing fit.

"Yeah."

"I'd staple her to a stick and teach the dog to fetch."

Even Buck laughed at that, and the Songster laughed, and Niles laughed too hard for too long, and for a moment it was just a bunch of guys getting drunk and stupid together.

"No, really." The Songster's voice came softly, and not only dark but dark and spooky settled back inside the car. Buck could hear the girl breathing in the back. At least he thought it was the girl. He hoped it was.

Niles lit a cigarette, cracked open the window, blew the smoke out. "Hard to say, Songster." He sounded clear and lucid as if he were making a report to the board of directors. Buck didn't know what to think. "Hide her somewhere until she decomposed. But if this one turns up missing, there are those other two, you know, and they saw us and heard our names."

"It would depend on how we killed her, huh, Niles?"

"Yeah, that's right."

"I don't like this, Songster," Buck said, feeling close to tears. "Let's change the subject, okay?"

"No," the Songster said. "More gin."

Maybe if he gets drunk enough, he'll just go to sleep, too, Buck thought, and reached under the seat for the other bottle.

The Songster spun the top off and drank. He passed it over to Niles. "What if she was found out on the main highway, hit by a car?"

"Good," Niles said. "Accident. No investigation, not even the girls she was with would disagree with that."

"Not *my* car," Buck said.

"Why not?" Niles asked.

"Because! Jesus! Because they have a way of telling things like that."

"They can only tell if there is hair and blood and shit matted on the underside of your car," the Songster said with dead calm. "If we just put her in the road and you very slowly, very carefully ran over her head, there wouldn't be anything on your car."

Niles giggled like a little girl.

"Not my car," Buck said. "You guys are sickos. If you want to go to jail for the rest of your lives, you go ahead, but I won't."

"Relax, Buck," the Songster said. "We're just talkin'."

"Yeah, well, let's talk about something else."

The Songster lit up a joint and passed it around.

"How come you hate women?" Buck asked him.

"I don't."

"Seems like."

"They're always out to get you all the time, that's all," the Songster said, and Buck heard him rip a piece of the cracked upholstery off the backseat armrest. "They either say things or do things . . ."

Buck remembered the tears in Cara's eyes when he told her he was leaving her and the kids. "I just can't do it anymore, Cara," he had said. "I love you. God, I love you almost more than my own life, but I can't do this day-after-day thing. I've got to break loose."

"Break loose then," she had said, "and come back when you're finished."

He wondered if she would still be there. He doubted it. It wouldn't be fair to show up again without intending to stay anyway. But that woman was a woman filled with goodness. She never hurt anybody. "You're wrong, Songster."

"No, he's not," Niles said, bringing his feet up onto the front seat as if ready to leap somewhere. "He's right. Every woman is out to get what she wants. If you're going her way, that's fine, but if you're not . . . hooo, boy."

Cara wanted a family. Cara wanted a house and a station wagon and to keep up with the Joneses. She wanted nice shoes all the time. Nice shoes. She spent money they didn't have on nice shoes. And as long as he brought home the paycheck, and bedded her regularly, and didn't embarrass her in front of . . .

"So what do you think this here little chippy wants, Niles?" the Songster asked.

"She don't want nothin' but a good time, Songster. Get high, get laid, get her college degree," Niles said.

"Wrong." The Songster spoke with such flat authority that even Buck wanted to believe him.

Buck cringed. He hated belligerent drunks. And the Songster didn't know what the hell he was talking about.

"All right, know-it-all," Buck said, his face flushing hot. He turned around in the seat and faced the Songster. "What does she want?"

In the diffused light that came from nowhere but was magnified by the snow, Buck could see the grin on the Songster's face pull his lips away from his teeth, slow and meanlike.

"She wants to suck our brains."

Niles groaned as if he'd just heard a stupid punch line. Buck would have liked to have smacked the Songster on the side of the head with the gin bottle, but the Songster stopped him by saying, "She wants to find out how to do that woman thing. She wants to find out how to *handle* us, how to *work* us, how to *do* us. She's trying to find out how to outlive us, how to have the last laugh at us. This woman is back here being so incredibly *female* it makes me want to puke. Women are only good for two things. Fucking and . . ."

"And what, Songster?" Niles asked.

"Never mind."

Buck grabbed the bottle from Niles and drank. This was going to be the longest night of his life.

ELISE PUSHED OUT THE DRIVER'S SIDE OF THE TALL TRUCK and stumbled as she hit the ground. She almost gagged. She felt like puking. Behind her she heard Farley's truck start, and it wasn't until it had roared out of the parking lot just as she was pushing through the front door that she realized he'd gotten away without giving her the forty bucks. "Horse's ass," she said under her breath, then pushed her way straight through, past the bartender's judgmental eyes, to the ladies' room.

Once safely inside the rest room, Elise looked at herself in the mirror. Some dance-sweaty girls were doing their hair and fixing their makeup. They all looked sweet and smelled good. Elise looked like a wreck. Her hair stood all on end; her face was flushed, her mascara smudged. She had no lipstick on at all, and her mouth hurt right at the corner where that idiot cowboy had been too rough.

The college boys were nothing like that. Nothing at all. They were nice and quiet and passive and grateful. This jerk was . . . well, he was nothing like the college boys. And he hadn't even paid her. Horse's ass.

She wanted to cry but stifled it as she repaired herself. Her emotions felt so thick she couldn't sort them out at all. There was anger, and regret, and confusion. There was jealousy and insecurity and inadequacy. There was a sense of being wronged and a wish that she belonged.

Whatever.

She worked over her face and her hair, straightened her dress, and then pawed through her purse to make sure everything was still in its place. Including the snub-nose .38 revolver her daddy had given her for protection. "Don't get mad, baby," he'd said. "Get even."

By the time she was finished, she felt fairly well settled down. Now the decision was whether to find Rebecca and get on back to Eugene or to sit in the bar and watch for a while longer, find another trick, or what. Somebody had to pay for that fine blow job she'd given that horse's ass.

She slipped into her attitude again and walked on out into the humidity, into the music, into the sea of colognes and cigarette smoke. She got a beer from the bartender, took a long drink, and rinsed Farley's taste from her mouth, then turned around, and as she did so, Rebecca made her unsteady way toward the rest room.

Elise put her hand out and stopped her. "Rebecca!"

Rebecca's eyes were slow to focus. She squinted at Elise, closing one eye, and Elise remembered she was wearing only one contact lens. With recognition, Rebecca's face screwed up in a drunken grin. "Elise! Hi! Isn't this a great place?"

Well, there went that idea. Elise thought Rebecca might try turning a trick or two, once she'd had a couple of beers and got into the swing of things, but Rebecca was too drunk to do anything.

"I've got to pee," Rebecca said, and lurched toward the bathroom.

What a fucked-up night, Elise thought. She worked on her beer until Rebecca emerged, her hair still messed, her makeup still blurred. "Come over to our table, Elise. This is a really fun place."

"I think we ought to go," Elise said.

"No. No, it's early yet."

"You better slow down or you'll get sick." Elise could just picture Rebecca puking in the Camaro on the way down the mountain.

"I never been sick," Rebecca said.

You've probably never been drunk before, either, I bet, Elise thought. "Half hour," Elise said. "We leave."

Rebecca smiled. "Okey-dokey, arti-chokey." And she smiled and laughed her way through the crowd back to a table on the far side of the room.

Elise sipped her beer.

The band returned from its break and started up with a rockabilly tune that flooded the dance floor.

"Wanna dance?" The voice was close and low and surprised Elise. She hadn't seen him approach.

"I don't dance," she said.

He looked her up and down, at those nice legs in that green dress with the open coat and said, "That's a shame. I see you drink beer. Can I buy you one?"

"Sure," Elise said without looking at him. *Be nicer to him*, she thought. *Maybe he has money*.

He brought her a fresh beer. She finished hers and traded him bottles. He leaned against the wall next to her. "I saw you leave a while ago with Farley."

She felt the color rise in her cheeks.

"You working?"

She turned and looked him square in the eye and tipped her beer to her lips. He looked like a nice guy, mid-thirties, clean-cut, fit. She drank a couple of swallows, then turned back without saying a word.

"I've got a little cash," he said, "and it's been a long time."

Maybe the night isn't a total loss, Elise thought, and she started walking toward the door. She turned around. "Coming?" she asked, and smiled as he galloped to her side.

Iced air froze her eyes as she stepped into the mountain cold. The thermometer must have dropped like a rock. "Where's your car?" she asked.

"Mmm," he said, stalling, zipping up his jacket. "Where's yours?"

Elise planted her feet. "What's wrong with yours?"

He looked down at his boots. "Baby seat," he said. "I couldn't do it with the baby seat looking at me."

She snorted, then led him over to the Camaro. She keyed the frozen lock, then opened the door. She was afraid the frozen leather would crack. He got in on the passenger side. "Oh," he said. "Bucket seats."

"I gotta see the color of your cash," she said, shivering.

He pulled out his wallet and extracted three twenties. "Will this get me laid?"

She took the cash and set it on the dashboard. Suddenly she felt a little romantic. He was a nice-looking guy who smelled good. She took hold of his big, redneck belt buckle and opened it, then his jeans. She kissed him, and he kissed her back, his hands warm and tender on her body. She took off her shoes and straddled him, and in no time she was earning every penny of that sixty bucks. She used every trick she knew, and the groans of pleasure from his throat told her that he was happy with his investment.

When he was finished, she tidied herself up. He took the twenties from the dash, and she snaked out a red-taloned hand and grabbed his wrist.

He very carefully pulled a different wallet from a different pocket and opened it. A silver badge glinted in the faint light.

"Thanks for the freebie," he said. "If I ever catch you hooking in this bar again, I'll put your talented little ass in jail."

"Baby seat," she whispered. "You jerk."

He laughed, then touched her cheek with his finger. She didn't give him the satisfaction of flinching. Her rage was overpowering. "You're good," he said. "And so young."

"Get out of my car."

"Go home."

"Get out!"

He got out, closed the car door gently behind him.

Elise waited a few minutes, then grabbed her purse. She put on her shoes. She stormed back into the bar, made her way to Rebecca's table. Rebecca wasn't there. Frustrated and furious, Elise looked around, then caught sight of the red dress on the dance floor.

Elise walked through the dancing couples and grabbed Rebecca's arm. "Come on, Rebecca, we're going home."

"Hold on there," Rebecca's acne-faced friend said. "Rebecca isn't ready to go." He smiled at her. "Are you, sweetie?"

"No, Elise," she whined. "Come on, you said a half hour."

"Girls, girls," the boy said, looking at his watch. "It's early. This bar don't close till two. Come on now," he said to Elise. "Sit with us awhile."

"No," Elise said. "We're going. Come on, Rebecca. Get your coat."

"Oh, my coat." Rebecca said, bringing her hand up to her mouth. "I don't know where it is."

Fuck, Elise thought. *I just ought to go on home and leave her here to pop his zits. This is the worst night ever.* "Where did you leave it, Rebecca?" she asked with exaggerated patience.

"Gee, I don't remember." She turned to the boy. "Do you remember?" Then they both started to giggle. He led them off the dance floor, back to their table. No coat there.

"Did you leave it at the bar?" he asked.

"That's it!" Rebecca said, laughing. "I left it at the bar. I think I did."

"*Get it*," Elise said, and hoped her voice sounded as dangerous as she felt.

The three walked through the crowd. Elise waited by the door while Rebecca and Dennis went to the bar. She saw them talking to the bartender, saw him shrug. Great. No coat. Minus zero weather, and she has no coat. Elise wanted to scream.

They wandered up to her, squint-eyed Rebecca looking like a little girl about to tell her mommy that somewhere she lost her coat. Elise just opened the door and walked out. A moment later they followed her, Rebecca wearing Dennis's sheepskin-lined denim jacket.

Elise led the way to the Camaro and got in. Rebecca and Dennis leaned against the car, kissing for a long time, long enough for Elise to get even madder. She settled her purse, put on her seat belt, and honked the horn. Rebecca jumped. She shucked the warm coat, opened the door, and slid in, minus the jacket, her teeth chattering.

Elise gave the drunken girl a look, put the key in the ignition, and turned it.

Nothing.

Tulie grew up in as normal a family as could be found in America. The youngest of four girls, she was loved, protected, and watched over by a caring family with few serious problems. That, in itself, carries its own pressures, and when Tulie became a teenager, her rebellion manifested in a fascination with bad boys in black leather.

She never quite fitted in with that crowd, with her preppy clothes, her scrubbed look, her long, shining hair. She didn't look anything at all like the other girls who hung around the zippers-and-silver-studs element, she didn't drink, and she didn't do drugs. She just smiled her straight-toothed Crest Kid smile, didn't say much, and quietly fantasized about one after another of the scraggly guys and quietly envied the hard-bitten girls. She wondered what it would be like to dress like that, to be like that, to act like that.

But Tulie was no dummy, and while she liked the outlaws, she knew they were dangerous. Big mistakes, life-changing, life-or-death mistakes, could be made in a heartbeat with bad boys.

"You're asking for it," her sisters had told her, more than once. "You're just asking for it, hanging around with those guys."

But bad boys turned her on. Especially Mike Cook. He'd

been quietly watching her, just as she had been watching him, and one day he made his move.

After school one May day Tulie stopped at the edge of a group of people in the school parking lot who had congregated around a couple of customized motorcycles. She admired the motorcycles and watched the guys talk about them.

Before she knew it, Mike, a tall, round guy with a red-blond beard and long, curly, tangled hair that was thinning on top, had his arm around her. She didn't flinch. At five feet nine, she just about looked him squarely in the eye. He smelled good, like aftershave and new leather. He smiled, and his teeth were in good shape, not like most of the guys. In fact, he was fairly presentable.

She smiled back at him, and that's all it took. They were a couple. He was her boyfriend all that summer and during her entire senior year in high school.

She liked Mike, liked him a lot. She liked to tease him; she liked the power she seemed to hold over him. With a single finger she could create a hard bulge in the front of his jeans and make his senses go south. He wanted her, wanted her bad, and she enjoyed that. She got away with teasing and then dancing away for about six months, holding him off, but then he started to get nasty about not getting laid.

He finally got his way, and the price of admission was a fresh Trojan and a bottle of José Cuervo Gold, and the place was his makeshift bedroom in the attic of his grandmother's house. Tulie got tipsy, felt recklessly sexy, went a little too far with the teasing for the amount of tequila Mike had ingested, and when he roughly pulled her jeans down and screwed her with no tenderness, on the hard floor, she felt betrayed. Then she got sick and threw up on his new motorcycle boots.

She forgave him, but she never trusted him or tequila again.

Mike brought out the mothering instincts in Tulie. He wore

black leather and torn jeans. Sometimes he shaved; sometimes he didn't. Tulie's parents tried to find something to like in him, but her dad ground his teeth every time Mike came to pick her up.

Their daughter's propensity toward bad boys was the only thing Tulie's folks could find to complain about. Tulie was a model student. She pulled straight B's, played on the high school basketball and volleyball teams, was tall and lean and nice-looking. She pitched on the local girls' softball team and took the team to the finals three years in a row. She took good care of herself and had nice friends. She was a good kid.

But this guy she took to dating . . .

Tulie never went off the romantic deep end with Mike; she knew he would drop her when he found something else he wanted to conquer. And so he did. She felt bad about it for a couple of days, but she was never in love with him. She had a rational way of looking at relationships and realized that her time with Mike had been a valuable learning process.

Tulie knew she would eventually find a mate. She would search him out, look over his financial statement, his credentials, assess his future, and then commit to a partnership of raising children and saving for retirement. It didn't sound like a particularly fascinating future, but it was what was expected of her, and it was what she expected of herself. It would be okay.

She looked at her parents and saw two hardworking people who found time to see the satisfaction in their lives, in their families. Tulie's dad had worked for the railroad since he was eighteen; her mom was a nurse. Her older sisters were all college-educated, and their home was paid for. Their parents led a life of hard work and low expectations, but Tulie figured if they could do it, she could do it. It wasn't a bad life. She'd had a good childhood.

So before she had to settle down to a life where everybody else—husband, kids—came first, she was going to do all the experimenting she needed to do. She wanted to get everything out of her system before she settled down, so that she could seriously and consciously commit to that sedate lifestyle with no regrets. She wanted to find out about the bad boys. She'd already found out about booze. She wanted to try marijuana. And she needed to lay to rest the troubling attraction she was developing toward some women. It raised a curiosity in her that couldn't quite be put aside.

Every now and then she saw an unusually attractive woman, and when she did, she felt what she thought the giggly girls in high school felt when they goofed over the boys. That infatuation, that "Isn't he *gorgeous?*" gushy feeling. She touched herself at night and thought about what their breasts would feel like, what it would feel like to press her breasts against another woman's breasts, and what it would be like to kiss another woman, to taste another woman.

But those were private thoughts, and she would never act upon them, never, ever. The idea of being gay scared her. If she were, she would never marry, never have children, never lead the normal, Republican life she had always seen. She'd rather hang with the bad boys while they drank lager and whiskey. And when they all turned and whistled at some nice-looking woman, well, Tulie would turn and appreciate her right along with them. Quietly. Privately. And then maybe she'd screw one of the guys in the backseat of his car and she would be thinking of the woman, long, smooth legs, small, pointy breasts, lightly powdered and scented, her hair long and sweet.

Going away to school was the ideal opportunity to make a few changes. She vowed to stay away from the bikers and the bad boys. She decided she didn't like the other women who hung around with that element; they were really sleazy, and Tulie was not. She didn't dress down; she was always well groomed; she thought more of herself than that. So for a while she had few friends. She just kept to herself, watched others, and assessed her feelings. She looked for a place in university society where she could step in and feather herself a little nest, something other than sports. Getting away from the bad boys was just a part of it. Tulie looked at these college years as her last opportunity to do all the experimenting, all the exploring she needed to do for a lifetime. Right after graduation she would find her mate and settle down.

And then Anna Marie fell in love with her.

Tulie first noticed Anna Marie in history class. Anna Marie was short, squarely built, and bookish-looking, with big brown eyes and large black-framed glasses. She wore her hair bobbed, wore no makeup, and dressed simply, in tailored blouses and slacks. She looked well tended, in a casual way. Tulie found her embarrassingly attractive and tried to keep from looking at her, but somehow she always found her eyes sliding over toward her. When the teacher said something funny, Tulie would look to see how Anna Marie looked when she smiled, when she laughed. She looked over to see Anna Marie frown, study, take a test. And whenever their eyes met, Tulie felt a thrill that made her face grow red, and she would look away, look down, want to sink into the earth.

Then one day, while Tulie was browsing the card rack in the bookstore, Anna Marie bumped into her.

"Oh, hi," Anna Marie said, and Tulie heard her soft voice for the first time. She had some kind of accent.

"Hi," Tulie said, felt her face glow with a blush, and hated that about herself.

"You're in my history class, right?"

"Uh, yeah." Tulie felt too tall, too trashed out. Her jeans

were worn through to the white; she had a torn sweatshirt on; her shoes were scuffed. She never went out in public looking like that. She'd been studying too hard, too long, and had walked down to the bookstore for a mind-refreshing break.

She ran her hands through her hair and remembered that she'd just had it cut short for convenience and wasn't sure how to make it look right yet. This was not the way she wanted to meet Anna Marie for the first time face-to-face.

Anna Marie wore a clean and ironed white blouse, tan slacks, and loafers. Her shiny black hair curled softly under at her jawline. She looked preppy, and that was attractive, too.

"That professor, he's funny. Do you like him?"

"Uh." Tulie was amazed at her reaction. Where was her glib tongue? "Yeah, he's all right."

They looked at cards in silence for a moment. Tulie didn't know what to do, so she did nothing.

"Want to get a cup of coffee?" Anna Marie asked. "I don't have any more classes today."

"Me neither," Tulie said, then turned and looked at her. Those eyes. "Yeah, okay."

They both put down the cards they were looking at and walked out of the bookstore and into the bakery next door. They got large cups of coffee and sat at a small table in the back. Anna Marie was orchestrating. Tulie was petrified.

Anna Marie was interesting. Born in Guatemala, she was given to an aunt to bring to the United States when she was ten. She grew up in New Mexico and was headed for medical school. She, too, was a freshman, but she was a straight A student, as, she explained, she had to be if she was to succeed in medical school.

Tulie was interested, but she was more interested in the flashing brown eyes and straight, even white teeth. They drank coffee and talked about their homes, their families, their classes, their impressions of Oregon.

They left the bakery and headed to Anna Marie's apartment, which was off campus. It was decorated conservatively, punctuated with the kind of festive prints, pots, and rugs Tulie associated with New Mexico. It looked just like Anna Marie.

They spent the rest of the afternoon talking and laughing on the couch, then walked back across campus to the cafeteria and ate dinner together. Tulie walked Anna Marie home after dinner, in the cool prewinter evening, and before they said good night, they agreed to meet for dinner again the next day.

Tulie went back to the dorm floating on air, and that both confused and scared her.

Within the week they had tumbled, giggling and half drunk on wine, onto Anna Marie's bed to look at photo albums. They stayed there, talking. Sometime someone turned off the light, and they kept talking, until they eventually found their way under the covers, where they held each other and talked until dawn. In the morning Tulie felt uncommonly shy as she untangled herself from a sleeping Anna Marie, brushed out her clothes, and left.

She stayed the next night with Anna Marie, too, although this time they held each other naked all night.

Lovemaking was a natural outgrowth of their friendship, and it was the softest, warmest, most loving experience that Tulie could imagine. Anna Marie was tender and sweet, soft and yielding.

Men were never like that.

They began spending much of their time together, and as Tulie had a roommate in her dorm, she slept over at Anna Marie's most nights.

But Anna Marie wanted to touch her in public, and Tulie didn't want her to. Anna Marie wanted them to be a couple, and Tulie didn't want that either. Anna Marie took a lot of women's studies classes, and when she talked about them, Tulie felt vaguely uncomfortable. And she hated the word *lesbian*. She was not a lesbian, never would be, and even if she were, she hated the word. It sounded so harsh, so final. Nor would she ever be bisexual. That sounded too clinical.

Tulie just wanted to go where the good times were, and right now they were with Anna Marie.

They argued over it.

"I'm a lesbian, Tulie."

"Well, I doubt it, but you can call yourself that if you want. So what?"

"There's no doubting it. And you're denying your true nature if you don't admit it."

"I like men."

"No, you don't."

She did and she didn't, but there was no use arguing the point when she wasn't sure of her convictions. She just wanted to be alone with Anna Marie when she could and stay out of the politics of it all.

But Anna Marie was political, and increasingly so.

Now and again Tulie longed for the biker bars, where at least she thought she was sure of who she was.

The first year went by so fast Tulie couldn't believe it was gone. Summer looked her in the face, and Anna Marie wanted her to get a job, move into her apartment, and stay the summer. Tulie's family wanted her to come home.

Tulie went home, but she missed Anna Marie more than she thought she would. Her phone bill skyrocketed with Anna Marie in Oregon purring into the phone for hours. Tulie, in Arizona, lay on her bed, tears leaking out of her eyes.

She went to her old hangouts, found some of the same old

guys, but they weren't as interesting to her anymore. They seemed to be crude and childish.

After a month she went back to Eugene and moved in with Anna Marie. They honeymooned in bed for three days. Then Tulie got a part-time job at a camera store, and Anna Marie kept up with her accelerated summer classes.

They settled into a nice domestic routine. Tulie was happy but protective of her privacy. She didn't want anyone to know she was involved with Anna Marie; she just wanted everybody to think they were roommates. Anna Marie found this funny and said that Tulie wasn't fooling anybody. Tulie even looked like a dyke, Anna Marie said, and Tulie got mad. She started to let her hair grow.

They celebrated their first anniversary. They went to New Mexico to have Christmas with Anna Marie's elderly aunt. They slept in Anna Marie's old room, and nobody thought anything of it. Tulie loved seeing New Mexico. She'd grown up in Phoenix but had never been to New Mexico. She couldn't get over how different it was. Their vacation was wonderful. It was almost like a real honeymoon.

She was afraid she was beginning to love Anna Marie.

And then a letter came.

Dear Tulie.

Dad has to go to Seattle on union business, so I'm going to tag along and we'll drive on up. We plan to stop and see you for a couple of days. Please make reservations for us at a convenient AAA motel. Cheap. We'll be there on February 16. Love,

Mom.

Tulie's heart hit her bowels.

"My folks are coming."

"Great. I'd like to meet them."

"They don't know about you."

"They don't?"

"Well, I mean, they know your name, they know you're my friend, but they don't know . . ."

"They don't know we're living together?"

"No."

"Well, so what?"

"Well, so there's only one bed in this apartment."

"You don't want them to know we're lovers?"

"No, I don't."

"Are you ashamed of me?" The hurt was already beginning to show on Anna Marie's face, and Tulie knew that it was only going to get worse.

"No, of course not. They're just . . . kind of old . . . they're my *parents*, for God's sake."

"So? I don't understand. Are you ashamed of us?"

"Kind of."

"Are you ashamed of you?"

"Yes."

"I won't be hidden. I won't be a dirty secret."

"Oh, you're not, you're not."

"You act as if I am."

"It's not you," Tulie said. "It's me."

Anna Marie hid her face in her hands. She took off her glasses and rubbed her eyes. She replaced her glasses, seemingly more in control. "So what do you want me to do?"

"I guess I'll move another bed in here and make it look like home."

"Tell them you sleep on the couch. Tell them we take turns." Tulie didn't like the tone of Anna Marie's voice. Anna Marie was hurt, hurt deeply. "Or maybe you want me to move out while they're here. Move out of *my* apartment so you can lie to your parents about your shame."

"Please don't," Tulie said.

"Don't what? How could you? How *could* you?" Anna Marie got up off the sofa and shrugged into her parka. She got her book bag and walked out into the cold Oregon winter rain.

Tulie sat in the cozy apartment, filled with her things and Anna Marie's things, the apartment that looked and felt like her first real home, and knew she had done damage to the only person who had selflessly loved her. She knew she had done Anna Marie wrong, and there was nothing she could do about it.

She wouldn't bring her parents here to meet her lesbian (oh, God, that word!) lover.

She would move out.

Pain grabbed fistfuls of her insides and squeezed. She didn't know she could hurt like this.

She arranged to move back into the dorm the following week. The intervening days were silent and awkward. Anna Marie stayed away from the apartment, spending much of her time in the library, Tulie imagined. Tulie slept on the couch. She was close to tears the entire time, but just as she thought she wanted to give it all up and go back to Anna Marie's warmth, she knew she couldn't make a life like this. She couldn't live with another woman; she just couldn't. Better to break it off now than later, when it would only be worse.

Anna Marie wouldn't understand. She could, perhaps, if she wanted to, but she refused.

Life turned as cold and rainy as the Oregon winter.

The university gave her a studious roommate who was quiet and kept to herself. It was just as well.

Tulie's parents got slowed up by snow in the Siskiyou Pass, and their visit turned out to be barely an overnighter. They would never have known about Anna Marie because they checked into the motel, took Tulie out for dinner, fell exhausted into bed, and left early the next morning for Seattle.

Tulie thought she would never recover from her breakup with Anna Marie. She prayed for that detachment she had felt when Mike Cook dumped her. How come she hadn't felt this way then?

She spent her nights crying into her bed, exercising, drinking, trying anything and everything to quell the hurt. Nothing worked.

She began going out with the bad boys again. And drinking. Anna Marie was wonderful, but there was nothing quite like a good, steamy, vicious fuck. She avoided Anna Marie when she saw her because the ache flared up, and she didn't want Anna Marie to see that.

Just when she thought she was getting better day by day, she saw Anna Marie with another woman, and the hurt seared her again. Soon she saw Anna Marie in the steady company of that other woman, and once she saw them holding hands.

She'd been replaced.

That was good for another week of heartache and sobbing into her pillow.

Tulie was into her senior year before they actually spoke again, and then it was with that personal discomfort that neither wanted to show. The caring still showed in Anna Marie's eyes, but by that time Tulie was on to other things.

Tom. Tom Sullivan.

Tom was part Cherokee and looked it. At six feet five he was tall enough to make Tulie feel small. He had black hair and deep set brown eyes with those high cheekbones and well-defined lips that made him look like a painting. His profile sometimes made her catch her breath. Like Anna Marie, Tom was a serious student, only instead of medicine, his interest was in law.

ELIZABETH ENGSTROM

Tulie vacillated between clinging to Tom like a life raft in her turbulent sea of unresolved sexual identity and holding him off at arm's length. She liked him a lot, but his intensity frightened her. He had intensity but no passion. He was ready to find his mate, one who could help put him through law school after he got his undergraduate degree, then settle down to raising kids while he worked his way up the corporate ladder with a future in politics after he'd paid his dues.

Tulie was in no hurry to tie herself down, unless she needed to be tied down in order to survive. Sometimes she felt so confused about life that she was out of control, spinning right out of orbit, headed for certain disaster. Doomed. Tom could just casually reach out with one huge paw and lay it gently on her shoulder, defining her purpose as wife, mother, and political asset, and that spinning would stop. Once and for all.

Wouldn't it?

Before she met Tom, Tulie traveled in a couple of different circles, afraid to make close friends, afraid to fall in love, afraid, even, of being too attracted to anyone. She was afraid to find a man, afraid to find a woman. She was afraid of pleasing her parents in lieu of being true to herself, she was afraid that her attraction to women was a passing thing, and she dared not do anything permanent. She didn't want to hurt again. She didn't want to cause pain again.

While Tulie lay in bed agonizing over the choices she was certain she would soon have to make, her college days sped past.

She met no men worth having for more than a night. And she didn't do one-night stands. She stayed completely away from attractive women. She thought seriously about dropping out of school, except that she didn't know what she would do if she did—work forever in a camera shop? In a bookstore? Marry a millworker and raise a half dozen kids?

There was plenty of time to be responsible. College was for observing, discovering, exploring, right? She hated what she saw. She didn't like what she saw in herself.

Why was life so simple for some people? Anna Marie, for example. Brilliant, beautiful, she had no problem replacing Tulie's affections. She was headed for Harvard Medical School, her life was mapped out in simple, straight lines.

Tommy, too. He would have no problem finding a girl with the right résumé to snap into his plans. His future was cookie cutter perfect, with all its edges even and tidy.

She met Tom the same night she met the Elise and Rebecca team, at a frat house party. Men swarmed over Elise and Rebecca in their almost clothes while Tulie sat and watched them in action. They were pretty good, she had to admit. Elise wore a sequined bustier and black jeans with diamond cutouts all over them. Rebecca wore a striped tube top and a short jeans skirt. They flitted and flirted and flattered until Tulie could hardly stand it. Tulie wore new jeans, loafers like Anna Marie's, and a vanilla suede shirt that revealed nothing. She just sat and sipped a diet Coke and watched the guys go nuts over the two anorexic girls.

"They're really something, aren't they?" It was a low, soft voice, coming from her left. Startled, she turned to see a tall man with too much black hair leaning against the wall next to her. She must have been very intent on the girls and their magical bodies for him to sneak up on her like that.

"Yeah. Hot."

He laughed, and he had big, white, straight teeth. She liked his laugh. She smiled and sipped her soda and went back to watching the two women wield their power over the simple college boys.

He slid down the wall and crouched next to her so they were on the same eye level. "I'm Tom," he said.

"Tulie."

"Want a beer, Tulie?"

She held up her empty can of diet Coke. "Diet Coke," she said, and he took it away. The Elise and Rebecca team had split up, Rebecca getting cozy with some nerd on the sofa. Elise still had a round of groupies.

Tom came back with a fresh drink and crouched down again. But Tulie didn't feel like talking. She drank her soda and got up to leave.

He walked her back to her dorm and got her phone number.

It felt good to be pursued by somebody normal for a change, she thought. He wasn't greasy or full of tattoos. He wasn't a short-haired woman with a stocky build. He seemed like a nice guy, just exactly the type of guy she'd want to bring home to meet her parents. Now if she had been living with *him* when her parents came to visit . . .

He called her the next day, and they went out for pizza. He never made any of the classic moves on her. He didn't try any of the juvenile moves on her either. They just went out, ate a pizza, went to a coffee place for cappuccino, had a few laughs and then he brought her back home.

A sure way to get under a girl's skin. Make no moves.

He made her feel good about herself, and she liked that. She was beginning to like him. A lot. They began to see each other regularly.

In the meantime, Tulie had actually met the Elise and Rebecca duo. They lived on the same floor in the same dorm. Tulie had dinner with them in the cafeteria a couple of times and they talked about Elise's idea of going up to Bend to a cowboy bar.

Elise wasn't Tulie's idea of friend material, but there was something magnetic about Rebecca, little, fragile, wide-eyed, innocent freshman Rebecca, that Tulie found irresistible. Tulie's interest was piqued, and she found that she said things to try to make Rebecca laugh. Tulie found herself trying to impress Rebecca. Rebecca responded, and Tulie found herself gushing and blushing like a freshman herself. She couldn't believe it.

Every day she vowed she wouldn't see Rebecca again; she didn't want to have anything to do with that part of herself, but every day she found herself lingering where she thought Rebecca might show up, and when she did, Tulie found out more about her schedule, so they could spend more time together.

If she admitted it to herself, she would have to say she was smitten. But of course, she would never do that.

Then one night over a cafeteria salad Rebecca announced that the long-discussed trip to Bend would take place the next weekend, and then she innocently put her cool, tiny, long-fingered hand over Tulie's. "Want to come with us?" she said.

Tulie blushed and quickly pulled her hand back and put it in her lap.

Tulie saw Elise kick Rebecca under the table; that made her smile and increased the attractiveness of a trip that sounded like a good time anyway. She wouldn't mind spending an evening playing tug-of-war with Elise over Rebecca. The timing was perfect because Tommy had to go to Seattle for a job interview and he'd be gone all weekend.

Cowboys. Circle dancing. Rebecca in a cowgirl outfit.

Tom was fun, but Tulie was ready for a good party. This trip, even if it did include Elise, sounded like just exactly what Tulie needed.

"Sure," she said, and she looked squarely at Elise's scowl and smiled.

"TOMMY?" TULIE SAID. "TOMMY, I THINK I'M GOING to be sick."

Buck roused as if from some strange dream. "Songster," he said, and his voice sounded like somebody else's, coming from some other world. He wasn't even sure that he'd spoken, but the Songster was already opening the door so the girl could hang her head out to puke.

Buck wondered if he'd been sleeping. He looked over at Niles, who calmly smoked a cigarette and blew the smoke out in a straight stream. Then Buck turned his head again and looked out into the darkness.

What a weird night.

The girl kakked up her dinner and her tequila, heaved a few more times, then the Songster hauled her in and closed the door.

"It's snowing," she said, but nobody answered her. "Come to me, Tommy," she said, pulling the Songster over on top of her.

"Who do you think she means, 'Tommy'?" Niles whispered.

"Don't know," Buck said.

"Think that's the Songster's real name?"

"Don't know," Buck said.

"I bet it is." Niles leaned close, spoke furtively. "I bet that's what he meant when he said 'she knows.' Remember he said that?"

"I remember," Buck said. The Songster didn't look like any Tommy that Buck ever knew before. He looked like more of a . . . well, hell, Songster fitted him just about perfect. He probably had another name, but that was between the Songster and city hall.

"Gimme a smoke." The Songster's face appeared between them, startling Buck.

"Hey, Songster," Niles said. "You don't smoke."

"Gimme one anyway."

Niles fished a crumpled cigarette out of a crumpled pack. "Is Tommy your real name?"

"No."

"Oh."

"Ain't that a new pack of cigarettes?" the Songster asked.

"Yeah."

"How come this one's all squished flat?"

Niles looked at the wrinkled pack. "I don't know. They just always are." He took one out for himself, then lit a match.

The Songster drew in on the cigarette, then blew the smoke out. He coughed. "Yuck." He rolled down his window and threw the butt out. "God, how can you do that?" He spit. "Fuck."

"Jeez," Niles whined. "You wasted one."

Tulie sat up, brushing her hair out of her eyes. "Tommy?" she said.

"Ain't nobody here named Tommy, honey," Niles said.

Tulie remembered where she was. "Oh, yeah," she said, still a little disoriented. "Hi." Had she been sleeping? Had she dreamed about Tommy?

Tommy was in Seattle, she remembered, with a little twinge of homesickness. If Tommy hadn't gone to Seattle, she wouldn't have gotten in the car with Elise, and she wouldn't be here with these guys.

Stuck here in a car in a snowstorm in the middle of God knows where with three drunken lunatics. What in the hell had she been thinking?

Her heart began to pound as she groped for clarity of mind. She rolled down the window and scraped some snow off the roof of the car, then amid complaints from the guys, rolled it back up again and rubbed the snow on her cheeks, on her neck. She let some melt in her mouth, rolled down the window again, and spit it out.

She was beginning to get a glimpse of her situation. It was not pretty. She must have been insane. Or drunk.

No excuses, Tulie. Just keep your wits and get through this night.

"Have a nice nap?" Niles asked.

"I drank too much," she said, but the more she sat up and tried to be sober, the better she felt. "What are you guys doin'?"

"Playing a game," the Songster said.

"Yeah? You guys got anything to eat?" She was thinking about hamburgers. Or pizza.

Buck passed back the bottle of gin.

One whiff made her stomach lurch. "What's the game?" She passed it over to the Songster and tried to settle as far away from him as she could.

"We were trying to figure out what to do with your body after we murdered you," Niles said.

Tulie laughed, a brittle, hysterical sound. Nobody else laughed. A cold trickle ran through her veins. "Jesus, you're kidding, right?" *Tom's in Seattle*, she thought. *Elise is a bitch. How long before anybody would miss me? How long would my body rot in this forest before anybody even knew I was gone?*

"Right," Buck said. "It was stupid. It was just a stupid game. A drunk's game, you know?"

Tulie felt sudden affection for Buck. Affection for Buck and intense relief. She'd played stupid, useless games before. "Yeah, I know. Wow. For a minute there . . ."

"So here's the new game," the Songster said, and his voice had that flat quality again, that creepiness. "First, before we ditch the body, we've got to know how we're going to kill her."

"Wait. Hold on. This is not a good game. Nope." Tulie's heart began to flutter again as she realized how desperately powerless she was in this situation. She needed to have an ally. A buddy. She needed to be one of the guys, and *soon*. Buck. Buck had common sense, and Tulie had brains. "Have you already worked out how to get rid of my body?"

"No," Buck said.

"We were still working on it," Niles said.

"Well, let's change the game. You guys are going at it all backwards. First we have to figure out the murder. Then, usually, the disposal of the body suggests itself."

"Good," Niles said.

"*If* this is just a game, then I suggest we murder the Songster," Tulie said slowly, turning the attention away from herself and reasonably confident that they'd never hurt one of their own. "He's not much good. Are you?"

A grunt from the Songster, as if she'd punched him in the belly.

"I don't know," Niles said. "We're all pretty tight."

"I'm the outsider, right?" Tulie asked, trying to appeal to them without being too intellectual.

"Yeah," Niles said.

"Well, that makes it all the more important that we plan it right, do it right, and don't get caught. See, if he's your friend, then we don't want him to die slow or painful, right? Not only that, but you guys don't need any alibi or anything if you kill me, but you do if you kill your friend. There's more to the game if we kill the Songster. It's more fun. It's more challenging." Tulie felt perspiration slide down the side of her face. She felt as if she were pitting her college-educated wits against a bunch of drunken apes, and her smarts wouldn't amount to a hill of beans if they really wanted to kill her.

"I don't know . . ." Niles said. "It don't seem right, planning on how to kill our friend."

"It's just a game, right?" Tulie asked.

"Right . . ." Niles didn't sound too sure.

"Okay," she said, feeling a little control. "For a game to be really good, it's got to be like for real. Like in Monopoly, if you think it's just a game, then it's not worth playing just to exchange little colored pieces of paper, but if you really *believe* for a little while that it's money, then that makes the game, right?"

"Well, yeah." It sounded as if Niles were beginning to come around. Thank God for speech classes, psychology classes, forensics . . .

"Okay," she said, liking the fact that she sounded very sober, very lucid, and not at all scared when her heart was pounding so furiously she had a hard time catching her breath, "here's the deal. The game is: We're going to kill the Songster and get away with it. Rule number one. We never again refer to this as a game. Okay?"

"I don't know, Songster, what do you think?" Niles asked.

"C'mon, Niles," Buck said. "What do *you* think?"

Attaboy, Buck, Tulie thought.

"I think this girl's got some funny ideas."

"Oh," Tulie said, trying to sound righteously indignant, "but it's all right for you guys to talk about killing me?"

"Well, all right," Niles said.

"Go," Buck said.

The camping feeling came again over Buck. They were having a good time after all. The Songster got laid, and by a feisty one, too. There were games and camaraderie. . . . it was okay. Nobody was going to get hurt; the Songster wasn't going to hurt the girl; it was going to be just fine.

"Okay," she said. "Who has an idea?"

"Hey, hey, hey, I know a joke," Niles said. "I need gin to tell it."

Tulie grabbed the bottle from the silent Songster and passed it up to the front seat. Niles took a drink. "There was a Japanese, a German, and a Polack got captured by the Arabs and sentenced to die." He spoke too fast, with not enough inflection to tell a good story. He sounded like a sixth grader. "They were given a choice, they could be shot, have their heads cut off or get injected with AIDS. The Japanese guy said they could cut his head off, the German said they could shoot him, and the Polack said he wanted to be injected with AIDS. So they took him out first, injected him, and he went back to the cell. The other two said, 'Jesus, man, that is the *worst* way to die.' And the Polack smiled and said, 'The joke's on them. I'm wearing a condom.' "

Buck laughed. "That's great, Niles. That's really good. Here. Gimme the gin."

Tulie had heard it before. She kept the pressure up. "Okay then, shall we infect the Songster with AIDS?"

"Maybe you already did," Niles said.

Or he infected stupid me, Tulie thought with a bowel-disturbing twitch. "Yeah, maybe. He won't know for a while, though, will he?"

The Songster fidgeted.

"So," she said. "What other weapons do we have on hand?"

"The bottle," Niles said.

"Too precious," Buck said. "Tire iron."

"Rock," Niles said.

"Tree limb," Buck said.

"Car," Tulie said.

"I've got a knife," the Songster said quietly, and everybody fell silent.

"Nah," Niles finally said. "Let's see it."

"No," Buck said. "I don't want to see it. If you have a knife, Songster, you just keep it hid."

"Just thought I ought to mention it."

Tulie pushed herself as far toward the car door as she could. She swallowed hard. Moisture collected in the inner corner of her eye, and she wiped at it. Tears or perspiration? She didn't know. The last thing she needed to know was that this guy had a knife. "Oooh, a knife. Nice and bloody. The victim's own knife. And the way he said it, you know that it's no pocketknife. You guys are really good. Well. Are we going to kill him with his own knife?"

"Could," Niles said. "But that's kind of . . . I don't know."

"Lacks imagination," Buck said.

"Yeah. It would be rude," Niles said.

"We could use it, though." Tulie egged them on.

"Yeah," Niles said. "We could hold it on him to make sure he did what we told him to do."

"What would we tell him to do, kill himself?" Buck asked.

"Hey, that's a good idea," Niles said. "We'd tell him to kill himself or we'd cut his balls off. And he would. He wouldn't want to live without his balls, would you, Songster?"

The Songster was silent.

This is not a good game, Buck thought. "Maybe the Songster mentioned the knife because he'll use it if we try to kill him. Maybe we ought to talk about something else because *I* sure as hell don't want to get knifed by the Songster. I believe he'd really do it, too."

"Fuckin' A," the Songster said.

"So we'll have to put him out of commission quick, before he can get to his blade," Tulie said.

"Well, you're the only one in the position to do that," Buck said, and it sounded as if he were getting involved in the game when he really didn't want to, didn't mean to, meant, instead, to put an end to this discussion.

"How would you suggest I overpower him?" she asked.

"Leverage," Niles said.

"Cuddle up to him and get his ear in your teeth," Buck said, laughing. "And if he moves, bite it off." Why the hell didn't he just say he didn't want to play anymore?

"Better yet, get your teeth around his Homer," Niles said, "and if he believes you'd bite it off, he wouldn't give you no trouble."

"His *Homer*?" Buck said. Everybody laughed.

"And then what?" Tulie asked. No way was she going to get any closer to the Songster than she was. No way.

"Then Niles ties his feet together with his belt," Buck said. "And I bust his fingers so he can't use his hands, and then we drag him right the fuck out of my car before anything else happens."

"Break his fingers," Tulie said. "That's good."

Niles lit a cigarette. "So far, so good. But how do we actually do the killing?"

"You mean, *who* will do the killing?" Tulie asked.

"Yeah, I guess that's what I mean."

"Who hates him the most? Who has the best motive?" Tulie asked.

"I don't hate him," Buck said. "He's a friend."

"A friend?" Tulie asked. "Hmm. You three don't act much like friends, not really."

"What do you mean?" There was a note of hysteria in Niles's voice. He *needed* to act like a friend. He needed to be a friend; he needed to have friends. Friends and loyalty are what life is all about.

"I don't know. You all seem to mistrust each other." Tulie knew she had hit on something.

"Well," Buck said, "I don't trust the Songster because I think he's a liar. And I don't mistrust Niles; I just mostly don't trust his judgment."

"What about you, Niles? Do you trust the Songster?"

"Sure, I think so, well, maybe if Buck doesn't trust him. I don't know, Buck, why do you think the Songster's a liar?"

Buck turned the key in the ignition and hit the windshield wipers. They moved the powdery snow off in big arcs. He killed both switches. Then he turned around in his seat and faced the shadow of the Songster in the backseat.

"You know that woman didn't leave on her own, Songster. You lied to me about that."

"Yes," the Songster said in that terrible Clint Eastwood voice. "I lied to you about that."

"What do you mean? Buck, what does he mean?" The hysteria in Niles's voice grew.

Buck turned back around in his seat and clutched the steering wheel. He wanted to be right, and now that he was, he felt terrible.

"Buck? Songster? What's happening here?" Niles was on the verge of whining. He couldn't stand having his best friends fighting.

"Yeah, c'mon, guys. Give up the mystery," Tulie said. The pressure in her chest had eased as the pressure on the Songster had grown.

Buck white-knuckled the steering wheel and ignored them. Let the Songster tell them.

But the Songster was typically, maddeningly, infuriatingly silent.

Buck took a deep breath. He was just about to tell them when the Songster finally spoke.

"Buck thinks he knows some things, but he's wrong."

Buck gritted his teeth.

"Buck?" Niles seemed to be pleading.

"I know what I know, Niles, and I saw what I saw," Buck said.

"Hmm," Tulie said. She felt events beginning to spin out of her control, and she didn't think that was necessarily a good thing. She wanted to bring them back on track. "This adds a little dimension to our project. Buck has a motive, or at least if he doesn't have a motive, he doesn't have a reason to *prevent* the Songster's murder. Right, Buck?"

Buck pounded on the steering wheel. "Any of that gin left?"

Niles handed him the bottle. He spun off the top, felt it fly off toward Niles, and he drank. The anger was building up in him so slow, so strong, so heavy that he felt he was going to bust. And he didn't even know what he was angry about, except that there were people like the Songster in this world, dirty people, bad people, and they were allowed to get along, side by side, with normal folks, with regular folks, with decent folks. It pissed him off. It pissed him off bad.

"Tension's pretty hot in here," Tulie said.

"Shut the fuck up," the Songster said.

Without thinking, Buck whipped around in the seat, knocking Niles on the side of the head with the gin bottle. He grabbed the front of the Songster's shirt and pulled him up until their faces were inches away. "You're shit," Buck said. He threw him back into his seat, turned around, and fumed.

Tulie shrank back into the corner of the seat. She'd gone too far. She had wanted to take the spotlight off herself, and she had done that, sort of, but now something else was brewing in this car. Something worse. Something smoldering was about to burst into flame, and when it exploded, she didn't want any of it to get on her.

That damned Elise. This was all her fault. *We should be trying to figure out how to kill her*, Tulie thought.

ELISE SLAMMED HER FIST ON THE FROZEN STEERING WHEEL so hard she thought she could have broken a couple of bones. She pumped the accelerator and turned the key again. Nothing.

"What now, Elise?" Rebecca started to whine.

"It'll start," she said through clenched teeth.

But it didn't.

A tap on Rebecca's window. It was her friend, Dennis. He opened the door and stuck his head in. "Got trouble?"

"Yes—" Rebecca began.

"No," Elise said quietly. "It'll start. It always does."

Rebecca began to shiver more violently.

"Here, hon," the boy said, and handed her his jacket. Then he went around to the front of the car. "Pop the hood," he said, and motioned with his hands.

With a growl Elise pulled the handle that unlatched the hood. He lifted it and was lost to view. Elise's long nails tapped on the wheel. Her breath plumed out like dragon smoke.

"Try it now," he called.

Nothing.

More tinkering. "Now."

Nothing.

He lowered the hood and came around to her door. He had his hands stuck in his pockets, and he was dancing with cold. "I'm going to go see if Ross is inside. He's good with cars. He'll be able to fix it." He smiled across Elise at Rebecca. "Warm enough, hon? Want to come wait inside?"

Elise wanted to eat glass.

Rebecca took a nervous look at Elise before answering. "No, I'll stay here. I'm okay."

"Be right back."

They both watched him go back into the building. Rebecca shivered. "Maybe we ought to go inside," she said.

"No."

"What's the matter with you, Elise? Haven't you had a very good time?"

Elise looked over at Rebecca. Rebecca's eyes didn't line up; she was too drunk. "No, Rebecca, I've had a shitty time, and I want to go home."

Rebecca opened the door and stepped out. "Well, I'm going in where it's warm. Dennis'll need his coat if he comes back out."

Elise watched her go, then sat in the cold dark car by herself. No way was she going to give her keys to some bozo cowboy. She sat there, her anger warming her up.

In a few minutes Dennis reappeared, wearing his jacket, leading two other cowboys. All three had brown beer bottles in their hands. They walked over to the Camaro and lifted the lid, without even looking inside at Elise. She sat, helpless, impotent, furious. They messed around and messed around, with her turning the key every time they told her to.

One of them went to another truck and brought back tools.

Elise was not happy about that. It increased her anxiety 1,000 percent. She got out of the car and went around to see what they were doing.

"What's up?" she said.

"Looks like your electrical system is shot," the big cowboy with the wrench said. "The alternator isn't getting any juice."

"Dead battery?" she said.

"Nope. Battery's got plenty of kick." He pointed at a ganglion of wires. "This system didn't just die. It rotted away." He moved back from the car and looked her up and down. "Where do you girls live?"

"Eugene."

"Eugene! What the hell are you doing way up here?"

"They came to have a good time, idiot," Dennis said, and the three men laughed.

"Yeah, well, it's not such a good time after all, is it?"

The big cowboy with the wrench moved toward her and lifted his arm as if to put it around her. Elise moved out of his way.

"Well," he said, "no matter how you slice it, you ain't going nowhere tonight."

"What?"

"Nobody's going to look at this car at this time of night in this cold. Mechanic I know opens his shop tomorrow around nine."

"Nine." Elise's mind began to whirl. There had to be another way. "Just exactly what is wrong here?"

"Near as I can figure." The cowboy got his arm around her and pulled her close. She let him. He smelled like some sweet cologne. They bent over the engine, and he tapped something with the end of the wrench. "This is bad. Need a new one. Until then you ain't going nowhere."

Options. Elise needed time to consider her options.

"Let's go back inside and I'll buy you a beer," he said. He lowered the hood, latched it, then led the way back into the bar. "I'm Ross," he said. "What's your name?"

"Elise."

"Elise. Fine name. Fine name." He held the door open for her, then shouldered through the crowd to a table. Rebecca reappeared and attached herself, squinty-eyed, to Dennis's side. "Somebody get Elise here a beer," Ross said, and within minutes she had one.

She sipped it and studied him. He was big, with short cut brown hair. He had nice brown eyes and a wide-open mid-western face. His teeth were clean and even and straight, and if he'd lost maybe twenty, thirty pounds and got rid of the chins, he'd be downright gorgeous. He wore a tan Stetson and a blue and turquoise plaid flannel shirt under his down vest. The shirt strained at its snaps close to his belt buckle. He wore what looked like new jeans and black lizard-skin boots. Big man. Big, gorgeous man. The kind of man that under different circumstances, Elise would have liked to have picked her up and carried her off to Nirvana. Maybe for a whole weekend.

"You belong to Triple A?" Dennis asked.

Elise nodded.

"That's no good," Ross said. "Same guy tows for Triple A owns the mechanic shop. He ain't going to come here and fix the car. Best he'd do is tow it to his garage, where he'd work on it in the morning."

"What are we going to do, Elise?" Rebecca was still whining.

"Is there a hotel?"

"There's a Motel Six and a couple of fancier ones," Dennis said.

Elise looked at Rebecca and shrugged. "No choice, huh? Well, we'll have to stay over, I guess."

Rebecca looked up at Dennis, and they grinned at each other. "All right!" he said.

Elise grabbed Rebecca's arm and stood up. "Can I see you for a minute?"

Rebecca's eyes hadn't quite focused before Elise started walking toward the women's room, pulling a stumbling Rebecca along behind her. It was getting late; the bar was thinning out. They slammed into the rest room, and Elise pinned Rebecca up against the wall.

"Listen," she said, "that cowboy is not going with us. You and I are sleeping in one motel room, and there will be only the two of us, do you understand?"

Rebecca began to giggle. Elise felt her blood boiling. In frustration, she let go and turned away. Rebecca began to laugh and slide down the wall. "I hate this place," Elise said. "I hate this bar. I hate this town."

"Then why did you come here?" A woman Elise hadn't noticed was combing her hair in front of a mirror.

Elise ignored her. "C'mon," she said to Rebecca. "Let's go find a place to sleep."

Rebecca held her hand out for Elise to help her up. She was still laughing. Elise pulled her up and then left the women's room, made a beeline through the cowboys and smoke back to the table. Dennis and Ross had their cowboy hats tipped together as they talked about something.

"Here they are," Dennis said with a smile.

Elise found herself flirting with him as she slid onto her chair.

"Dennis," Elise said, "can you give us a ride to that motel?"

"Sure," Dennis said. "But we have to take Ross's truck."

"Why?"

"Because Dennis came with me," Ross said. "But it isn't far away."

"Okay," Elise said, and stood.

"Just relax," Ross said. "I'm not finished with my beer yet."

Rebecca sat down on Dennis's lap, and they began to kiss. Elise rolled her eyes and tried to be patient. She ought to be worried, but she wasn't. She had her wits, and she was no dummy. She also had long fingernails, fast feet, and that revolver. She wasn't worried. She was just pissed.

Ross finished his beer and another one after that. He seemed to enjoy himself, the music, Dennis and Rebecca making out, Elise fuming by his side. He just seemed to want to kick back, put one cowboy boot up on an empty chair, hook one thumb in that big silver belt buckle, and swig his beer, Elise and her green dress ornamental at his side. He was in control, he was the big shot, and everybody had to dance to his tune.

Elise endured it, but she wasn't going to dance to it. She couldn't believe she had found him attractive. She hated guys like this. Power trippers. Assholes.

Eventually he swallowed his last, belched, put a big linebacker's hand on her thigh, and said, "Well, I reckon it's time we hit the road."

Elise already had her coat on. She stood up and slung her purse over her shoulder. She watched Ross carefully as they made their way out of the bar yet again. He walked all right. He seemed sober enough to drive. It was a good thing Dennis wasn't driving. He and Rebecca were holding each other up.

Ross unlocked the passenger side of his big Chevy pickup and Elise climbed in. Her naked thighs stuck to the frozen seats. She moved over on the bench seat, and Dennis got in beside her and pulled Rebecca up and into his lap. Ross climbed in, big and warm on the other side.

"The nearest motel will be just fine," Elise said.

He started the engine, then turned on the lights and the

heater, which blasted frigid air onto their legs. Rebecca squealed. He backed out of the lot too fast, bouncing them over the frozen ruts, then turned right.

The town was deserted. Its stoplights looked eerie changing for nobody in the winter night. Elise saw the Motel 6 sign a couple of blocks ahead; if she'd known it was that close, she'd have walked there.

"There," she said to Ross. "Motel Six."

They drove right by.

Elise sighed and took a firm grip on her emotions. "Where are we going?" she asked.

No response.

Rebecca giggled, and Dennis whispered something else to her.

Elise took a deep, exasperated breath.

Ross kept driving, through darkened neighborhoods, where houses sat close together, and then out into farm country, where animals looked like dark rocks littering the pastures, and huge rolls of hay looked like strange, round, snow-covered sheds.

Elise realized that she hated Oregon. She'd be safer in a big city, where there were people all around. Nice people. City people. People who wore suits to work. Professional people. Good Lutheran Minnesotans. Like at home. Minneapolis. What the hell made her think she wanted to move to Oregon?

They kept driving, farther and farther into the countryside, past a feed store, past a little country store, past stands of trees that might be postcard beautiful another time. In the daylight. In the Camaro.

Then miles and miles of snow fields. No lights, no houses, no streetlights. Only the eerie light that seemed to come from the snow itself.

Finally Ross slowed the truck, turned at a rock covered with red reflectors and drove up the long gravel driveway of a little farmhouse with no discernible neighbors. A woodpile stood between the house and the barn. Sheep milled about in the barnyard, quietly watching them. A black-and-white dog stood up on the porch, stretched, and walked over to the truck, wagging its tail.

"What is this place?"

"Home," he said. He parked the truck right in front, turned it off, and opened the door. He leaned over and scratched the smiling dog's head. "This here is Fletcher."

"Hi, Fletcher," Rebecca said.

Elise didn't know what to think or what to do.

Dennis opened his door and was trying to help Rebecca down on the ground without her falling out of the high cab.

Ross jumped out and held his hand out to help Elise.

"C'mon in," he said.

Up until the time Buck was four years old, his name was Don. Donald. Donald Dwayne Hanson. Up until the time Buck was nine years old, he had an identical twin brother, Ron. Ronald Wayne Hanson.

When the twins were four, their parents took them and their two older sisters from their nicely groomed two-story California neighborhood home to a family reunion in Oklahoma. They stayed in a run-down motel, and their parents argued the whole time. These were their mother's relatives, and dirt-poor, ugly relatives they were. On the Sunday afternoon that they were there, after sweltering it out in a church that smelled like sweat and old-lady perfume, the twins were cut loose to run off all their energy down by the river. The parents and all the weird cousins came down with potato salad and beans and macaroni salad. There was fried chicken, too, although Maizie, the twins' oldest sister, called it "some kind of fried animal," and none of the Hanson kids would eat it. So while the twins went running around, getting muddy on the riverbank and giggling to themselves about everything odd, one of their ugly Okie girl cousins came down to play with them.

Her presence was so odd they just stared at her. She was tall, and her legs were covered with scabs. Her hair was dirty, and they were mesmerized by this sight. They began to follow her around. Finally she announced to the group at large, "Lookee them young uns, just starin' with their fool doe-eyed faces."

"Buck-eyed," Maizie said. Maizie was old enough to know the difference between a buck and a doe.

"Huh?"

"Buck-eyed, not doe-eyed."

From then on they were known as the Buckeyes. They loved it. It was far better than being known as the twins. Don and Ron, the Buckeyes. Eventually they both became known as Bucky, and together as the Bucks.

The Bucks did everything together; they even fought with their mother to let them dress alike. Identical in almost every respect, right down to the freckles and the cowlicks, they enjoyed confusing people. They shared a bedroom, plans, opinions, everything. They planned to go through life together side by side, even marrying a pair of girl twins and living next door to each other.

After they'd been navy pilots.

After they'd seen the world. After they'd made all the money they'd ever need.

After they'd bought all the Lego in the world. And had a basement vault full of Butterfingers.

In the meantime, they were filled with the wonder and adventure of life and spent all their time with their heads together, discussing things. All things.

They discussed their sisters; they discussed their teachers, their parents, and the grasshoppers in the vacant lot across the street. There was much in that vacant lot to discover and discuss. There were friends and enemies. Bullies and sissies. They believed they could carve out their futures however they wanted, and they designed their lives over and over and over again as they discussed everything. There were no secrets; there were no private thoughts. Not between them anyway.

One morning when they were nine years old, in the third grade, Ronnie woke up crying. Don called his mother up to their room. She felt Ron's forehead, frowned, and told Don to go ahead and get ready for school. He ate breakfast with his dad and sisters while his mom called the doctor. He went to school, but he just stared out the window. He'd never been to school without Ronnie before. It wasn't the same.

When Don came home from school, his dad was home. Don's heart clutched in his chest. His dad was never home during the day. Never. His dad met him on the front porch with a very scary expression on his face, took Don's little hand in his big one, and they sat together on the living-room couch. Don knew the bad news; he just knew it.

But to hear his dad say it was so awful; it was the awfulest thing in the world. It was worse than anything he could ever hear in his life. He covered his ears. He screamed to keep from hearing the sound of his father's voice and that word *meningitis*, but his dad just hugged him, and eventually, they cried together.

Nobody missed Ron the way he did. They all said they did, but they didn't talk about him anymore, they just went on with their lives. Dad went to work, Mom made breakfast and cooked dinners, and it was as if the place Ronnie used to occupy had just sealed shut. They had excluded Ron from their lives, and that ignited the pilot light of anger in Don. It wasn't fair. He started having everybody call him Bucky again, the nickname that had fallen away when the boys started school, because that way, whenever anyone talked to him, they talked to both of them. He wanted Ronnie with him for the rest of his life, and that was one way he knew he could do it.

Buck made straight C's for the rest of his schooling. In high school he went back to the name Don, dated girls, and went to football games. He made both the JV and varsity wrestling teams, and the coach got him into the boxing ring a few times, but Don didn't like boxing very much. He got too carried away with it. He couldn't remember his moves when some-body started punching him, and he just wanted to retaliate. Rip. Tear. Hurt. Kill. *That's not sport,* his coach said, and that was the end of that. He went through the motions of life and school and finally graduated, but there was a hole in the world by his side, and its name was Ron.

Eventually the pain of losing half of his life lessened, and he thought less and less frequently about Ron. The weight of Ron's absence was always there, clinging thickly to his chest, but that weight became normal; it became a part of who Don was.

He went to a community college for a year, raised his grade

point average, and applied to Northwestern University in Chicago. To his surprise, he was accepted. He thought that getting out of California, getting away from the family he increasingly despised, would free him. But it didn't. He was still the same person. He was still trying not to do any of the things he and Ron had planned out for their lives. It would be bad if he did. To do those things by himself would make him a traitor.

In his junior year he met Cara Singleton, a nice girl, a pretty girl, a flirtatious girl who took charge of their relationship from their first date. Don was very willing to let Cara run their lives. She helped him with his study schedule; she made sure he went to the dentist, that he wrote to his parents, that he paid his fees on time. Instead of going home during the summer, he and Cara got an apartment and stayed in Chicago.

Midway through his senior year she began to make wedding plans, and he did nothing to stop her. One night when her plans were reaching the point of no return, Don left the apartment alone and walked down to the Lake Michigan shore. He walked and skimmed stones over the water, trying to think, trying to sort things out.

In the end he decided he could do a lot worse than to go through life with Cara. He didn't love her the way she loved him, but she was a good woman, not prone to the silliness of most of her peers. She was a solid girl, with good sense, and she would make a good home for him. He would find work as a civil engineer, and she would be a fine wife.

When these things were settled in his mind, he went home satisfied, and she continued unabated, making plans for their future together.

He was graduated with a degree in civil engineering and went right to work for the Illinois State Highway Department.

The wedding took place, and all their relatives showed up. They took a three-day honeymoon in Wisconsin.

Cara continued her studies in journalism until the inevitable missed period.

Cara's excitement over the approaching birth matched the intensity of Don's fear. As long as it was just Don and Cara, there was freedom. There was freedom to pick up and drive to Indiana; there was freedom to move across country; there was freedom to quit his job and travel Europe . . . or any one of a zillion things. They could live like bums, and nobody would care. He could even go off by himself for a while if he wanted to, or needed to.

But a family! Bring a child in, and the whole idea changes. Now there had to be food and shelter and clothing of a particular standard. This was lifetime responsibility. In his mind was the horror of a little carbon copy of the family he had grown up in: two girls, twin boys, and parents in charge of the family grief—a grief they wouldn't share. A family that couldn't share anything but the outward image of perfection while the infrastructure rotted.

Don felt the walls closing in on him, and he didn't know what to do. He hadn't meant for Cara to get pregnant; she hadn't meant it either. It was an accident. He was not prepared. But she slipped into motherhood preparation as easily as he had slipped into her that night without a rubber, and he found that he couldn't even voice his fears to her.

They would lie awake at night, holding hands, staring at the ceiling, and Cara would go on and on about the baby, and Don's chest would tighten until he could barely breathe. It was all he could do to stay in bed and listen.

But he managed. And when the child was born, he was there, in the delivery room, loving Cara. She had worked so hard for this child he was ashamed of his feelings.

And when he held his newborn son, something like the winding of a clock took place in his chest. A Hanson child. His child. Grandchild of his parents', nephew of Ron's, an actual living piece of his own flesh. He was awed. And instantly devoted.

And sometime that first day of the baby Cara mentioned that since Don and Ron had been genetically identical, this baby was as much Ron's as it was his.

They named him Kaiser Ronald. Don found a new purpose in life. He worked for his son. He was eager to go to work, eager to advance, eager to provide well, eager to have his son respect him. And when the day was finished, he couldn't get home fast enough to bathe him, feed him, change him, play with him, stare at him.

When Kaiser was walking, Cara threw away Don's condoms. For a week Don just held her in bed, while he considered the next step. He was following in his father's footsteps. Did he want that? No, but he didn't want Kaiser to grow up an only child either. His greatest childhood memories were of him and Ron together. So one night, as if the decision had made itself, he began to stroke her side, and nine months later they had Cecelia Karen.

They should never have had the second one. Again Don was overwhelmed by the responsibility of it all, and while he adored his baby girl, he somehow didn't have the time to devote to both of them, so he didn't devote much time to either of them. He began to resent them, and he hated himself for those feelings.

Cara was mystified. She talked to him at night, gently, letting him know that she loved him and the children loved him, no matter what. All he had to do was keep himself safe and happy and the family would be just fine. "Take care of yourself," she kept saying to him. "Get what you need. Take care of yourself."

But that was easy for her to say. She didn't have to deal with the State of Illinois Department of Transportation. She didn't have to face the errors that he made because he was distracted trying to figure out how he was going to keep a check from bouncing because they were living beyond their means. She didn't have to work with a boss who was increasingly becoming a son of a bitch. She didn't have to commute every day. She didn't have to spend eight hours a day with fiendish coworkers who would stab him in the back in a minute if it would further their careers and with the slacker career civil servants who did the least work possible in order to get by in their secure jobs.

Every day at the office Don's sense of fairness was compromised, and he hated it.

Don spent his life hating his job, resenting his children and loving his wife, longing for the simpler times when he and she could just run off together for the weekend without a worry.

She said she understood, but she didn't, not really. She just stayed at home, playing with the children.

And then one night, after they'd gone to bed, she turned to him. "I talked with your mother today."

"Oh?" That was odd.

"She told me something peculiar."

"What?"

Cara snuggled up to Don's side. He put his arm around her and loved the feeling of her cradled next to him. "She said that you used to want to have everything even between you and Ron. And if it couldn't be perfectly even, that you didn't want any."

Don smiled. He remembered. He remembered throwing tantrums over things not being even between them.

"Honey?"

"Hmm?"

"Do you think you need to be even between Kaiser and Cecelia? And that if you can't be, you don't want to spend time with either one of them?"

"No, I don't think so." But Don's face got hot. "How did you happen to talk to my mom?"

"I called her."

Don sat up in bed, upsetting the cuddle. "Why?"

"Because I'm pregnant again."

Don was speechless.

"And I think you're going to leave us."

He never thought it, he never *really* thought it, until she gave voice to it. He *was* going to leave them, he knew it. Cara and his two—three babies. Cara, whose face was more familiar to him than his own, Cara, his lover, his friend, his sweetheart. Cara, who knew him better than any other person ever could. He was going to walk out on her and their children.

Torment raged inside him. He couldn't reassure her, he couldn't say anything. He swung his feet out of bed and pulled on a pair of sweatpants, then went out to the kitchen and popped open a beer.

He could hear her crying in the bedroom, and no matter what foul names he called himself, he couldn't make himself go back in there. He was a coward, and he hated himself.

He sat at the kitchen table in the dark, drinking the beer, for a long time. Then there were cool hands on his shoulders, and she kissed the top of his head. He leaned his head back into her soft stomach, into the baby growing inside.

"How?" he asked. "We're careful."

She sighed. "I don't know, Buck," she said, and the use of that name settled his soul. She massaged cool fingers across his hot forehead. "I feel like saying I'm sorry, but it's not my fault, and I'm really not sorry."

Don felt those fingers work their tension-melting magic. He *was* sorry. He was sorry all the way through his soul.

"Will you stay with me until the baby comes?" she whispered.

He nodded, then brought her around to sit on his lap. She hugged his head, he hugged her, and while neither one of them understood what forces were shaping their lives, they accepted them as forces beyond their control.

The knowledge that he was leaving became a clear glass box around Don. The children changed from normal, joyous children to creatures that were either solemn-eyed and quiet or shrieking, desperate for his attention. He tried to act as if nothing were different, but he couldn't fool them.

His heart ached for Cara. She went about quietly making arrangements for herself and the children. She didn't include him in any of the plans; she asked him no questions, she never asked his advice or opinion. He ceased to exist as a part of her future and therefore was only a temporary inconvenience as a part of her present.

A million times he wanted to take it all back, to heal everything, have his Cara and his children back, but even as the words were on the tip of his tongue, he felt the call of freedom, the unwrapping of his bonds, and he knew it was mere months away. He wanted Cara, but he didn't want the package she came with, even though he'd given it to her.

He died thousands of little deaths. Every time Kaiser asked a "will you someday" question, Don lied to him. Every time Kaiser wanted to make a long-range plan, like going to Disneyland, or talked about the family when the baby was born, Don wanted to cry.

But he maintained. He kept his job at the highway department, he paid the rent, he added to his retirement account. He did everything he had always done.

One day in March he received a call from his neighbor. Cara had fallen. They had taken her by ambulance to the hospital. He was needed.

He dropped his pencil, grabbed his coat, told his secretary, and drove like a maniac to the hospital. He was so scared. He was so afraid. He must have been crazy to want to leave her, he loved her so much, he loved her *so* much!

The admitting clerk directed him, and a nurse coming out of her room met him as he was about to go in. "Mr. Hanson?" He nodded. "A moment, please?"

Don calmed himself while the nurse had the obstetrician paged. He sat on the edge of the chair in the waiting room, wanting to see Cara, dying to see Cara, wanting to know if she was all right, but the nurse wouldn't tell him anything.

Finally the doctor arrived. "Mr. Hanson," he said, looking official with a lab coat over a shirt and tie, "I'm Dr. Ambrose."

Don stood up. They shook hands, then sat down on the plastic couch.

"Your wife took a terrible fall. She was carrying Cecelia down the steps, apparently, and tripped. The little girl is downstairs in the pediatric wing. We're taking a look at her, but it seems as if she only got a bump on the head, a bruised arm, and a scare."

Cecelia. Don hadn't even known she was involved. His heart pumped for his baby girl.

"Cara?"

"Cara's another story. We're trying like crazy to save the baby, Mr. Hanson, but to tell you the truth, I don't think we're going to, and it's not far enough along to survive outside the womb. She took a hell of a tumble, you have to understand. She's got a broken arm, and she's in a lot of pain. We dare not give her too much pain medication because we don't know the internal damages yet."

"Can I see her?"

"Yes, for a short—"

A nurse ran around the corner, her heavy breasts bouncing wildly in her white uniform. "Dr. Ambrose?"

The doctor turned.

"It's Cara Hanson," she said, and from the look on her face, Don knew it was not good news.

Both men rose. "Stay here," the doctor said, and Don wanted to scream. Now he knew what it meant to pace in a waiting room.

Two hours later he was holding Cara's pale hand in her hospital room. She'd lost the baby, her arm had been splinted, and she'd been shot up with Demerol until she was woozy and barely conscious. She was conscious enough to cry, and she held on to Don's arm and sobbed.

He cried, too, giving vent to terrible pain, a deep well of shame.

When she had gone to sleep, he went down to the gift shop, bought Cecelia a stuffed elephant, and took it to her. She grinned when she saw him, and he played with her for a while. The nurse told him the bandage on her head was just covering a scrape, and it didn't appear there was anything to worry about. She thought Cecelia would go home the next morning.

Don went home and fixed dinner for himself and Kaiser. Kaiser slept with him that night. He wiggled and wiggled until Don held him close.

Cecelia came home the next day, but Cara was in the hospital for a week. The internal damage was minor, but the broken arm required surgery and a metal plate bolted to both good ends of the bone. It would take at least eight weeks in a cast.

Don ran the household by himself, taking time off work, finding a sublime pleasure in seeing that the kids were clean and the house was together, that meals were nutritious and on time. It was a facet of his personality that he hadn't known existed, and he liked it.

But it was only for a week or so.

When Cara came home, she was weak and gaunt and had dark circles under her eyes. He put her to bed and fed her chicken soup and corn muffins. He made her stay put for three days and let the kids in to sit on the bed and talk to her for only an hour twice a day. The fourth day she didn't ask his permission; she just got up and began to do for the family.

Don went back to work.

They didn't talk about it. They didn't talk about the fall—Don never found out what happened—they didn't talk about the baby; they didn't talk about the future. They didn't make love, and after she was healed, they didn't hold each other in bed anymore. She was preparing herself, he knew. He didn't blame her. And as much as he wanted to tell her that he'd changed his mind—as much as he wanted to tell her he'd stay with her, hold her, walk through life with her—he wasn't sure that he did, and until he could be *absolutely* sure, he wouldn't raise her hopes.

The cast came off. She was again fully self-sufficient. He knew she was self-sufficient because she never once said it was her fault that the baby died. She never once said it was his fault, although he felt as though it were.

The supervisor at work had singled Don out as a scapegoat for his own inadequacies.

The kids were shrill and messy.

Life was back to normal.

One night in bed Cara said, "We'll wait for you, you know. We'll always be here if you want to come back." He pulled her close, swallowed his unworthiness, and kissed her neck, buried his psyche in her maternal wisdom.

The next day he dressed for work, but instead of taking the car to the train station, he walked to the freeway on-ramp, stuck out his thumb and got a ride going west. He was too much of a coward even to say good-bye.

He took a succession of day jobs, invented a history, affected a country boy accent, bought a backpack and a sleeping bag. He slept out, mostly, finding showers here and there, taking a room during the winters. He didn't care much for the South, or the far North, and always headed west. California didn't suit him. It was too close to home, family, relations, commitments, expectations, responsibilities. He took back the nickname Buck, loving the anonymity it afforded. He circled Oregon and Washington a couple of times, ever resisting the impulse to send postcards to Cara and the kids.

He was surprised at the type of people he met on the road. He expected to find retarded, stupid, or brain-damaged people. Alcoholics. Drug addicts. Bums. But they all were people. They all longed for things that seemed to be out of reach. Many were highly principled; many were crooks. He felt an odd kinship with all of them, except for those who pined away for families. There were those who had lost their spouses to disaster or divorce, who cried for them, and talked incessantly about how lucky everybody else was to have a wife or kids. Those people made Buck nervous. He dared not confess to them because he knew he'd done wrong. He'd done Cara, his best friend, wrong. He'd done those adorable, helpless children wrong. He was a loser, a bad egg, a joke.

He was a winner only when he was with others whose sins matched or surpassed his own.

He embraced the code of honor they all lived by. It was an ask-no-questions code. It was a live-and-let-live code. Nobody blew the whistle on anybody else; nobody wanted to know anything about anybody, nobody told anything about anybody. It was a solitary existence, and it drove some of them a little bit nuts, but Buck dived into the anonymity and loved it.

And then he landed the painting job in Eugene, Oregon.

Niles zeroed in on him right away, and that was fine with Buck. Niles had a good heart, and he was loyal to the tooth. He also needed somebody to help him look after himself, and Buck fell easily and readily into that role. This was the perfect kind of responsibility to take. Help someone help himself. Not like kids. Kids were totally dependent, needy. Niles was just a little bit needy, and if Buck walked out of his life at any time, Niles would get along just fine.

Buck enjoyed Niles. Niles was sleeping in an abandoned car under the bridge. He was the one who knew about the night watchman who let him take showers at the mill at night.

Then came the Songster, needy in his own way. The Songster told the two of them about the boxcars—he could have told everybody, or nobody, but for reasons Buck never understood, he told only the two of them—and the three lived each to his own personal boxcar, almost like roommates in a very strange apartment house.

Buck knew that the Songster, too, sought out those whose sins paled his, and while Buck never told anyone about Cara—not until the camping trip anyway—the Songster knew that Buck had skeletons in his closet. Just as Buck knew about the Songster.

But the Songster was dirtier. Much dirtier.

BUCK JUMPED OUT OF THE CAR AND SLAMMED THE door. Snow fell softly, muting whatever sounds there could be out in the woods. He watched the moisture in his breath steam out and concentrated on steaming out all his anger.

He took deep breaths, the fresh air tasting faintly of something bad, like dogshit. Maybe he'd become so used to the nasty smell of the inside of the Pontiac that fresh air smelled bad. He smiled wryly to himself. That'd be just about right. Live in crap long enough, and it begins to feel like home.

He closed his eyes and leaned against the car. He felt the cold metal behind his back, felt the wet as the snow melted and soaked into his shirt and the top of his jeans. He took another deep breath and listened. He thought if he were blind, he would still know when it snowed. He could hear it. There was no other silence quite like it.

He opened his eyes and looked around. If it hadn't been so dark, he'd have walked down to the lake, watched the big flakes as they fell on the water, floated for a moment, and then smooshed out and became part of the lake. He always thought it was an odd sight, snow at the edge of water. A snow-covered beach. He remembered his whole family going out to the mountains in the winter so the California kids could play in the snow. He and Ronnie would crouch down next to a little trickle of a stream and watch it melt the snow. They'd set snowballs in the middle of it and watch the lacy patterns as the cold water slowly ate away the snowball.

Flakes fell on his eyelashes. He stuck out his tongue and caught a couple.

Snowballs.

He swiped a handful from the hood of the Pontiac and packed it tightly. His fingers began to feel the icy, wet cold through their insulation layer of alcohol, and he could visualize them turning red. When he got back into the car, they'd ache.

He remembered snow-crusted mittens and socks.

A snowball fight. He'd like to throw a snowball right into the Songster's stupid face. He'd like to bust his fucking nose.

He walked over to a tree, tucked the snowball up on a branch, and unzipped his pants. He emptied his bladder, and just as he finished, he heard the car door open.

"Oh, God," Tulie said. "It smells sane out here."

She stood with her back to him, arms out and face to the sky. He could hear her taking deep, ragged breaths. She took a few steps away from the car. He took his snowball from the tree, took careful aim, and whacked her right in the middle of the back.

She screeched, ducked, and a moment later a snowball came back over the car toward him. The darkness was an added handicap; Buck couldn't see the snowballs until they were almost to him. He scratched a couple together quickly and lobbed them over the car, then ducked and ran around the back of the car and to a tree behind.

He could see her still crouched next to the car, making snowballs and throwing them over the car. But he was behind her now, in perfect position for an ambush. He quietly put together an arsenal and piled them up by his tree. When he had a few, he attacked.

She screamed, that wonderful girlish trill, and ran around the nose of the car, but not before he'd nailed her at least four times.

Then the front passenger door opened. The sickly yellow interior light illuminated the filth and nastiness of the Pontiac that Buck had forgotten about. For a moment he and the girl had been little kids again, clean and pure and lost in the joy of a snowstorm in the woods. Then Niles stepped out, and Buck remembered that he was an adult, an adult with history and shame.

"Whatcha all doin'?" Niles asked as he lit up a cigarette.

A snowball sailed through the air from the front of the car and took the cigarette right out of his mouth.

"Hey! Ow!"

Buck started to laugh. God, she had a deadeye.

"I'm still the champ!" she shouted.

"Hey, shit, you hurt my lip."

The girl laughed at Buck's laughter, making Buck laugh harder.

"Hey," Niles said. "Not funny. Hey, who threw that?"

That made them laugh even harder, and soon the two of them were laughing at each other more than anything, and they heard Niles begin to chuckle as he wanted in on the joke, and that made them laugh harder yet. Tears ran out of Buck's eyes. He was weak and helpless, and it felt so good. God, that felt good.

"Hey, where are you guys?"

Tears ran down Buck's frozen cheeks. He could see Niles standing there, illuminated by the car's interior lights, hearing disembodied laughter in the woods. Buck picked up a snowball and threw it at Niles, hitting him in the arm.

"Hey!" He turned toward Buck.

Then the girl threw one that hit him in the back.

"Stop!"

Buck threw another and the girl threw another, and Niles jumped inside the car and slammed the door to get away from them.

Then the light was gone, that dirty yellow, that nicotine-tainted light that showed the ratty interior, the smelly carpeting, the rotten seats, the Songster.

The Songster.

The light wasn't gone for long. The Songster opened his door and got out, not even bothering to go to a tree before unzipping his pants and letting that used beer fly.

Buck lost his joy. So did the girl. He heard her footsteps crunch through the snow toward him. "That was fun," she said.

"Yeah," Buck said, and he began to feel protective and brotherly toward her. He wanted her to stay away from the Songster; he didn't want anything to happen to her, not here, not in his car, not ever. She was a bright girl with a good future, and he wanted to save her from the fucked-up kind of life he had led. He wanted to save her from the fucked-up kind of guy he was, the Songster was, Niles was.

She came closer, and he could smell her perfume as it steamed off her in the cold. She laid a hand on his arm. "Take me home," she whispered.

Some weird alarm went off in Buck's head. Something about women dividing men. Something about brothers sticking together no matter what. He realized that he and the Songster and Niles all had been friends before she came along, and suddenly he and the Songster were at each other's throats, and that didn't need to be. That didn't need to be. They could live in peace and harmony, and Buck could just turn his head away from the Songster whenever he needed to. He didn't need to judge the Songster. He couldn't. He'd never see this

ELIZABETH ENGSTROM

girl again, but he might be living and working with Niles and the Songster for a long time yet.

He shook her hand off his arm and said, "It's cold out here, I'm getting back in."

"Please," she said, her fingers digging into his throwing arm.

But Buck didn't want any women telling him what to do. *That's how it starts,* he thought. *You do something nice for them and suddenly the wheels are in motion. A guy gets ground to dust under one of those wheels.*

His attitude disgusted him.

"Get back in the car before you freeze." Buck bent down and scraped together a loose snowball. He tossed it casually over the top of the car, and it hit the Songster right on the back of the neck.

"Fuck," the Songster said, and turned around. He spotted them and ran toward them. The girl made some kind of sound and went running off into the woods. Buck stepped out of the way, and the Songster chased after her. They'd probably screw each other in a snowbank, he thought.

Buck snorted, walked back around the car, and got in, feeling as dirty as the Songster, as dirty as Niles and his cigarettes, as dirty as the yellow light of the broken-down Pontiac. He heard that girl squeal again, but it didn't sound the same. It ticked off another little alarm in his head, but he turned it off. He shut it down.

His heart pounded. He had had it within his power to help that girl, and he hadn't. Did that mean if the Songster hurt her that it was his fault?

Fuck.

He put his mind right off it. He tried to think they were playing in the snow, although the Songster wasn't exactly the playing-in-the-snow type of guy.

Buck wondered if they'd get snowed in here at the campground. He tried not to listen for the girl in case she was in trouble. Instead he listened to Ronnie in his memory as they lay on the top bunk of the rented cabin in the mountains, watching the snow fall.

"What if we get up and it's ten feet deep?"

"What if we get up and it's so deep we can't get out?"

"Yeah, can't push the door open."

"And the windows . . . We'd have to slide the window open and then dig out, tunnel out from the window up to the surface."

"The car'd be buried."

"We'd starve."

"Nah. We've got lots of food."

"But we'd be here until spring. We'd have to hunt."

"Set traps."

"Think Dad brought a gun?"

A gun. What a profound thought. It silenced them both as they wondered if their father had brought a gun and what it meant if he had and what it meant if he hadn't. If he had, he was a hero. If he hadn't, it meant his family would starve to death.

"Let's go ask."

They jumped down from the bunk beds and ran through the cabin and down the stairs to where their parents were talking quietly by the fire.

"Dad, Dad!" they both shouted. Each one wanted to be the first to ask the question.

"Did you bring a gun?" Ronnie asked.

"A gun?" Their father smiled. "No, why?"

"You *didn't?*" Suddenly he wasn't the protector they had always thought he'd be.

"No. I don't believe in guns. You boys know that."

"But in the wilderness . . ." Buck said.

"Survival . . ." Ronnie said.

Their parents laughed, and the boys put their tails between their legs and went back upstairs to bed.

Even today Buck thought his dad should have told them that he had guns, lots of guns, elephant guns and tiger guns and crocodile guns. All the guns they would ever need, but they were packed away safe and wouldn't be unpacked unless they were needed. That would have saved the vacation.

Instead the brothers were disappointed in the trip, in their parents, and maybe a little bit disappointed in life.

If Kaiser asked me a question like that, Buck thought, *I'd tell him the fantasy.*

But Kaiser would never ask a question like that because Buck had robbed him of that privilege.

Suddenly what his father had done on that snowy day seemed insignificant, compared with what Buck had done to Kaiser on this snowy day and every other snowy day since Buck had let his own personal yellow streak—uglier than any the Pontiac company had ever made—ruin the little boy's life.

TULIE SAW THE SONGSTER SPIN, AND SHE KNEW HE wasn't going to chase after Buck. She ran for the woods, hoping the Songster would lose interest. She could hide out there, flapping her arms and trying to stay warm, until morning.

But he kept after her.

Tell us about that woman.

She picked up the pace, grateful that she had been an athlete, because now she felt she was running for her life.

That woman didn't leave on her own.

Cowboy boots were not the best thing for running, but her strengths were youth and fear. She clomped through the snow, her breath rasping in her throat, which was still sore from throwing up all that beer and tequila and chips and stuff. It was hard to see; she had to be sure to pick her feet up high and keep moving.

I got a knife.

She ran down by the lake, the words echoing in her head, squirting adrenaline into her bloodstream. She could hear the Songster right behind her. She made a quick right turn into the thick of the woods, but it was too dark to see where she was going. She was afraid of falling and breaking a leg or something.

She had no game plan.

. . . what to do with your body after we murdered you.

She ran through some tangled undergrowth that brushed against her face and pulled at her clothes. She stopped and listened and tried to think. She'd get lost out here. She'd fall and break something. She had to get smart.

Her heart was hammering so loudly she thought the Songster would find her by following the sound. She listened and heard his footsteps coming along the lake path.

She hid around the rough-barked back side of a huge lodgepole pine and tried not to breathe hard. Light globes danced in front of her eyes as her lungs screamed for a deep breath. She wondered if her white blouse would give her away. To her eyes, it glowed.

The Songster was walking, and breathing hard as he caught up to her hiding spot.

. . . after we murdered you.

Tulie held her breath.

Before we ditch the body . . .

Tulie tried hard to believe she was blowing this out of proportion. Had anybody actually confronted her? Threatened her?

. . . we've got to know how we're going to kill her.

This Songster guy was bad news. She knew bad boys, but this guy was way out of her experience. He was really bad news. In a league of his own. No telling what he would do to her out here. He had a problem with women.

I got a knife.

He had a knife. She'd gotten drunk, gotten stupid, gotten loudmouthed, and now . . . now she'd put herself in just exactly the wrong place at the wrong time.

I'm the outsider, right?

He could just slit her open out here in the woods, where nobody was going to come until spring. Where he and those good old boys would just wisp away like dreams back into the underbelly of society.

He walked by.

Her heart began to slow down. Her breathing became more regular. She wished she had something to smash him on the head with, but she didn't, and she didn't want to take the time to look for something. Besides that, her hands were frozen, and she just wanted to get the fuck out of there.

She waited until he was a good distance past her. Then she took a deep breath and crashed back through the brush, stumbling and losing skin from her hands until she was on the trail by the lake again. Then she ran, full-tilt boogie, for the car. Those guys had to help her now. They would help her now.

The car loomed up out of the shadows. Tulie dashed with all she had left in her, ran around to the driver's side, jerked open the door, and squeezed in next to Buck, pushing him into the middle.

She fumbled for the keys, but Buck grabbed them out of the ignition and held them away from her, in front of Niles.

"He's trying to kill me," Tulie gasped.

"Kill you?" Buck said. "No, he's not."

Would you kill for me?

Tulie's heart tried to seize up. "He is, *he is*, let's get out of here, Jesus Christ, let's get out of here!"

She looked at Buck's face, just inches from her own, then at Niles's. They both showed the same disbelief. They thought she was nuts.

Then the Songster came up to the window, and Tulie screamed. She lunged across their laps and tried to hit the locks on the doors.

"*All right!*" Buck said, and hoisted her back up to a sitting position. "You just settle down."

The back door opened, and the Songster got into the car behind Niles.

"Niles, get into the back," Buck said.

"Why?" Niles whined.

"Because I said so," Buck said. "Just do it."

Niles opened the door, got out, slammed the door, opened the back door, shouldered the Songster over, slid in, and slammed the door again. Tulie could feel Niles pouting, but she didn't care. The Songster was right behind her. She climbed over Buck's lap into the passenger seat. She didn't want the Songster to be grabbing her throat from behind.

"Okay," Buck said. "Are we settled now?" She didn't answer him. "Jesus Christ," he said.

Tulie was freezing. Her hands were frozen and numb. She had ridiculed Elise for not wearing hose, and here she was in a short skirt with cotton boot socks on under her boots and nothing on her legs. *Stupid, Tulie,* she thought for the zillionth time that night. Her knees ached, they were so cold.

She was so scared she thought she would just fly apart. She thought she and Buck had made some kind of spiritual connection during the course of that snowball fight, but she was wrong. He wasn't her ally at all. *Guys stick together,* she remembered, and the thought didn't comfort her at all. She was out of options.

No, she wasn't. She had one left. One good one. She was smarter than these guys. She just had to keep working them until the goddamned sun came up. When daylight hit, things would be different, she knew it. All-night parties always get sane when the sun comes up.

"My lip is swelling up," Niles said. "She hit me with a snowball, Songster."

"You're becoming a real pain in the ass," the Songster said. "Women. Women in general are a pain in the ass."

"*I* threw the snowball at you," Buck said.

"Don't matter," the Songster said.

"She thought you were trying to kill her, Songster," Niles said. "Were you?"

"No," he said softly.

"See, stupid?" Niles said. "Jeez, you're dumb for a college girl."

"I could see it," Buck said. "I could see why she would think that."

Relief squeezed tears out of Tulie's eyes.

"He's killed before, and more than once, haven't you, Songster?" Buck asked.

Silence.

"C'mon," Buck said. "It's time to tell the truth."

"HEY, NO WAY," ELISE SAID. "YOU WERE GOING TO take us to a place where we could spend the night."

"*Voilà!*" Ross said.

"No, I mean a motel. We're not going into that house with you guys."

"Then you sleep in the truck," Ross said. Fury burned brightly in Elise. With great reluctance she got out and followed them into the house.

"Who lives here?"

"I do," Ross said. Elise nodded as she looked around. It looked like a place where a man lived by himself.

Dennis and Rebecca disappeared immediately.

"Take off your coat," Ross said. "Stay awhile."

Elise took off her coat and wished she had jeans and a sweatshirt to wear. The green machine was a little too hot for this situation. She didn't want to ignite anything here. She dropped her coat and her purse onto a torn vinyl recliner.

"How about a beer?"

She nodded, and Ross brought her a beer; then they both sat on the couch. Elise picked at the stuffing that was coming through on the arm. The coffee table looked as if it hadn't been cleaned in a month. It was covered with trash, empty bottles, overflowing ashtrays, one gray sock, a splat of what looked like dried macaroni and cheese, a coffee cup with something growing on top of the dregs, and a hammer. A mess of newspapers was in a corner where an easy chair should have been. The lampshades were cockeyed, the walls empty except for a picture of a Ferrari that had been torn out of a magazine and taped to the wall by the television.

"Been single long?"

" 'Bout a year," Ross said. With a grunt he pulled off a cowboy boot, flexed his toes, then stretched out and put the other cowboy boot in her lap.

Elise grimaced and took hold of the boot while he pulled his foot out.

"Rub my feet," he said.

"No! God, get off me." She pushed his foot off her lap.

"Hey, now, that's not very nice," Ross said, then sipped his beer and looked at her out of the corner of his eye.

"I don't have to be nice to you."

"Well, now I'm extending all sorts of hospitality to you," Ross said. "A rescue when you were stranded, a warm place to spend the night, a cold beer . . . You could be nice."

Elise picked at her fingernails. The fresh polish was chipping off her forefinger nail.

"Now I figure a motel at this time of night would cost you and your friend upwards of forty dollars." Ross sipped his beer, drawing out his words. "I don't know what you were charging those guys back—"

Elise jumped up off the couch, but Ross was quick. He grabbed her arm and pulled her back down.

"Ow, ow, let me go."

"Just sit here nice, now, and hear me out."

"Let me go."

"You going to sit here nice?"

"Let me go."

"You going to sit here?"

"Ow! Yes."

He released his grip on her. Fear began to creep up Elise's back.

"Now, as I was saying"—his voice continued to be calm and gentle—"I figured you weren't charging more than about forty bucks for a quickie in the parking lot."

"I don't know what you're talking about."

"Don't take me for stupid, Elise; that makes me real mad. You know you were hooking at that bar, and I know it, and everybody else in the whole goddamned bar knew it." His voice began to rise. "So don't act like I'm *stupid!*"

She went back to picking at her fingernails. Now two of them were losing their polish.

"So, for the forty bucks you'd spend on a motel room"—his voice was back to low and gentle—"I figure you could be real nice."

"I don't think so."

"Oh? Why not?" He smiled, looked genuinely interested.

He was being too reasonable, too soft, too quiet, too sweet-sounding. That softness scared Elise more than ragged violence. This was an unknown quantity. She wasn't used to it, didn't know how to handle it.

"It's different."

"How so?"

"Well, for one thing, when I choose a guy in a bar, it's my choice. This is not my choice. You are not my choice. You're holding me against my will, and that's kidnapping."

"So who's going to call the police?"

Elise cringed. He must have seen her leave with that cop. She was such a fool.

"Who's going to yell rape?" He said it so softly Elise could barely hear him. Those icy fingers zipped once again up her spine. "You?"

"Nobody's going to get raped here," Elise said. *This is good,* she thought. *Just keep him talking. Keep him drinking and talking, and soon it will be morning. Maybe if he drinks enough, he'll just go to sleep. Then Rebecca and I can jump in that big redneck truck of his and hustle our little asses right out of stupid Bend and back to Eugene. Back to the university.*

The dorm room suddenly seemed cozy, comfortable, homey, and so very far away.

"Your friend seems real nice," he said. "I think she's being real nice to Dennis."

"She's a Mormon," Elise said, sneering. "Mormons are like that."

Ross laughed, startling Elise. She turned and looked at him. He wasn't bad-looking. She had that flash of attraction again. Under other circumstances, they might get along real well.

"Hey, you're funny. You're a funny girl." He finished his beer, got off the couch, and went to the kitchen. "How's your beer?"

She still had half a beer left. She didn't need any more beer. She needed her wits. "I'm okay."

"So," he said as he walked back into the living room and flopped down next to her on the couch, "you're funny, you're pretty, you're probably smart, you go to the university, right?"

Elise pretended to drink and nodded.

"What are you doing turning tricks up here?"

"It's something to do. Something different. I need the money."

"You don't look like you need the money."

"Yeah, well, looks aren't everything."

"I've got a little cash."

"Sorry."

"Why are you being like this? What is wrong with me? I know I'm not ugly. I'm not a bad guy. Why won't you play?"

"Because I don't like your way. I don't like that you brought us here the way you did. I just object to your entire . . . your entire . . . you. I just object to you. If this is how you seduce girls, I bet you haven't gotten laid in years."

Ross laughed again, a big, genuine laugh. He was enjoying himself, and that made Elise mad. What right had he to enjoy himself at her expense? And where the *hell* was Rebecca? What must that girl be thinking?

Ross took a long drink on his beer, set it down on the coffee table, and then stretched, long and hard. He seemed to be completely comfortable and at ease, and that made Elise even madder yet. "I've never quite understood people like you," Ross said.

Keep him talking, Elise thought. "Oh? What kind of people is that?"

"You know. You're always drinkin' that lizard wine, gripin' about the taste, then sittin' on your butts, waiting for the good things to happen to you." He got up and went into the kitchen. She heard the refrigerator door open, and in a minute he came back with a loaf of bread under his arm, a bag of Doritos under the other, a cutting board with a knife, and some cheese in one hand and two jars of mustard in the other. He cleared a space on the coffee table with a swipe of his forearm and set the food down in front of them.

Elise struck what she hoped was a thoughtful pose. The food was a good sign. She was beginning to feel a little better about being here. Ross was an okay guy; he was just a cowboy, a redneck who'd had a lot of beer to drink. He wasn't going to hurt her. He sat down, opened the bread, smeared mustard on one piece, and laid slices of cheese over it. He offered it to her, and she took it.

"Lizard wine?"

"Yeah. Russians drink it. They think it makes them live

131

longer." He finished a sandwich for himself, stuffed it into his mouth, chewed a mouthful, and washed it down with a beer.

"Does it?"

He shrugged. "They think it does. And they live a long time. So, that's the question. You know that wine made out of lizards can't be very tasty, right? So does the lizard wine really make them live longer or do they live longer because they drink this nasty shit believing that it's good for them?"

"I don't get it." Elise bit into her snack. Her stomach immediately growled. She was hungry, but then she was always hungry. A sandwich like this would be a three-day allotment of calories.

"Don't get what?" Ross asked through a mouthful of sandwich.

"Why do you say I'm drinking lizard wine?"

"Come on, Elise. You're too old for the rebellion-against-the-rich-parents thing. That's what you're doing, you know. You've got some resentment stuck in your head, and you're going to act it out if it kills you. And it might, you turning tricks in the parking lot like that. Lizard wine, that's all it is. It tastes terrible, but you keep right on doing it because you think it's good for you, but you know what?"

She didn't answer.

"Those Russians, they die anyway." He swallowed the last of his sandwich with the last of his beer. He belched and sat back on the couch.

Elise thought she had perhaps heard something profound from a Bend cowboy, and she couldn't believe it. She hoped she'd remember it tomorrow, because it sounded like something worth thinking about, even though she didn't take it personally. Instead she began picking at that forefinger fingernail again. All three coats of British Red Coat were almost off that nail. It looked terrible.

"So, Elise, my lovely," Ross said, scratching his ample belly, "how about that roll in the hay?"

Elise laughed. She toyed with her sandwich. "I don't think so, Ross."

"Why not?"

"You're not my type." Elise smiled.

"What? I'm not a whore?" He reached over and grabbed her upper arm in a vise grip. Her sandwich tumbled to the floor, and fear flashed through her. "C'mere," he said.

"No!" Elise hit him in the chest, hit him hard. She felt like a bird fluttering at a window.

He started to laugh.

She reached over and grabbed the knife from the cutting board and held it out.

"Whoa," he said, releasing her. He held his hands up in surrender. "Take it easy."

"You just leave me the fuck alone, you hear?"

"Yeah, sure, I was just trying to get friendly."

"*I'm not interested.*"

"Okay, okay, just put the knife down."

"I think you better take Rebecca and me to one of those motels now."

"Come on, Elise, I'm not going to hurt you."

"I think you should take us."

"Okay, if you want to. Get your coat. I'll go get Dennis."

Elise stood up, and Ross grabbed her wrist so hard she heard bones crack. The knife fell to the floor.

"Think you want to play rough with me, you little bitch?" Ross's lips stretched tight over his teeth. His eyes narrowed into little slits, and Elise was completely helpless. He had one hand around her screaming right wrist, and she was totally subdued.

She took steps backward as he approached her. She stumbled into the coffee table, and he held her up by that wrist, that one wrist that hurt so bad tears began to leak out of her eyes.

"Please . . ." she said, and her voice choked.

"Please? Are you begging me? I think I like that. Let's hear a little more. Come on, just a little more, Elise, you hoity-toity tart. Think you're too good for me, huh?"

"Please don't hurt me," Elise said, the sobs beginning to shake her. For once she wished she weren't so small. He was such a huge, monstrous, overpowering menace. Her knees were shaking, from both fear and the pain in her wrist, and it wasn't going to be long before she fell on the floor. Maybe she ought to go ahead and screw him.

Only she had a feeling he'd be mean. She didn't want mean. She couldn't do mean. "Please." It came out as a whisper.

He laughed, spittle hitting her on the cheek. She was still backing up; he was still acting the bully, holding her up by the wrist, enjoying the role, beating up on a little girl.

"You're breaking my wrist."

"Oh, yeah? Sorry." He let go of her wrist, and then with one stubby-fingered hand in the center of her chest, he pushed her.

She flew across the room and landed against the recliner. She grabbed her purse strap as she slid to the floor, the green machine sliding up and over her hips.

"Ooh, isn't that nice," he said, and stopped to admire her bared crotch.

In a flash she knew what to do.

She scooted down flat on the floor and spread her legs, inviting him.

He unbuckled his belt.

With her good hand she moved her purse out of the way.

"Come on," she whispered. "Hurry."

"Oh," he said. "I've heard about girls like you. Like to play rough, eh?"

She nodded, breathing hard, trying to make it look like lust instead of disgust. While he was getting his jeans off, she slipped the catch and put her left hand around the .38.

She pulled it out and aimed it at him, her hand shaking.

He saw it and laughed.

She pulled the trigger, and the gun made an amazingly loud noise. The bullet smacked into the wall behind him.

For a moment she thought she'd missed.

But there was a small black hole on his shirt pocket, like an ink stain. He touched it, and red trickled down his front, staining his plaid flannel shirt. Then blood began to flow, spread down over his belly, masking the plaids, turning the whole thing blackish red. He touched the sticky stuff with his hand, looked at the red smeared on his hand, looked at her. "You bitch," he said softly, wonderingly.

Then he gasped for breath, his mouth opening and closing like a fish. He took a few steps toward the couch and fell down on it.

Elise scrambled to her feet. Her wrist was swelling. It was broken for sure. She pulled her dress down and ran down the hall. She had to find Rebecca, and the two of them needed to get out of town. Now.

BRENT AND MERRY HAD BEEN HIGH SCHOOL SWEET-hearts. They lived only two blocks from each other in the small Idaho town populated entirely by members of their own faith. Mormons. Right after high school graduation, Brent went to Paraguay on a two-year mission, and his letters to Merry were filled with the joys of missionary work and the torture of being away from her, worrying about her, wondering if the temptations that came her way were too strong for her to resist.

But Merry was true blue. She had found her life mate and was idling at the University of Utah, studying home economics, waiting for Brent to return.

When he got back, wedding plans whirled, and they were married in their temple, sealed together for all time and eternity.

Three years later Merry was in tears every month, when the Lord had again found her unfit to bear Brent's children. A barren woman is a worthless woman, she was convinced, and while Brent had a good job and provided well for her, she was unfulfilled. All her friends were having a baby a year. A blessing a year. One of her friends from high school had five already. Five wonderful little souls had been brought into this world through them. Five delightful personalities had to wait no longer for a good family to care for them, to bring them up with the right ideas about family, home, God, and country. It was their Christian duty to have children, lots of children.

Brent was the wage earner and an elder in the church. Merry was to be the head of the home, but it was a cold and lonely home.

In an emotion-charged conversation in bed, Brent finally agreed to adopt another man's child.

Merry got to work. She was going to find herself a child, and she was going to do it now. Quick, before Brent changed his mind.

She found a six-month-old girl, daughter of an eighteen-year-old girl who was forced to give the baby up when she was arrested for armed robbery. Merry and Brent got custody and their attorneys drafted the adoption paperwork so fast the juvenile delinquent mother's head swirled.

She signed.

Rebecca was theirs.

Within two months Merry became pregnant.

Merry set Rebecca aside while she awaited the arrival of her first "real" child.

Brent and Merry produced four natural children, but if genetic counseling had been a reality in those days, and if the Mormon Church would have ever allowed such a thing, they would have stopped with the first one. They had four boys, each a year apart, each one a little less mentally efficient than the previous one. The fourth had Down syndrome. At first Merry and Brent eschewed birth control, knowing that the Lord wouldn't have given them these challenges if they weren't up to them. And the children were indeed a blessing. But lots of work. Lots and lots of work. Finally, in another tear-filled, emotional conversation in bed, Brent agreed to a vasectomy.

Merry and Brent, along with Rebecca's help, set about raising four retarded children. The Mormon elders called the boys "charmed" and continually told Merry and Brent how lucky they were to be blessed with four of them.

Merry and Brent agreed, but in their hearts they longed for normal, rough-and-ready boys Brent could wrestle with, kids who would go to school and come home with wonderful pictures for the refrigerator magnets. Children who would date and drive and go to proms and marry and bring home grandchildren.

Instead what they got was a lot of work and a lot of heartache. The little gifts were so small, the little moments of gratitude were sweet, but they were so fleeting . . .

Rebecca loved her brothers but hated that they were so needy. She couldn't understand why they couldn't do the things that came so easily and naturally for her. Eventually she came to realize that they were disadvantaged, "special" her mother called them.

While Merry tried desperately to balance the hard work against the sweet zinging moments of satisfaction, Rebecca found only the hard work and none of the satisfaction. School brought peace because it got her out of the house and away from the diapers and drool. And she went to church, because at church someone else baby-sat. She could be with her friends.

She went to church on Saturday mornings, twice on Sundays, and Wednesday nights, too.

And the more she heard, the more she wanted to hear. She wanted to understand why her family was different. She wanted an explanation and forgiveness for her constant resentment. She wanted to believe that going to church was not just a selfish method of getting out of the house but a worthwhile activity, worth the extra work she knew she was piling on her mother while she was gone, worth the light in her father's eyes when she told him where she was going. Church was her only acceptable avenue out of the house, and she bought it, whole-sale.

When Brent and Merry decided the time had come to let Rebecca know she was adopted, they sat down with her after her brothers had been put to bed. Rebecca, sensing a serious conversation, never got beyond hearing them say that she was a "special gift" to them. *Special* to Rebecca meant "retarded." She was horrified to think that she was going to become like her stupid brothers. She never heard the adoption part.

She was twelve years old before the topic arose again, and when she finally understood that she was adopted and had no genetic connection with either her parents or her brothers, she smiled and laughed and hugged and thanked her parents with a glee that frightened them. The lifting of that burden made a new and more carefree child of her.

With the profound realization that nothing was as it appeared to be, she began to question everything about their lives, particularly their religion. She thought that maybe being Mormon was a genetic condition as well.

One calm summer Wednesday evening as Rebecca walked to her youth group meeting at church, she ran across her friend Carolyn Adams, who was just standing near the entrance of the church.

"Hi," Rebecca said. "What are you doing?"

"Waiting."

"Are you coming in?"

"Are you kidding? I hate all that church shit. We have to take seminary in school and go to church twice on Sundays. I'm not going Wednesday nights."

"Where are you going?"

"Home. As soon as my parents leave. They go out on Wednesdays, so I wait until they leave, then I go home." Carolyn looked at her watch. "They should be gone by now. Want to come?"

"What are you going to do?"

"I don't know. Hang out with my brother and his friends."

"Okay," Rebecca said, succumbing to the seduction of deception, and they walked the two blocks to Carolyn's house.

Carolyn's brother, Mark, was flopped on the couch, watching television. Another boy was standing next to the couch, juggling three pairs of folded-up socks. "Rebecca, this is Mark," Carolyn said as she pushed Mark's feet off the couch and sat down. Rebecca sat on the edge of a recliner. "And that's Calvin."

Calvin stopped juggling long enough to look at her. "I know you," he said. "You go to Kennedy High?"

Rebecca nodded.

"I graduated last year," Calvin said. "And you were there then."

Rebecca nodded. "I'm a sophomore now."

Calvin went back to his juggling.

"You guys get a movie?" Carolyn asked.

Calvin pulled a paper bag out from behind a chair. "And a six-pack." He handed everybody a beer, then plugged in the movie. *Star Trek.*

"Not *Star Trek* again. You guys," Carolyn complained.

Calvin said, "Scoot over." Then he sat in the chair next to Rebecca, pulled her back toward him, and, with a lurch, reclined the chair. She found herself lying snuggled next to him, his arm around her shoulders.

Calvin shuffled them a little bit. "Comfy?"

She nodded, her mind filled with things other than *Star Trek,* which she thought was a pretty good movie.

Cutting church was like cutting school, and now she was drinking beer and sitting so close—touching, practically lying down—with a guy, not even a senior, but a graduate! She could barely breathe. She sneaked a look at his profile. He had a few pimples along his jawline, and it looked as if he could use a shave, but his profile was good. He looked over at her, smiling, and he had great eyes and a nice smile. He was so close. She'd never been that close to a boy before.

Not boy. Man. She saw black hair on his arms. He was a man. She smiled back, then settled down to see what the evening would bring.

That was the last Wednesday she even considered going to church. She hung out with Carolyn and Mark and Calvin on Wednesday nights for a couple of months, and then she just hung out with Calvin.

She wasn't quite sixteen yet, so her parents didn't let her date, and they certainly wouldn't want her to be dating a guy who was almost twenty, but he called her every night, and somehow they found time to be together.

Rebecca thought she was in love for certain. When he kissed her, she felt things. When he touched her, she wanted him to touch her all over.

She thought of him all day long. During English class she daydreamed of being his wife. She wrote his name on her books. She was the envy of the other girls because she had a boyfriend, and he was already out of school and had a job at the video store.

Some of the snotty girls thought she was too young to have a boyfriend that old. Rebecca ignored them.

When school let out for the summer, she and Calvin had a lot more time to spend together. Rebecca was old enough to have personal responsibility, and her mother was so busy with the boys that she was happy to have Rebecca out of her hair. They whiled away long, hot days at the park or the pool or riding their bikes on the long country roads. They talked about their futures, they talked about important things, and he made her laugh.

One Wednesday night, long after any guilt over skipping church had evaporated, long after deception had become a habit, Calvin met her at Carolyn's with a long kiss and a sleeping bag. "Let's sleep out," he said.

She called her mother and told her she would be staying the night at Carolyn's. No problem. Her mother had other things to worry about.

Calvin hefted the sleeping bag, and Rebecca brought the paper bag with corn chips and two quarts of beer. She was developing a taste for beer. They walked up the street and along the mountain road into the farm country. They cut through a pasture and laid the sleeping bag out on a hill over-looking their simple little town. Rebecca was so excited by the thought of being alone with Calvin for an entire night, of sleeping with him, of waking up with him, of wrapping her arms around him and being held all night, that she was sub-dued. It was an awesome undertaking. So adult.

They drank the beer and ate the chips in relative silence, sitting side by side, Calvin with his arm around her.

When he began to kiss her, Rebecca thought it was the most romantic thing in the world. They scooted into the sleeping bag, and he lay on top of her, and it felt as if he belonged there. And when he began to take off her clothes, she let him. She was hot and woozy from the beer and the juices he whirled up in her, and before she knew it, he had his pants off and was putting something warm and hard and strange in her hand. She rubbed it, and he moaned. She liked that. She rubbed it harder and faster, and then she felt his fingers moving in her, and she moved around to accommodate him.

Then he slid over on top of her again and slid inside her,

and it didn't hurt, it didn't hurt at all. It felt strange. She felt full and uncomfortable, but it didn't hurt.

He moved back and forth, and Rebecca felt as if she were watching the whole thing rather than experiencing it. Just as she was about to ask him to stop because it was starting to hurt, she was starting to get sore, he moaned and moved faster and groaned loudly, then collapsed on top of her. He kissed her cheek and rolled off. He pulled her close to him and nuzzled in her hair. In a few minutes he was asleep, his warm breath scented with beer, his eyes moving underneath peaceful lids.

She'd done it. They'd done it. She was Calvin's now, and she was very happy.

In the morning she was shy, with dew in her hair and her makeup caked in the corners of her eyes. But Calvin didn't notice any of that. He woke up with his penis hard, and she was still slippery and sticky from the night before. He slipped it inside her from behind, and with both arms wrapped around her waist, he made love to her again, and this time it felt good. Real good.

Carolyn was unimpressed when Rebecca told her.

"He's a flake," she said. "Just don't get knocked up."

Pregnant.

Of course, she knew she could get pregnant, and she had to do something about it. Now. Because in the cold light of day, what they had done was insane. What on earth would they do if she got pregnant?

She went to the drugstore, gritted her teeth, and bought condoms, acting as if it were a completely normal thing. Nobody said anything. Nobody noticed. She made Calvin wear one each time from then on, but it was too late.

When her period was a day late, she panicked. She couldn't concentrate on school; she didn't want to see her parents; she

143

ignored her brothers; she didn't want to see Calvin or Carolyn or anybody. She went to church and prayed that she wasn't pregnant.

When a week went by, she went back to the drugstore and bought a home pregnancy test. This time she didn't care if anybody noticed. If she was pregnant, they'd all notice in time anyway.

It came up positive.

She cried.

When she finished crying, she was resigned to the idea that she was going to have Calvin's baby, and a sense of calm peacefulness came over her. She felt she could tell her parents, she could tell Calvin. They could get married. It wasn't the best of situations, but they would make do. They would make do.

Before she told her parents, she stood in front of the full-length mirror in her bedroom and looked at herself. She smiled. Her freckled nose wrinkled up, and her teeth showed. They were nice teeth, not perfect, but they were okay. One front one crossed over the other front one, but the rest of them looked all right. Her brown hair hung straight down to her shoulders, and thick bangs ended just at her bushy eyebrows.

She took off her clothes and looked at her small breasts, her thin frame, her long, skinny legs. She touched her stomach, put her finger in her belly button. Calvin's baby. Inside. She smiled at herself with the secret that nobody else but she knew. It was a secret that would affect lots of lives, and she was the only one who knew it.

For now.

She put on her clothes and went to talk to her parents.

Her father cried.

Her mother said, "So you're following in the footsteps of

LIZARD WINE

your stupid, slutty whore of a mother." And then she cried and prayed to be forgiven for the things that she had said.

After the original storm of the announcement was over, the house was silent for a couple of days. Rebecca felt in charge of her life for the first time. Then her parents called her into their bedroom for a private meeting.

"Rebecca," her father began, "we've prayed about this situation, and we've come up with what is really the only workable plan."

Rebecca smiled. This was so like him, to have a plan.

"We've prayed about it and prayed about it," her mother said, suddenly pious after her inexcusable initial outburst, "and we've discussed it with the church elders."

Rebecca's face flushed. She didn't know they would be discussing it with others, although she realized they would, now that she thought about it. The church people controlled their lives, controlled their thoughts.

"You'll have this child," her mother said.

"Of course I will," she said.

"And we'll put it up for adoption."

"Adoption?" Rebecca was astonished. "No way."

"It's the only reasonable thing to do," her father said. "We want you to finish high school, go to college, get an education, find a nice boy, perhaps someone in one of the professions, settle down, and have a good life. Keeping this baby would be two strikes against you before you even have a chance to start."

Rebecca's resolve began to harden into a knot in her stomach. "I'll think about it," she said.

"You do that, honey," her father said. "Have you talked to the . . . boy, the . . . father yet?"

"No." Rebecca chewed on the inside of her mouth. She didn't want to have to tell Calvin.

"It's just as well. Why don't you hold off on talking to him for a while, and you think about what we've said. We'll talk again about this tomorrow, okay?"

"I won't give it up," she said.

"We'll talk about it tomorrow," her father said.

"*I won't.*"

"We think it would be best," her mother said.

Rebecca looked at the woman who had raised her and suddenly she was a stranger. These people weren't happy to have a grandchild because it wasn't of their blood, their Mormon blood. These people were strangers to her, and she would not let them control her life and the life of her baby either. "I think you're afraid I'll give birth to a normal baby. You're afraid that I can do it when you can't."

Her mother's hand slapped her so hard and so fast Rebecca had no idea it was coming, and when it was over, she wasn't sure what had happened.

"Someday, Rebecca," her mother said through tight lips, "you will need to depend upon your Lord. And He will be there for you. Until then you are a minor—you are *only* fifteen years old, for God's sake—and you will do what we say because we know what's best for you at this age and you do not. The Lord took you away from your irresponsible mother and gave you to us to raise as we see fit. You will have this child. We will not let you murder it. You can stay here if you like—it is not *our* shame—or you can go away, as you wish. But you will have this child, and it will be given to a family who is prepared to raise it. And that is the *end* of the discussion." Merry's face was white and looked old. Her hands trembled in her lap as she whirled her gold wedding band around her finger over and over and over again.

Rebecca rose and walked out of the room, leaving the door open behind her. She went into her bedroom, closed and

LIZARD WINE

locked the door, picked up a pillow, and held it to her chest while she cried and thought about what was happening to her.

The next day she packed some things, and her father drove her to his sister's house on a farm in the middle of nowhere Idaho. She hadn't told Carolyn; she hadn't told Calvin. She was ashamed. What had been a wonderful experience with the boy she loved and a fabulous secret had been turned into shame by her parents.

"We'll tell your friends there was a family emergency and you had to go out of town," her dad said. "Now it's up to you to write to them and make up whatever story you see fit."

Aunt Louise was just as Mormon as the rest of them, but she seemed to understand Rebecca better than her parents did. Aunt Louise gave her a long hug and a kiss on the forehead and said, "You take Van's old room, honey," and Rebecca was free to unpack and lie on the bed and cry or read or do whatever she wanted to. About an hour later her dad called his good-bye up the stairs, and Rebecca came down and gave him a hug. Then she went back to her room.

Aunt Louise came up with soup about an hour after that. Rebecca was poking through Van's chest of drawers. The picture of him, looking so grown up in his navy uniform, was on the dresser. She loved her cousin Van. When they were kids, he always played with her. Even though he was older, he played fair, and he was fun. She was happy to be in his room with his baseball pennants and his skis and Van stuff. His dresser drawers smelled like him, and it made her feel sad that those childhood times were gone.

"We'll clear all this old stuff out and make it your room," Aunt Louise said.

Rebecca didn't have anything to say.

Aunt Louise sat on the edge of the bed. "Now then," she said. "tell me about this boyfriend of yours."

Rebecca smiled, then started to cry. "Calv," she said. "He's sweet."

"I'm sure he is." Aunt Louise held out her arms, and Rebecca fell into them and then sobbed out all her pain and confusion. Aunt Louise just held her and rocked her. "Everything's going to be all right," she said, and Rebecca believed her.

At dinner Uncle Mo said that the Lord was looking out for each of them and that what He says goes. Rebecca groaned inwardly and figured Uncle Mo was part of her punishment. Eight months of Uncle Mo.

She spent a lot of time reading. Van had a whole bookcase filled with science fiction novels, and Rebecca lay on his bed reading, sometimes a book every two days. When she wasn't reading, she was thinking.

And she thought that her mother seemed to know an awful lot about her real mother. In just over two years Rebecca would be eighteen, and she would look up her real parents.

Aunt Louise made an appointment with a doctor. She held Rebecca's hand on the big sofa and told her what to expect from her first pelvic exam. Rebecca was horrified.

She threw up her dinner the night before the exam. She couldn't sleep, tossing and turning. She felt sick. She was too sick to go, she'd tell Aunt Louise.

She wanted to tell her now. In the middle of the night. It was important.

She got out of bed, and her nightie stuck to her. She turned on Van's bedside reading light and almost fainted. Her bed was covered in blood. Warm, sticky blood.

"The Lord hath spoken," Uncle Mo said.

Aunt Louise drove her to the hospital an hour away. They gave her medication that made her woozy, and she stayed the next day and another night.

Rebecca sat on the edge of the high, stiff hospital bed,

holding Aunt Louise's hand, as she waited for her father to pick her up and take her home. While she waited, Aunt Louise talked to her. She talked about being the daughter she was supposed to be. Subdued, obedient, chastised. Rebecca realized that in part she was all those things. And in part she felt she had rocked the boat enough for her young life.

"Just feel the Lord's presence when you need Him," Aunt Louise said, holding her hand. "And soon you'll begin to feel His presence when He needs you. Be grateful, child. The Lord has saved you. He has saved you from eight months of Uncle Mo." They both laughed, and Rebecca felt overwhelming affection for her aunt. "He's saved you from stretch marks and falling in love with a baby you couldn't raise. You've been saved from falling out of step with your schoolmates and making a premature mess of your life."

She was right, Rebecca realized. They sat quietly then, on the edge of the hospital bed, holding hands, thinking. Most of all, Rebecca realized, she had been saved of eight months of boredom, eight months of Van's room, thinking about him and what a good son he was, and herself and what a terrible daughter she had become. She was saved from the pain and discomfort; she was saved from the embarrassment her family would have to suffer; she was saved.

She hugged her aunt Louise, and the tears wet her aunt's cotton dress. Then she sat quietly while Aunt Louise prayed.

Rebecca never saw Calvin again. She went to church as she was asked. She felt she had survived a very close call, both in her personal life and with her family relations. The Lord had seen to her in her time of need, just as her mother had said. Just as her father had said. Just as Uncle Mo and Aunt Louise had said. She owed the Lord. She owed Him.

She finished high school, and none of her friends was the wiser, although Carolyn asked some questions that were pointed and accusing, and Rebecca looked her squarely in the face and lied.

When she turned eighteen, she asked her mother about her birth parents, but her mother professed to know nothing. Rebecca went down to the county courthouse and filled out a form. If they wanted to be found, she could find them.

When it came time to pick a college, Rebecca realized the time had actually come when she could be free of her family, her friends, and the entire small-minded community. She chose Oregon. Oregon was about as far away as the University of Utah, but everybody else was going to Salt Lake City. Going to the University of Utah or to BYU would seem only like an extension of high school. Rebecca needed to get out of town. She needed to get away. She needed to get far away. She needed to find out if the Lord would follow her to Oregon or if He lived only in Mormon territory. Her parents, seeing that Rebecca had her mind set on Oregon and was not going to change, no matter what, finally agreed.

She breathed deeply when her parents hugged her a final good-bye at the Eugene campus, got into their van for the trip home. At last she was out from under them, the hard work of her simple brothers, and their suffocating religion.

She hadn't been in her new dorm with her new roommate for three weeks when a letter came. It was a copy of her original birth certificate. With the names of her birth parents.

Suddenly Rebecca wasn't sure she wanted to look them up at all. She put the certificate in a drawer and forgot about it.

Oregon. College. Elise.

Her immediate need was to cut loose, explore being Rebecca in an unfettered environment. She wanted to find out what the University of Oregon held in promise, and while she felt she could bide her time in tasting all of its delights, she was eager to get a small start.

As fate and overcrowded student housing had it, her room-mate was a senior. A senior who had seen, tasted and done everything the university had to offer.

Rebecca felt like wide-eyed putty as Elise slowly turned her from a country bumpkin into a college woman.

After a month Rebecca never wanted to go home again.

TIME TO TELL THE TRUTH.

Tulie felt the dark feelings in the car deepen. She watched Buck take a pull on the almost empty tequila bottle, but she didn't figure it made much difference: Nobody was getting drunker; nobody was getting sober. The tension was growing, though, and people were getting mean.

The air in the car was stifling. Niles kept his window cracked so that theoretically his cigarette smoke would curl out the window, but the car was full of the stuff. The windows were fogged. But more than that, the air in the car was full of unspoken statements, declarations, challenges and insults.

The air had coagulated around them. Tulie felt as if she were choking on a clot of it.

Niles lit a cigarette, and the stream of smoke blew into the front seat.

"Enough smoking, Niles," Buck said. "God, it's *awful* in here."

"That ain't the only thing in here that's awful." It was the Songster, his voice low and menacing.

"What's the matter, Songster?" Niles asked.

"Buck," the Songster said. "Buck's suspicion is about as smelly as your stupid cigarettes."

Buck's knuckles showed white in the dimness of the car. Tulie's heart began that hammering again. *Oh, God, not again.*

"If you're so lily white, Buck," the Songster said with a sneer, "what are you doing here with us?"

"I never said I was lily white." Buck spoke through clenched teeth. "I just ain't a killer, that's all."

"Yeah, well, I am, and I admit it. I ain't proud of it, but I admit it."

Tulie didn't want to hear any of this. She didn't want to hear any of this at all.

"Tell us," Buck said. "Let's hear it. You're so eager to impress us with this new knowledge of yourself, let's get down to it. Just how bad are you, Songster?"

"It happened a long time ago, Buck," the Songster said softly. "A *long* time ago."

"Then tell me what happened with that woman," Buck said. "What happened with that woman?"

"It ain't your business," the Songster said.

"He's accusing you, Songster, you gotta defend yourself," Niles said.

"I don't have to defend myself against some suspicious little shit." The Songster spit something from his tongue, real or imagined. "I know who I am."

"Like I don't?" Buck's grip on the steering wheel tightened.

"Yeah," the Songster said. "Like you don't."

Tulie thought that if she just sat back and stayed quiet, they would forget all about her. She slid around and rested her back on the car door, and she could see Buck in the driver's seat and she could see Niles and the Songster in the back. She wished Buck would just turn the key and fire up this old hunk of shit and back out of this park and head back to Eugene. There would be no more talk about this boxcar woman; there would be no more talk about murdering one another; there would be no more tension among them.

But Buck wasn't firing up the car, and the tension was there to stay. *Just stay cool*, she told herself. *Just be invisible.*

"Okay," Buck said. "Let's get down to it."

"What do you mean, Buck?" Niles asked. "Songster, what does he mean?"

"He wants us to tell him if he's a man or not."

Niles snorted. "Well, of course he is. He's a gentleman. C'mon, Songster, that ain't what he's talking about. Buck?"

"I'm talking about telling the truth, Niles. The *truth*, Songster." Buck turned around in his seat and leaned back against the door. He laid his hand across the seat back in what seemed a casual motion. Tulie looked at the pale outline of his head in the October night light.

"The truth shall set you free," she said, then wished she hadn't.

"*So?*" The Songster challenged her.

"So . . ." Tulie said, casting about for something to say, something, anything, to get the spotlight off her. *Be smart, Tulie*, she said to herself. *The best defense is a good offense.* "So, let's everybody tell the truth."

"About what?" Niles asked.

"I don't know," Tulie said. "Whatever. We'll just be honest. About everything."

"What if somebody's not?" Niles asked.

"He'll die," the Songster said, and everybody believed him.

"Jesus," Tulie said. "Listen. I have a question for Niles. How come you agreed to help Buck kill the Songster when you and the Songster are supposed to be such good buddies?"

Niles fidgeted, and Tulie could feel his discomfort.

"Because it was a game." Buck answered for him.

"Yeah," Niles said.

"You're speaking for Niles?" the Songster asked.

Nobody spoke.

"I've got another question," Tulie said. "For you, Buck. How come you're so angry? I don't mean right now. I mean, you're an angry kind of guy, and I want to know why."

"He's afraid," Niles said.

"Very good, Niles," the Songster said. "Buck is angry because he's afraid. He doesn't like to be afraid, but he can't help it, and that makes him mad."

"What makes him afraid?" Tulie asked.

"He's afraid that he can't cut the mustard," the Songster said.

"What mustard?" Niles asked.

"*Any* mustard."

"That's not true, Songster," Buck said, but he knew they were right.

"The mustard that counts," the Songster said.

Buck took a pull on the tequila. It was almost gone.

"Hey," Niles said, "I got a question for the girl. How far would you go with one of these games?"

"All the way," the Songster said.

Tulie said nothing. She wanted the attention on somebody else.

"I got a question for the Songster," Niles said.

"Good," Tulie said, then bit her lip. *Shut up*, she told herself. *You started it; now let them carry it.*

"Songster. How come you carry a knife?"

"He's afraid," Buck said, then hooted, because it was the

absolute truth. "He's afraid, so he hides behind that dangerous look."

"What's he afraid of?" Niles asked.

"Women," Buck said. "He hates women because he's afraid of them."

"Hey, Songster," Niles asked softly, "when you killed that woman, did you use that knife?"

"Yeah."

No apology, no hesitation, no remorse. Tulie's skin seized up.

"That very *same* knife?" Niles couldn't seem to believe it.

"Yes, Niles," the Songster said condescendingly.

"Okay, Songster," Buck said. The atmosphere in the car had thickened. Everyone was speaking softly. "The truth. How many women have you killed?"

The Songster ran his fingers through his hair, ran his hands over his face. "Three."

Tulie's hand clenched the door handle so hard her knuckles hurt. She wanted to run, but she knew that running was the worst thing she could do. She wanted out of there. She wanted out of there real bad.

"Tell us," Buck said.

The Songster lit a joint and toked deeply. "Why?"

"I want to know why you said you were going to have to kill this girl because she knows," Niles said.

"Knows what?" Tulie asked, a slight note of hysteria in her voice.

"Relax," Buck said. "Nobody's killing nobody here. We're just talking."

"Remember, Songster?" Niles pressed.

"I remember."

"What did you mean? What does she know?"

"How to steal my soul. Women know that thing."

"That's stupid," Tulie said. Jesus Christ, why couldn't she keep her mouth shut?

"Shut up," he said.

"What *is* it with you and women?" Buck asked.

"Yeah," Niles said. "What *is* it?"

"Nothing *is* with women," the Songster said. "I just feel better when they're not around."

"Some woman did you wrong once, huh?" Niles said.

Silence.

"Aha," Buck said. "The truth."

"Just shut the fuck up," the Songster said. "You guys have no idea."

"Then tell us," Niles said. "Tell us why you want to stick that knife into this girl."

Tulie's heart started to pound again. She took a fresh, slippery grip on the door handle.

"Tell us," Buck said, "why that woman never left your boxcar on her own."

"Yeah, and why you yelled for your mama when—when, you know, when you were humping this girl," Niles said.

There was barely light in the car, but when the Songster slipped his blade out and held it high, it glinted. He turned it back and forth, as if admiring it. Tulie heard it as much as saw it, and it made her feel light-headed. "Now," he said softly. "Shut the fuck up. All of you."

Tulie knew the Songster had had enough grass, gin, beer, and tequila to do just about anything, and they were all within easy reach. She hoped they all would just shut up, as the Songster had suggested, but she knew they wouldn't. She closed her eyes hard and tried to remember about praying.

"Put it away, Songster," Buck said.

The Songster moved, and the knife disappeared. Tulie breathed a sigh, but just because it was out of sight didn't mean it was off their minds. The Songster was as good at offensive maneuvers as anyone she'd debated in high school. "Just wanted you all to know that Gloria was close by," he said.

"Gloria?" Niles said. "You named your knife? You named it a girl's name?"

"The only girl ever understood me."

This is way too weird, Tulie thought. *I should have gone to Bend with Rebecca and Elise.*

She consciously willed her muscles to relax. She let go of the door handle. She took deep breaths; she felt her head clear; she felt the heat steam off her; she felt her cramped fingers loosen from the door handle.

"How long you had that knife?" Niles asked.

"Long time."

"Yeah, but how long?"

"Friend gave it to me when I was fourteen."

"Fourteen years old? Wow."

Tulie didn't want to hear any of this. She wanted the sun to come up. She desperately wanted this night to be over. But there was no evidence of light anywhere. Being on the west side of the mountains, they would get the last of the morning light, and if there were dense snow clouds, this night might last even longer.

"Is that the knife you used to kill those women?" Niles asked.

"Yes," the Songster whispered.

"Tell me it was self-defense," Tulie said just as softly, knowing there was no way it could have been. Not three of them.

"It was accidental," the Songster said.

Buck snorted. "Accidental! Accidental, my ass. Three of them, Songster? Three accidents?"

"I ain't defending my actions to you," he said. "I done my time."

"For *one*," Buck said.

The Songster said nothing.

"You got two more to account for," Buck said.

"Don't have to account to nobody," the Songster said.

"Maybe you have to account to us," Buck said.

"Yeah," Niles said.

"Yeah," Buck said. "Maybe that's what this is all about after all. Maybe it's time you owned up and did a little penance."

"Did what?" Niles asked.

Everybody ignored him.

"It would do you good," Tulie said, seeing the perfect opportunity to turn the spotlight full force on the Songster.

"I ain't telling you guys nothing."

"Maybe you keep doing it because you *don't* tell nobody nothing," Niles said.

"Bullshit."

"C'mon, Songster," Tulie said gently. "Confess. Get it off your chest."

"Sure. Like I could trust you assholes."

"Sure you can," Tulie said.

"You can trust me, Songster," Niles said.

"Well, I don't think you can trust *me*," Buck said. "I say you should be tried for killing those other two women."

"Songster on trial," Niles said. "First tell us about the woman you did time for."

Silence hung thickly.

"Were you friends?" Tulie asked.

"She was a whore."

Nobody spoke.

"I picked her up on the street. She was really ugly, you know. I mean, I can't imagine anybody wanting to fuck a woman who looked like that. And that's when I wanted her. She wanted fifty dollars."

"Fifty dollars!" Niles couldn't imagine a fifty-dollar lay.

"And we went to her room in this lousy hotel, you know the kind."

None of them knew the kind.

"We got up there, and she started to get stupid."

"What do you mean?" Niles asked.

"I mean she had a bad mouth. I didn't want any bad mouth. I wasn't in the mood for any stupid remarks from an ugly whore."

"Like what, Songster?"

"It doesn't matter, Niles. Jesus." He rearranged himself on the car seat, and for a moment Tulie wanted to stop everything. She didn't want to hear it, didn't want to know it. "Drop the subject, Songster," she wanted to say. "Let's have some fun instead."

"Hey, what the hell am I doing anyway?" the Songster said. "I don't want to tell you guys this stuff."

"Yes, you do, Songster," Buck said.

"Don't you want to make up for it, Songster?" Niles asked. "Don't you feel bad?"

"I'm not proud."

"What drives someone to murder somebody, that's what I want to know," Buck said, pissed off and wanting to cut to the chase. "What could be so threatening that someone would kill somebody else?"

"When you get there, you'll know," the Songster said, his voice back to that low, menacing whisper.

"I thought we were going to put the Songster on trial," Niles said.

"I can't judge him," Buck said.

"I'll be the judge," Tulie said. "I'm the woman."

"I'll be the lawyer that asks the questions," Niles said.

"Guess you'll have to be the executioner, Buck," the Songster said. "Maybe you'll find out what it takes.

"I need tequila," the Songster said. Buck passed the bottle to him; he drank, opened the car door, and threw the empty bottle out. Cold wind blew snow inside, and Tulie hoped it would blow a little sanity, a little reality, a little normality inside, but then he closed the door and coughed, and the thick air closed around them again.

Niles cleared his throat. The trial was about to begin.

ELISE STOPPED HALFWAY DOWN THE HALL. SHE LEANED against the wall and closed her eyes. Her right fist opened and closed as she willed her breathing to slow down, willed her heart to return to normal. If she didn't take it easy, she was going to pass out from hyperventilating. All she could think was: *I can't believe I shot him. I can't believe I shot him.*

She resisted the temptation to slide down to the floor and lie there. She closed her eyes, squinted hard, then opened them. She ran a hand across her forehead. Cold sweat. She'd heard about that, read about that, but this was the first time she'd ever experienced it. Her teeth began to chatter, and she wondered if she was going into shock.

She straightened up and felt momentarily dizzy. *This is not the time to get weak and feminine, Elise.*

All four doors in the hallway were closed. She pushed on

the first one, and it led to a bathroom. She turned on the light. A bare bulb illuminated the small stark room. The broken light cover sat on the toilet tank. It was a bachelor's bathroom, with no toilet paper and a heap of smelly, mildewed towels in the corner by the tub. The shower curtain hung off half its hooks, and the sink probably hadn't been cleaned in the year that Ross had lived there by himself. Elise went inside and looked at herself in the toothpaste-speckled mirror.

A pale, freaked-out version of herself looked back at her. She used the toilet, fishing a used Kleenex out of the overflowing wastebasket to use for toilet paper. Then she splashed cold water on her face and grimaced as she used the only towel hanging on the loose towel rack. It was damp and smelly.

She gingerly touched the blue swelling at her wrist. It didn't hurt very much, although it would. When she settled down, it would hurt like holy hell.

The face that looked back at her from the mirror was now a little more like the standard version. She took a deep breath and felt better. She could cope. She could engineer an escape for her and Rebecca.

Rebecca.

Elise turned off the bathroom light and stepped back into the hallway.

The room across the hall from the bathroom had a weight bench and some boxes in it. The next room was completely empty, except for a cable hookup that snaked out of the wall and coiled up in the middle of the room.

Ross's bedroom was behind the last door. She pushed it open and saw Rebecca and Dennis asleep on a single mattress on the floor. They both still had their clothes on. There was a pile of Ross's laundry in the corner, a lamp on a stack of books, and a blanket with its edging coming off hung over the empty curtain rods for privacy.

A full-length mirror was mounted on the opposite wall, and Elise started at the sight of herself. At first she thought it was someone else. She hardly recognized the thin, wasted thing in the tiny dress. She looked terrible.

She wanted to go home. She was ready for a good cry.

She said a short prayer of thanks that the shot hadn't wakened Dennis. She went over and grabbed Rebecca by the arm. Rebecca's eyes opened and rolled around and then closed.

"Rebecca, wake up, come on, we've got to go."

"What?" Rebecca focused on Elise. "Oh, hi," she said.

"Come on. We've got to go. Don't wake up Dennis."

"Why? Where?" Rebecca sat up and rubbed her eyes. "Is it morning?"

"No, we're going anyway. Come *on*." Elise found Rebecca's shoes by the door and handed them to her. Rebecca stood up, unsteadily, then leaned against the wall to put her shoes on.

"What's going on?"

"Nothing. Just hurry." Elise went back into the living room and found her coat. She picked up her purse, put the gun back in it. When she turned around, Rebecca stood in the hallway, her eyes wide open and fixed on Ross.

"Better get Dennis's jacket, or you'll freeze."

"My God, Elise, is he dead?"

"I think so." Elise turned and looked at Ross again. He was slouched sideways on the couch. He had that look, that Eddie look, that bluish gray pasty look. The wound in his chest no longer oozed blood.

"Did you shoot him?"

"Yes, now let's go."

"You shot him? My God." Rebecca walked over to the body. "He didn't bleed much."

"Rebecca, we've got *to go*."

"Yeah, no kidding."

"Go get a jacket."

Rebecca obediently went to the back room while Elise walked over to Ross and felt in his jeans pockets for his keys. When she wrestled to put her hand in the pocket to fish them out, Ross slipped over sideways.

The back of the couch was covered in blood.

She felt the acid rise up the back of her throat. The blood smelled raw. It looked thick, reddish black. She stood up, closed her eyes, and took a deep breath. Then she looked again at the lump of keys in Ross's jeans and went after them.

When she pulled them out, she whirled around and found Rebecca right behind her.

"My God," Rebecca whispered.

"Dennis still asleep?"

Rebecca nodded.

"Let's go."

"Shouldn't we call someone?" Rebecca asked.

"Let's just go," Elise said.

They went out the front door into the softly falling snow. Elise unlocked the truck and got in, then slid across and unlocked the passenger door. She turned the key, and the truck roared to life. She let it idle for a moment while she thought things through. She wanted to peel out of that place and drive a hundred miles an hour back to Eugene, but she couldn't do that. She couldn't do that. She had to be calm. She had to be in control. She had to have a plan.

What about going back to the bar for the Camaro?

Bad idea.

She put the truck in reverse and backed gently out of the driveway, adrenaline racing her heart the way she wanted to race the truck. She turned on the lights and the heater and headed slowly and inconspicuously out of town, hunched over the steering wheel, one eye on the speedometer. She did not want to be stopped.

She did *not* want to be stopped.

"We should go to the police," Rebecca said.

"I know we should. But I have to think about it first."

"Think about what? If we don't go to the police, and they come after us, we'll go to jail."

Elise didn't know what to do. "They'll throw me in jail anyway," she said. "Nobody would ever believe it was self-defense."

"Was it?"

"Of course." But the way she said it wasn't convincing. She knew Rebecca wasn't convinced, and she didn't think she was convinced either. She could have gotten out of the situation without using the gun. She could have let Ross screw her, for one thing. That would have handled the situation just fine. That's why she couldn't go to the police. They'd talk to Farley, that horse's ass; they'd talk to Dennis. There's no way she was innocent. No way. Especially since she had screwed one of Bend's finest and tried to charge him sixty bucks.

Nope. No way.

Her parents would shit. Paul would hire the best attorney money could buy; maybe that would work. The prosecutors in a jerkwater town like Bend might not be a match for a high-powered, expensive Minneapolis attorney.

She drove slowly through the darkened, snow-silent town, keeping her bad wrist in her lap, trying to imagine the one phone call she would be allowed to make. "Hi, Daddy?"

"Hi, baby."

"Daddy, I'm in trouble. I'm in jail for murder."

Paul would never let on that he was shocked. He would scarcely miss a beat. "Did you do it?"

"Yes, Daddy, but it was self-defense. He was trying to rape me. I shot him with the thirty-eight you gave me."

"I'll be right there, baby. We'll get you out, and then we'll talk about this."

He would come, bail money in hand, as fast as United Airlines could get him there. And she would have to face him. And tell him. She'd have to tell him what she had been wearing, what she had been doing. The cop. She'd have to tell him about the cop. She'd have to tell him about the guys in the bar, about leaving the Camaro and going to Ross's house with him. She'd have to look her daddy in the eye and tell him all those things, and it would be just like Eddie coming back to haunt her, only it was worse, it was far worse, because she had actually killed Ross.

Elise's heart pounded so hard and so fast she thought she was going to faint. She slowed down, knowing she couldn't drive too slowly or she'd get stopped.

She did *not* want to be stopped.

This was her karma. She'd run out on a dead body once before, and now she was doing it again. Maybe this was her chance to get straight about it all. Turn herself in. Confess. Break the chain.

"We've got to go to the police, Elise," Rebecca said quietly. She seemed lost in that sheepskin jacket. "What you've done is wrong, and not reporting it is worse. It's a sin."

That was the last thing Elise wanted to hear: Mormon crap out of the mouth of a thirteenth grader. "Like you've never sinned," Elise said. "Like what we came to Bend to do was not a sin in the eyes of your stupid church."

Rebecca started to cry. "Please, Elise, let's not make this worse. Let's go to the police. *Please*."

"Shut up, you silly bitch," Elise said. "I'm trying to think."

Rebecca probably had a loving, forgiving family and church

congregation that would hug her and kiss her and cry for her and listen to her confession. They would lavish praises on the prodigal daughter who had seen the error of her ways and come back into the fold. Not only that, but Rebecca hadn't pulled the trigger.

Elise *had* pulled the trigger. And she had no such support group. They would fry her as sure as shit—if not the state, then her family. She had no right to spit on everything they stood for and then expect them to spend all their money on her defense in a murder trial. Especially when she was guilty.

She wanted to drive off the nearest cliff. She wanted to pull the .38 out of her pocket and put a bullet in her head. She wanted to dump Rebecca by the side of the road and take off for Canada. She could be in Vancouver by noon.

She looked at the speedometer and lifted her foot off the gas. *Too fast for such a cold night. Don't want to get stopped.*

She looked over at Rebecca, who was crying softly, her head turned toward the window.

It didn't really matter what she did, Elise realized. Rebecca would call the police at her first opportunity. There was no outrunning this.

"Okay," she said.

"Okay what?"

"Okay, let's go get Tulie, and then we'll go home and call the police."

"Really?"

"Yeah. I can't run from this." Elise felt tears trickling down her cheeks. Funny, she couldn't feel them coming out of her eyes. She laughed, a harsh bark, and suddenly she did see the tears, and she could barely see anything else, as everything haloed and the snow came down harder and faster. "I've been wondering what to do after school," she said, and then the tears began to choke her. "Guess I'll go to prison." She sobbed then, and even she couldn't tell if she was laughing or crying.

Rebecca laid a calm hand on Elise's leg, and then she said one of those stupid things that people say to other people when they don't know what else to say. "You've got to find the Lord, Elise," Rebecca said.

Elise coughed, sniffed, rubbed the wetness off her face and from under her nose with her bare hand. "Yeah," she said, the only suitable response to a statement that lame. She'd been right. Rebecca *would* call the police at her very first opportunity.

Well then, Elise thought, *that narrows the choices, doesn't it?* She pressed the pedal to the metal, felt the big truck roar in response, and they headed for the campground.

NILES WAS THE LAST CHILD BORN TO AUDREY GRIFFIN, the pregnancy and birth that put paid to her childbearing years. He had eight predecessors. When Niles was born, the oldest boy was fifteen. Audrey was only thirty-six. None of the children had ever known a father.

When the obstetrician told Audrey that her baby factory days were finished, she was thrilled. She wasn't dumb but somehow always failed to make the connection between those hot, urgent passions in the dark with another nine months of belly. She never could remember to take the pills or don the diaphragm. Never to have to think about that again gave her a newfound and dangerous sense of freedom. She stuck a bottle in the baby's mouth and smiled. Three weeks later she was hitting the bars, depending on the kids to see to one another.

Clementine was eight when Niles was born. She claimed her baby brother as her own, and the other kids thought that was just as well. Clementine stopped going to school; she stayed home and played with the three youngest kids, Niles and the two sisters just older than he. But Niles was Clementine's. She changed him, bathed him, scrounged food for him, and played mommy. The role suited her well. She and Niles lived in a pleasant fantasy world that included none of the roughness and violence of their crowded conditions, their neighborhood, their mother's behavior.

When Niles was four, he woke up in the middle of the night to hear his mother yelling. He moved over in the bed, but Clementine wasn't there. Men were in the house, and loud footsteps. Then Clementine screamed and began to beg and cry. Niles pulled the covers over his head and cried.

In the morning Clemmy was gone. One of the older kids said that her father had taken her to live with him, and all the other kids were jealous. They didn't know that any of them had fathers, not really.

But Niles didn't care anything about fathers. Clementine was his real mommy, and he wanted her back. He wanted her back so bad he couldn't eat, sleep, cry, or get to the toilet in time.

And he was beaten, humiliated, and tormented regularly for not being able to do those things.

He dreamed about Clementine. He dreamed that she was there, her long black hair pulled back from her face and fastened with bobby pins, her bangs shining, wearing that flannel nightie, the one she'd found in the poor box and mended herself. In his dream she smiled at him and reached up with her soft little hand to touch his cheek. Then big, rough hands came around her waist and pulled her from him. She screamed and cried, reaching for him . . .

Niles always woke up crying. "Clemmy." he'd say, "Clemmy!" he'd yell to the night, and one of the older kids would throw a pillow or a shoe at him. He'd stick his thumb in his mouth and pull on the frayed edge of the pillow while he tried to muffle his hicking. Tears leaked out of his eyes and ran across the bridge of his nose.

Occasionally one of the older ones would lean down, pat him on the head, and say, "Don't worry, baby, she'll come back for you someday."

Everybody in the family fended for himself, and they expected him to as well. Eventually he did.

It wasn't until Niles himself was around twelve years old that he became aware of his surroundings as they related to others of his age. The Griffin family, such as it was, lived in an old mobile home behind an abandoned sawmill in a little backwater Montana town. Someone, probably one of the older brothers, told Niles that the mill and the property their home sat on used to belong to their grandfather, their mother's father. She inherited it when he died, so all she had to do was come up with enough money every month to pay the electricity and the taxes, which weren't much.

Apparently she was able to keep that much together.

Audrey Griffin drank. She drank a lot.

Niles grew so tall that he stopped getting hand-me-downs; that meant he got no new clothes at all. That is when he realized they were poor. The knowledge struck him slowly, like all other knowledge, but it brought with it a terrible shame. If they hadn't been poor, maybe Clementine would still be with them. If they hadn't been poor, maybe his older brothers and sisters would be nicer to him. If they hadn't been poor, maybe they'd all have a father.

Money was power, he could see, and the Griffins didn't have any at all.

When Niles was fourteen, Audrey had another fit of conscience and tried to go on the wagon. These times were famous among the elder siblings, but Niles had no real awareness of them until this time.

She got up one morning, made breakfast for Niles and the three sisters and two brothers still living at home, then went about cleaning. She cleaned the whole trailer, did the laundry, cooked a real dinner, set the table and all. She did a lot of kissing and hugging and crying while she did her work, all the while smoking and drinking coffee.

Niles didn't know what to do. He didn't know how to act. The Audrey he knew slept until noon, got up frowzy and grumpy, sat, bleary-eyed and puffy-faced over a cup of coffee and an ashtray full of cigarettes, then dragged herself to bathe, dress, and then she was gone to work, for the night, and sometimes for several days in a row.

Niles also discovered, in early adolescence, that they lived in a small town. He had friends who visited Helena, Butte, Great Falls, and Billings, and through them he learned about tall buildings and busy streets.

There weren't any busy streets in Hightown, Montana. And his friends said there weren't any falling-down old deserted mills in those big cities either. Or any broken-down old trailer houses where all nine kids slept in practically one room. Niles was ashamed.

But when Audrey got sober and started to pay attention to the kids, the kind of attention filled with guilt and promises of silver linings in those ever-present gray clouds, Niles's shame began to evaporate. He knew hope. He thought maybe if she loved him enough to hug him and cry over his head, that she would love him enough to buy him some new jeans, move them to a real house, one with some flowers in front instead of weeds filled with dogshit. Maybe she'd get them all a father. And maybe she'd go get Clementine back.

Audrey stayed sober just long enough for Niles to blossom in her sunshine. She got up early, spent time with him, went to work with a song on her tongue, and came home before midnight. They dressed up on Sundays and went to church, Niles and his mother, and Niles raised his hands in the air when they all sang, and tears ran down his face and he felt that something even better than Clemmy's coming back had happened to his life.

Audrey brought home a nice man for dinner a couple of evenings, and on the weekend the three of them went camping, all sleeping in one tiny tent. The man, Jack was his name, taught Niles to fish, and they even fried up and ate the tiny fish Niles caught. They told jokes around the campfire and drank hot coffee with milk in it, and it was the warmest and coziest Niles had ever felt in his life. He wanted to stay at that campground by the river forever.

The other kids scoffed at Audrey's latest behavior, her most recent stab at sobriety, but Niles believed in her. He believed in something for the first time since Clemmy had been stolen from him.

But it didn't last. Everybody, even Audrey, knew it wouldn't last.

And when she came home after a three-day binge, hungover and ashamed to belligerence, Niles went over to his sister Marjorie's house. Marjorie was twenty-two and had a husband and two kids of her own. He stayed with her for a year. He stayed there until Marjorie's husband threw him out.

At fifteen years old Niles Griffin was on his own. He was skinny, slow, and absolutely alone.

By the time he was seventeen, he had been in and out of a half dozen foster homes and an equal number of youth facilities. His was not a behavior problem, but he was fairly dim and totally apathetic. He wandered through life with no enthusiasm at all. This grated on most people.

Until he met Lisa Stevenson.

Lisa Stevenson was definitely a behavior problem. She was in the same group home as Niles, having served her time at a home for young women. The people at the group home were helping her find a job and become readjusted to the outside world. Lisa was almost eighteen.

Niles noticed Lisa looking at him a lot, but he wasn't much interested. He just went to church every Sunday and minded his own business. He swept floors, washed dishes, peeled potatoes, did laundry—whatever he was told to do—and he kept his eyes to himself. Now and then he'd look up, and there would be Lisa, her bright eyes boring holes into him, her thick brown hair shiny and pulled up into a ponytail, her painted fingernails drumming some tattoo on the arm of her chair, her teeth chewing gum a mile a minute. When she saw him looking at her, she smiled, and her glossy red lips parted to show teeth whiter than any teeth he'd ever seen. They were crooked with the two front ones crossed over each other, but they were white. And her eyes were the darkest blue he'd ever seen. Dark, dark blue.

He didn't care much for Lisa. She had a smart mouth. She was always talking and giggling with her girlfriends, and Niles kept his head down, certain that they were always talking about him. Not that he was important, but she was always looking at him, so he figured she thought about him.

And he began to think about her.

Soon he began to look at her openly. He'd just lift his head and look around, and she'd be there, smiling. He'd try to smile back. Sometimes it worked; sometimes it didn't.

One night he felt something in his bed. He turned over, and there she was. "Clemmy?" he asked, sleepy and confused.

"Lisa," she whispered, and her long fingernails played in his hair and on his face, and her lips opened and took his in. He jumped when he felt her tongue, but she settled him down, and soon he was exploring her crooked front teeth with his tongue, and her hands were hot and on his private parts. He exploded at her touch, but she was willing to wait for him, and it wasn't long before they were bucking and thrashing in the bed, Niles mindless of his roommate, concentrating only on the extraordinary things she was saying and doing to him, wanting desperately for it to last longer, longer, longer.

But of course, it lasted barely a minute.

He lay there, like a stunned frog, while she slipped out of bed, into her nightie, and out the door.

In the morning he thought it was the most wonderful wet dream he'd ever had. Then he smelled her perfume on his pillow, and her stickiness was still on him.

He lifted his head higher that day and smiled openly at her. She smiled back.

He wanted her to come back every night after that, but she came back only now and then. Niles didn't see any pattern to her nighttime visits; he only assumed she came when she could.

With Lisa's interest in Niles, Niles became interested in life. His interest spilled out of his bed and into other activities in the group home. He even looked at the bulletin board where job opportunities were posted, thinking that if he got a job, he and Lisa could get married and move out.

Then one day a runner came and told him that the supervisor wanted to see him. "Me?" Niles asked. He'd never been called to see the supervisor before.

Niles slowly put away his cleaning tools, dusted himself off, and went to the supervisor's office. He'd never spoken with the supervisor face-to-face before. Niles had never been in his office, except to vacuum.

He knocked and opened the door. Lisa sat in a chair, and she did not look happy.

"Come in, Niles," the supervisor said. "Sit down."

Niles sat, his belly full of grit.

"Lisa here is in the family way, Niles. Now I know that neither of you is yet eighteen, but the state has a policy about things like that."

In the family way. Niles had no idea what he was talking about.

"The reverend has consented to perform the marriage ceremony this Sunday after divine services. Fortunately both of you will turn eighteen before the baby is due. You will have to leave the center when you turn eighteen. Am I making myself clear?"

Niles heard only "marriage" and "baby." He looked at his feet. He was going to get to marry Lisa, and the center was going to have them move out on their own. It was like a dream come true. He looked at his feet and smiled at them. They were going to have a baby.

"You know, of course, this is a direct violation of the rules. If you refuse to do the manly thing here, Niles, and marry this girl, then we will have to file criminal charges against you."

Niles looked up alarmed, not understanding at all.

"You will marry the girl?"

Niles nodded. He looked over at Lisa. She smiled with satisfaction, but she didn't smile at him.

"That's all then," the supervisor said. "I suggest you two make some plans."

Lisa stood up, and Niles followed her out the door.

"Married?" he finally managed to say.

"Just to name the baby, Niles, that's all. Sorry." And she turned on her heel and walked away.

Just to name the baby. He never figured that out. She never came back to see him at night.

They were married by the minister in the supervisor's office, with the supervisor and his secretary as witnesses. Lisa avoided Niles after that, but whenever he could, he stole looks at her swelling belly and he'd shake his head. He really couldn't figure it all out.

He sneaked around and listened when she talked to her girlfriends. The baby was going to come on September 8, he heard her say. His spirits soared when he thought about it. He felt light when he thought about being a daddy, about having a baby. He thought about poor Audrey and all his brothers and sisters who never had a daddy, and it was no wonder, if that's all it took. But he was going to be a good daddy to this baby, to Lisa's baby, to Lisa and his baby.

Lisa turned eighteen in July, one month before he did, and when the girls began to cry and made a flurry of going-away-party preparations, Niles realized that she was leaving without him.

It had happened too fast. He wasn't prepared. He didn't have an outside job. They didn't have an apartment. He felt caught in the headlights of an onrushing life, completely unprepared for his responsibilities.

He didn't know how to face her.

But after the party, before he began sweeping up and tossing all the cake plates and ribbons and baby wrapping paper into the garbage, he went to her room, where she was zipping the last of the baby gifts into her suitcase.

Her roommate saw him, got up off the bed, and brushed past him into the hallway.

Niles and Lisa were alone, and Niles had no words for her.

"Fun party, huh?" Lisa said as she finished zipping, then sat on the bed and looked at him. He recognized that look. All the same emotions were tornadoing her, too.

Niles nodded.

"I'm going to live with my brother and his wife," she said.

Niles nodded, and a tear slipped down next to his nose. He took a deep, ragged breath, pleased to discover that tears relieved the pressure. He had been afraid he was going to explode. He coughed and turned away, wiping the moisture so she wouldn't see it.

"In Indiana," she said. "Indianapolis, isn't that a silly name? Indianapolis, Indiana?" She looked down at the suitcase, fingered the zipper pull. Then she wiped her cheeks with both long-nailed hands, and Niles saw moisture there, too.

"Can I come?" he asked.

She smiled at him, then shook her head. "I'm sorry, Niles. This wasn't exactly what I had planned. Not that I had a plan, exactly . . ." She sniffed, rummaged in her purse, found a tissue, and blew her nose. She looked up at him with reddened eyes. "I thought I had a plan, but I wasn't thinking too clearly, I guess."

"I can't come?" He didn't understand. They were married. They were a family.

"No," she said slowly. "Forget me, Niles. I'm trouble." She blew her nose one last time, pulled a pocket mirror from her purse, fingered at her eyes for a moment, then shut it, snapped her purse closed, and stood up.

Niles lifted her suitcase and carried it out to the house van, idling by the front door.

Lisa thanked him, touched his cheek with a finger, then bundled her belly into the front seat and closed the door. She never looked back.

Niles stood in the driveway and watched the van disappear around the corner. He never saw her again.

On his eighteenth birthday he was given a little zippered bag and told to pack his things.

Once again Niles was on the street. But this time he knew a few things.

He knew that women would use him and then hurt him.

He knew that things that felt real good were usually trouble.

The problem that he wrestled with included both the great feeling of sex and the trouble he was sure it would cause. So he began a little ritual. Every day he would do something he hated. Every day he would torture himself just a little bit, so when he found some sex, he could indulge himself, and perhaps in the eyes of God a balance would be struck.

He hitchhiked to Great Falls, found a home in an abandoned car, and found work in a foundry. His job was to grind the mold burrs off cast metal parts. It was a good job, but he couldn't wait to get through for the day, because then he would find himself something terrible to do, like hit himself on the toe with a hammer. That was a good one because he remembered it every time he took a step for three days. Or one time he volunteered to clean out the garbage cans at the plant. He had to climb inside them, and the stench almost choked him. But he cleaned them, scrubbed them down with soap and water. Penance in advance. Then he was always ready to get laid, if the opportunity ever presented itself again.

A grizzled old foundry foreman named Fitch was Niles's

first supervisor. Fitch was a muscled, hard worker. He had dozens of different baseball caps, and he always wore one, wiry gray hair sticking out from underneath it like feathers around his ears. He didn't seem to like Niles very much at first, but as Niles just concentrated on doing his job and doing it right, pretty soon Fitch spoke more softly and kindly to him. Now and then he'd put a big, meaty arm around Niles's thin shoulders, and Niles fantasized that Fitch was his dad.

One Friday night Fitch invited Niles out for a beer after work. Niles smiled widely and nodded. "Sure," he said. "Sure."

When the whistle blew, they cleaned up and walked across the street and down a block to a tough bar filled with smoke and black leather. There were beards and fists and muscles and scars and the stench of unwashed males. Fitch looked right at home. Niles looked around, wide-eyed.

"Don't stare, kid," Fitch said. "You look like a geek."

Niles didn't know what else to do, so he lowered his eyes and only took sly glances around. Nobody seemed to pay any attention to him.

Fitch brought two frosty beers to the table. He picked his up and held it. Niles picked his up, and they clinked mugs. "To the future, kid," Fitch said, then drained half his beer. Niles took a tentative sip. It tasted good. He drank.

Fitch pulled a pack of Camels out of his shirt pocket, shook some out of the hole, and offered them to Niles. He took one. Fitch slipped one into his mouth, then pocketed the pack. "Ever smoke before?"

Niles shook his head no.

"Ever drink beer before?"

Niles smiled shyly and shook his head again.

"Ever gotten laid?"

Niles looked up and nodded enthusiastically. Fitch roared with laughter. "Good. Good. Well, here." And he lit Niles's first cigarette. Niles coughed, sputtered, and burned with embarrassment, while Fitch and those around them laughed. But determined, he kept at it until he could take a small drag and pull it into his lungs with only a minor catch on the way down. The beer helped. He watched Fitch and the other guys as they became caught up in the camaraderie of the tavern, and he tried to imitate their easy handling of cigarettes and beer.

He had a great time and fell down the stairs when they left.

In the morning he awoke headachy, with a terrible taste in his mouth. He sat up and found himself on a couch, fully clothed, with a brown and tan afghan thrown over him. The only thing he could remember from the night before was Fitch putting his heavy arm around Niles's shoulders and saying, "Know what I like to see in a man? Loyalty. A man's got to have loyalty in his soul or he ain't no man."

Niles got up quietly, found the toilet, and peeked into the bedroom. Fitch was snoring. He even wore a baseball cap to bed.

Niles remembered that it was Saturday, and he went back to the living room and turned on cartoons quietly, then looked in the kitchen for some cereal. There wasn't any. There wasn't anything in the cupboards but a half-empty package of spaghetti noodles. The refrigerator had a can of applesauce, five cans of beer, and a half carton of cigarettes.

Niles took the applesauce, a beer, and a pack of cigarettes back to the living room.

When Fitch finally got up, he found Niles, drunk again, with five empty beer cans on the table before him, a spoon in the applesauce jar and two cigarettes going at the same time in the ashtray.

Fitch hitched up his pants, adjusted his hat, put on his shoes, walked to the corner grocery, and bought more beer, more cigarettes, more applesauce and a package of sweet rolls. He came back to the apartment, and the two of them made a day of it.

From that day forward Niles felt a bond with Fitch, a loyalty so deep he thought he could hide within it forever. He followed Fitch around, did whatever Fitch told him to do, worshiped Fitch, and gloried in his presence. He knew that the others laughed and that sometimes even Fitch laughed at him, but he could take it. Nobody had ever been his friend before, not like this. Everybody else either resented him, used him, or downright ridiculed him. Not Fitch. Fitch brought out the best in Niles.

They went to bars together, they went to whorehouses together, and soon all of Niles's belongings were behind Fitch's couch, and he had moved in. He cleaned Fitch's apartment, washed Fitch's clothes, did everything but the things the guys at work sniggered about and hinted that he did. It was a joyful penance, and sometimes Niles felt guilty because life felt so good. He thought perhaps the laundry and the dishes weren't enough penance for the fun he was having, but he didn't seem to have too much time to do other things. He just hoped it was enough to appease God.

Niles had found a home, a friend, a job, and a life. He blossomed. He felt more intelligent, wittier. He was able to carry on conversations with people. He found that he had opinions. Niles began to fall in love with life.

One summer afternoon, after Niles had been living at Fitch's almost a whole year, some of the workers at the foundry had a picnic. They brought wives and girlfriends, children and elderly parents. Niles wanted to play softball, and he wanted Fitch to play, too.

But Fitch wouldn't. He just sat on the bench, drinking beer. And later he wouldn't discuss it either.

After that, Niles began to look at Fitch out of the corner of his eye to catch him unawares, and he noticed that Fitch looked different. He looked older suddenly. He was thinner.

"Fitch." Niles finally confronted him at home one night. He'd polished off half a bucket of Kentucky Fried, but Fitch hardly ate anything. He had dipped a roll into the mashed potatoes and gravy, taken a bite, taken a bite of chicken, then had lit up a cigarette and turned on the television.

"Huh?"

"You aren't eating. You're losing weight. How come you're not eating?"

"Not hungry."

"C'mon, Fitch. Is there something wrong? Seen the doctor?"

"Nothing's wrong. Don't nag me."

Niles knew now, and panic began a slow rise. "C'mon, Fitch," he whined. "Tell me. What is it?"

Fitch turned to him, and Niles saw fear.

"You wanna know? Okay. Here." Fitch pulled up his T-shirt. There was a lump the size of a walnut on the back of his shoulder. It had a tuck in it, a dimple. "Satisfied? Want more?" Fitch was angry and Niles was scared. He pulled his shirt off. There was a great pink growth on his left breast, the size of a silver dollar. It was smooth and looked cold and hard. It dimpled way down in the center, like a doughnut. "Fucking woman's disease, Niles. Got another one coming up on the top of my head. Now what? Now what? Jesus Christ, you make me crazy."

Niles was stunned. He knew about lumps. He knew about cancers; they had safety and health training films at work. Usually they were a time for the guys to hoot and holler and make fun of the actors, but Niles paid attention to them.

Fitch had cancer. Breast cancer, and it had spread. Fitch was going to die.

"Fitch," he said, his hands flopping around in helpless gestures. "Fitch, you've got to go to a doctor."

"It's too late." Fitch snapped the brim of his cap farther down over his eyes. "It was too late two years ago."

"Two years?"

Fitch opened a new beer and drank half of it down.

"You've had that lump for two years?"

"Enough about it."

"Don't you want to live, Fitch? Don't you want to work no more? Don't you want to be with me? Don't you love me, Fitch?"

Fitch slammed the beer on the coffee table so hard that its rim left a dent. *"It's too late!"* He pulled off his cap, ran his fingers through his hair, then repositioned the hat. "Leave it alone, Niles."

"I—I don't know what I'll do when you die." That feeling that he was going to explode built up inside Niles again.

"Listen to me." Fitch stood up and turned off the television set.

He suddenly looked shrunken. Niles could see the disease. It was all around him. It was all through him. How could he have not seen it before?

"You are all right," Fitch said. "You will be all right." Fitch sat on the coffee table, his knees touching Niles's knees. His sincerity forced Niles to look into his yellowed eyes. "When I die," Fitch said, "you'll just come in one morning and find me dead in bed. You'll call nine-one-one, and they'll take care of everything. You'll just take over this apartment. Nothing needs to change. You just move my stuff out of the bedroom and move your stuff in. You pay the rent every month just like I do. That's all. You keep the job at the foundry. It's a good job. And you don't drink too much and don't pick whores up off the street. You'll be all right, Niles. You'll be all right. I mean it."

Then he got up, went into his bedroom, and closed the door.

Niles looked up at the ceiling. "God, I'll do anything if you won't make Fitch die," he said. He stood up and began to pace. "I'll cut myself. I'll cut my feet off." He didn't think God wanted him to do that because then he couldn't do much else. "Better than that, God, I'll . . . I'll stay after work after everybody else has gone home and I'll sweep up and clean the toilets." That didn't sound like something God would want him to do, either. That sounded like something the boss would like him to do. It didn't seem like something that would keep Fitch alive one extra moment. "No, no," he said. "Wait. Don't hang up, please. I'll think of something."

He resumed pacing. He reviewed everything he knew about God. It wasn't much. He had gone to church a few times with Audrey, and then, when he was at one of the youth homes, they made him go. He was supposed to put money in the little dish they passed up and down the benches. So God liked people to go to church, and God liked money. "I will go to church every day, and I will give You all my money." He stopped to think. "Except for what I need to live. And I won't drink, and I won't smoke, because I know You don't like those things, and I won't screw whores anymore. Just please let Fitch live."

And Niles put on his coat and went out, hoping he'd stumble upon a church. He didn't. He just wandered, wondering why all the bad things in the world had to fall upon his head and wondering how he would handle all the bad things if he didn't have Fitch for a friend.

He hated the thought of giving up sex, but he knew if he

didn't have sex anymore, he wouldn't have to do those other things that he did to himself.

He wanted to fall to his knees in the middle of the street and implore God to release him and Fitch from all this torment. The pain was unbearable. This time he was certain he would explode. He would do whatever God asked—if God would only *ask!* In lieu of God's direct requests, Niles would give up women, booze, cigarettes, go to church, and give them all his money.

"So, God," he said, "You better see that Fitch gets well."

But Fitch didn't. Soon he began to cough.

Niles found a church and went twice a day.

Fitch began to take off work at noon every day. Niles borrowed money to give to the church.

One day, when Niles came home from work, Fitch was in bed. His face was damp and pale. He didn't want to talk to Niles, so Niles let him sleep. And in the morning, just as Fitch had predicted, he failed to wake up.

Niles knelt by his bedside and cried. Then he dialed 911, gave them the information they asked for, and went to work. He bought a pack of cigarettes on the way, and after work he stopped at his favorite whorehouse and had a go at Marylynne. Then he bought some beer and went back to *his* apartment. He moved Fitch's things out of the dresser drawers and closets, put them in a bag to take to the church, moved his things in, shook his fist at God, and decided that if God didn't care about him, he didn't care about God.

Something inside him didn't like the way he was acting, but he ignored that. He wasn't interested. He cried himself to sleep every night, he missed Fitch so badly, and sometimes when he cried, he said Fitch and sometimes he said Clementine, and sometimes he didn't even know the difference.

He didn't have much luck finding new friends either, so

when a group of kids his age started paying attention to him, Niles went along with them. He had a vague feeling they were laughing at him behind his back, but he ignored that feeling, too. He didn't care anymore. He didn't care about anything. He paid his rent the way Fitch told him to, and he went to work, but he spent the rest of his life being mad.

It was the self-appointed leader of this group of kids, Hombre, he called himself, who recognized Niles's anger and began to capitalize on it. Soon the group had Niles stealing things for them, and in return Niles received recognition, friendship, belonging, and a piece of the action. He knew Fitch wouldn't approve of the things he was doing, but every time he had an attack of conscience, he would look up at God and say, "I don't care. I don't *care.*"

It was only a matter of time before he got caught robbing a liquor store. The job had gone just as Hombre had planned it, but Niles had tried to cram an extra bottle of vodka and an extra carton of cigarettes into his coat. He dropped the cigarettes, went back to retrieve them, and that was just the wrong thing to do at the wrong time. He heard the sirens and froze. Hombre and the rest scattered like cockroaches. He just stood there with the goods.

His boss bailed him out, lent him the use of the company attorney, and went to court with him to help plead his case. The judge took into account Niles's background, his mental capacities, and gave him a thirty-day sentence in the county jail and five hundred hours of community service.

Niles did his time quietly. When he got out, he got a schedule for his community service, and he performed every hour cleaning the county library without complaining. He shrugged off Hombre and that crowd, and he worked harder than ever at the foundry.

When all his debts were paid, he thanked his boss, quit his

job, packed what few things he wanted to take with him, left the apartment key on the counter, walked down to the highway, and stuck out his thumb. He never wanted to see Montana again.

As time passed, Fitch's face began to blur and then fade. Niles could no longer remember anything about Clementine except her name. He marked the passing of the years in terms of his daughter's age. He didn't know, exactly, that what he and Lisa produced was a girl, but somehow he knew it all the same. And he didn't know when she was born, either, but he celebrated her birthday on September 8 every year.

He visualized the girl—Little Lisa he called her—to be kind of skinny, bony, perhaps, like him, with long, soft, luxurious brown hair like Lisa's, and those dark, dark blue eyes. He hoped she had Lisa's softness and Fitch's personality. On September 8 of every year he spent an entire hour thinking about her, thinking about Lisa, wondering, imagining where they'd be, who they'd be with, whether Lisa had ever married and found a dad for Little Lisa. He marked her sixteenth birthday as a special one and even bought a little cupcake, put a candle on it, and sang "Happy Birthday" to her. Thinking about Little Lisa usually made him happy, but now and again an overwhelming sadness that they might never meet would attack him, and he would cry.

He drifted from job to job during those years, keeping himself out of trouble, afraid that there would be no friendly boss to go in front of the judge for him anymore. The Hombre types were drawn to him like metal to a magnet, but he just put his head down and walked harder, faster, worked cleaner, ignored them and their temptations. He drifted from Idaho to Washington, to Oregon down to California and back to Idaho again, never really settling down, never really finding what he could call a home.

Until he landed that painting job in Eugene, Oregon, and found Buck and the Songster. And the boxcars.

Niles fixed his boxcar up with a bed, a dresser, a night table, and lots of blankets. There was even a little rug on the floor. Buck had a mattress and a cooler, but the Songster just had a nasty sleeping bag wadded up in the dusty corner of his boxcar.

The boxcars. Free rent, and nobody bothered them. Quiet, out in the country. Niles liked it. It was like the Songster said, a place where you could look out over nothing but peace and tranquillity. It was a place he could call home for a long, long time.

"OKAY," NILES SAID. "SO LET ME GET THIS STRAIGHT. You've admitted to killing three women, right? And you did time for one. So we're going to put you on trial for the other two? What's the trial for if you already admit it?"

"He needs to be punished," Buck said. "He needs to be heard, judged, and sentenced. That's the law."

"We've got no proof," Niles said.

"We've got his word," Tulie said. "And he wants to tell the truth." She wanted to get the information and turn him in to the police. This type of scum had no business being alive.

"Oh, yeah, right," Buck said. "He wants to be *delivered* of his sins."

"Do ya, Songster?" Niles asked.

The Songster lit up another joint.

"He's not going to tell us anything," Niles said.

"You have to ask questions," Buck said, "if you're going to be the prosecutor."

"Yeah? Like what?"

"Like, was the woman you did time for the first woman you killed?" Buck asked.

"No," the Songster said.

"How old were you when you killed the first time?"

"Fourteen."

"Wow," Niles said. "You just got that knife brand-new and you used it, huh? Did you get the knife in order to kill that woman?"

"No. It just happened. It was an accident."

"And nobody yet knows who killed her," Niles said with reverence. "Wow. Unsolved mystery. Who was it?"

"A whore."

"Jeez," Niles said. "You hang a lot with whores, huh?"

"They're the best and the worst of women, all on one street corner," the Songster said without exhaling, his lungs full of marijuana smoke.

"I like them, too," Niles said, then snickered. "If you know what I mean. Know what I mean, Buck?"

The Songster let his breath out with a rush.

"I want to hear about the one in the boxcar," Buck said, ignoring Niles. "I don't care about something that happened thirty years ago. That woman never came out of that boxcar under her own power, Songster, and that was only a few months ago."

"It was an accident, I told you." the Songster said.

"An accident!" Buck hooted. "You knife a woman with that

huge gut ripper there and you say it was an accident? *Another* accident?"

"Shut the fuck up, Buck," the Songster said. "It was an accident." He toked long on the joint, and the car settled into that wavy silence. "I'm not sure exactly what happened, except that she wanted to play rough. She liked that. And when I pulled out the knife, she liked it even more."

"Yeah, sure, a woman who gets turned on by a stranger in a boxcar with a knife?" Buck scoffed.

"It could happen," Tulie said in horrified fascination. "Go on, Songster."

"She wanted it."

Tulie felt her heart turn over. It could have been her, hanging with the rough trade. Her emotions began to slosh. Terror and compassion.

"What bullshit," Buck said. "She begged you to kill her, is that it?"

"No, she just wanted to be hurt a little bit. Lots of little bits. It just got out of control."

"*You* got out of control," Buck said.

"No kidding," Niles said. "So did you kill her in passion or in cold blood?"

The car was so quiet for so long Tulie wasn't sure the Songster had heard the question. She felt hot tears pushing at the back of her eyes. "Don't know," he finally said.

"You *must* know," Buck said. "Did you consciously plunge that knife into her because of who she was or what she said or did, or when you were yelling for your mama, did it just accidentally get caught in her throat?" There had to be explanations for things like this. Somebody had to understand it completely. There had to be cut-and-dried, totally rational thought processes behind something like that. Somebody had to understand it, either the Songster or some shrink, but *some-*

body had to understand it. Somebody had to. And who better than the killer himself?

But here he was, saying he didn't understand it at all. Buck couldn't stand it. He needed to know that somebody could, would, someday understand what he did to Cara. He needed to know that *some*day *some*body would explain it to him. To Cara. To Kaiser.

He slammed his hand on the steering wheel. Again. And again. Somebody had to know just exactly what the fuck was going on.

"Hey, Buck," Niles said. "Settle down, okay?"

"I liked it," the Songster said calmly, and Tulie's attention snapped back from Buck's anger to the Songster's gruesome confession. "I liked the little nicks and cuts and little drops of blood all over her. She liked it and I liked it, and I liked that she liked it. It just got a little rougher and a little out of hand. I just kept cutting her a little deeper, a little more often. She started to not like it so much, and then she started to struggle, and I liked that even more, and Gloria liked it even more than that."

"Gloria?" Niles asked.

"His stupid knife," Buck whispered through clenched teeth.

"The rougher it got, the better we liked it, until I could see—"

"See what?" Niles asked.

"I could see that I could *really* come to like it. She was going to steal my soul with that stuff. She had to go."

"There are other ways to ditch a woman," Buck said.

"It was more than that. I didn't know she had to go until after. Then I saw how it had to be that way. It was, like, meant to be that way. I don't know."

"So what did you do?" Niles asked.

"I put her in her car and drove it to Roseburg and left it."

"No," Niles said. "I mean, what did you do? How did you kill her?"

"I don't even remember it, Niles," the Songster said softly.

"Did you cut her throat? Did you gut her?"

"Niles," Buck said.

"Small wound," the Songster said. "Clean."

"Yeah, but *where*?"

"Shut up, Niles," Buck said. "We don't want to hear where."

"I do," Niles whined.

"I sliced her heart in two, Niles," the Songster said as if reciting poetry. "Silently."

Tulie felt those tears threaten to cascade over her lids. She blinked quickly to hold them back, felt her breathing turn ragged, hoped that didn't give her away. She felt as if she'd known that woman. She wanted to go home.

"Jesus," Niles said almost reverently. "And how do you feel?"

"I'm not proud," the Songster said.

"So this first one, this one when you were fourteen," Buck said. "Was she trying to steal your soul, too?"

No answer.

"Do you know how stupid that sounds?" Buck pressed.

No answer.

"Tell us about the one when you were fourteen," Niles said.

"I don't want to talk about that."

"Then what about the other one?"

"I don't want to talk about that either."

"You're pathetic," Buck said. "For a while there I thought you were dangerous, but you're just pathetic." He wasn't afraid of the Songster anymore. The Songster couldn't hurt him. The Songster was just a sad case, a sorry, sorry mental case. Buck was finished with the Songster. He could find a much better class of friend. Hell, even Niles was a far superior class of friend.

"Don't you judge me," the Songster said.

"*I'm* the judge," Tulie said, pleased that her voice sounded solid. She was going to take charge of herself now, if not the situation. "Has all the evidence been submitted?"

Silence.

"Well, then," she said, speaking carefully, feeling tense, each nerve ending sniffing the air for danger, "you're guilty, there's no question of that, is there?"

Silence.

"The only thing for me to do here is to decide your sentence." Tulie took a deep breath, her heart pounding. "I think you're a pretty miserable guy, Songster. I think if you've killed three women so far, you'll keep on killing women, and that's unacceptable. You're a menace. I say you should die. Be put out of your misery."

"Fuck you," the Songster said.

"Okay, Buck," Niles said. "You're the executioner."

Tulie let out a long whisper of air. The spotlight was back on the Songster again.

"He's a pussy," the Songster said.

Tulie felt Buck tense to the breaking point. The air thickened, and she was sorry she'd started this. There didn't seem to be *anything* she could do to fix the situation; it was just plain bad. No matter what.

Buck turned his head to look at the Songster.

Gloria glinted.

Tulie's stomach lurched.

Buck's lip curled away from his teeth.

Kill him, Buck, Tulie thought.

"You're dirt," Buck said. "You should be eliminated. Not put out of your misery, but eradicated like a cockroach."

"Fuck you, too," the Songster said. "Just try it."

Buck shouldered the Pontiac door open and twirled out in one smooth motion.

Without warning, Tulie's head was jerked backward as the Songster had her hair in his hand and he was dragging her backward over the seat. It felt as if her scalp were being pulled right off her skull. She cried out, a strangled sound that scared her more than anything.

Her neck was stretched so far backward that her boots slipped on the car seat as she tried to stand up in order to keep him from breaking her neck. Then she saw the blade of the knife, and she tried to swallow and keep quiet. *Oh God*, she thought, *Oh God, Oh God, Oh God.*

Buck pulled the Songster's door open.

"Try it, you puke," the Songster growled, "and I'll give this bitch's throat a big red smile."

Oh, God.

Headlights wavered through the trees and the sound of a big truck engine filled the woods.

The inside of the car was silent except for the pounding of Tulie's heart. Tears squeezed out of her eyes and trailed toward her ears. Her breath sucked raggedly in and out over her stretched neck.

"Forest ranger," Buck said.

Gloria disappeared, and the Songster released her hair.

Tulie tried to pull away fast, but her neck hurt. She leaned forward, releasing a couple of sobs, then opened the front car door and stumbled out.

"Cops," Buck said, standing in the doorway. "Get back into the car."

She waved him off, coughing, tears falling down her cheeks. No way she was getting back into that car. The ranger would take her home. And arrest the Songster. He threatened her. He assaulted her.

In the back of her mind her sister's voice said, *You're asking for it, hanging with those guys.*

Tulie didn't care. It had gone too far. She wanted out. Perspiration ran down the bridge of her nose and trickled into the hot tears of fear and frustration. She slapped them off her face, felt her throat for damage. "Asshole," she said. She leaned over and spit words into the backseat. "Fucking lunatic."

Buck got back into the car. Tulie heard him tell the Songster to put the dope away.

That was what she'd tell the ranger. They have dope.

She watched the headlights wave around crazily between the trees as the vehicle bounced over the deep ruts and potholes in the road. Her knees went wobbly with relief.

"Get back in," Buck said again. "It's the cops."

"Good," she said, wiping tears from her face. "I'll talk to them out here."

"*Get in the car,*" Buck said. "You'll get us all arrested."

"I haven't done anything," Tulie said, and walked away from the car. She intended to get inside that ranger's truck and get the hell out of there. And she wouldn't mind if the forest ranger pulled the shotgun from his rack and sent a double load through the Songster's belly just for kicks.

Ross's truck lurched to a stop next to them, and Elise opened the door and dropped heavily out of the driver's seat into the snow, holding one hand with her other.

"Elise!" Tulie said with surprise. She didn't know if this was an answer to her prayers or another complication. "Come on. Let's get out of here."

"I have some decisions to make," Elise said. "I'm not quite sure what to do."

Complication. Shit. Of course, she was going to be a complication. This was Elise.

"You don't want to stay here," Tulie said. "Come on."

Rebecca came around the nose of the truck and stood, denim-jacketed arms folded over her chest.

"Come *on*," Rebecca said. "Let's go."

"I don't know where to go yet," Elise said, standing her ground.

Tulie grabbed Elise's arm, then let go when she saw Elise wince. "Let's just get the hell out of here," Tulie said. "These guys are nuts. They're drunk, and one of them has a knife."

It was the wrong thing to say. Elise had both Tulie and Rebecca begging her to drive them away. Elise was in control. Elise was the queen. She had the spotlight.

"Elise," Rebecca whined, "it's cold."

Elise walked over to the Pontiac.

Niles opened the door. "Well, well," he said. "The ladies are back."

Buck opened the driver's door and stood up, resting a forearm on the snowy top.

"I'm not getting back in that car, Elise," Tulie said.

"Suit yourself. I'm not going to stand out here in the cold."

"Elise—"

Niles slid back into the car. Rebecca followed him in and closed the back door. Elise held the front door open, but Tulie stood her ground. "I'm not getting back into that car with those guys, with that asshole, with that lunatic."

"I won't let him hurt you," Buck said.

"Yeah," Tulie said, but her resolve was melting.

Elise said, "Coming?"

Tulie wasn't going to stand out in the cold by herself either. "Can't we just go?"

Elise started to get into the car.

"Then give me the keys to that truck."

"It's open."

"I'll need heat. Come *on*, Elise. Don't be—"

ELIZABETH ENGSTROM

"Don't be what?" Elise stared Tulie down. "I'm not giving you any keys. There isn't enough gas. Either get in or stay out and freeze. I don't give a shit either way."

I hate this night, Tulie thought, but realized that she'd hate it even more alone out in the cold. "Shit," Tulie said, and Elise backed out. Tulie slipped into the front next to Buck. Elise got in and closed the door. The car stank. Tulie was freaked out about the Songster behind her. He radiated some kind of evil energy; she could feel it. She shrank down into the seat.

Let Elise take the spotlight. Surely the Songster would find her infinitely more entertaining. She wondered if Elise would get behind something like the Songster's little nick-for-blood sex game.

"What's the matter with your wrist?" Buck asked.

"It'll be all right," Elise said.

"Where'd you get that truck?" Tulie asked.

"Elise shot some guy," Rebecca said. "It's his truck. We've got to go to the police."

"It was self-defense," Elise said.

"Jesus, Buck," Niles said. "We're surrounded by 'em. The Songster kills women by accident, and this here hooker kills men in self-defense."

"You *shot* some guy?" Tulie couldn't comprehend what she was hearing. She sat up straight. "What do you mean, you *shot* some guy?"

"It . . . it just happened," Elise said, hugging herself.

"Something like that doesn't just *happen*, Elise," Tulie said. "My God. Who *are* you people?" She ran fingernails through her hair, raking her scalp. "Come on, tell."

"Elise on trial," Niles said, and even Buck barked out a laugh.

"There's nothing funny about this," Elise said. "I'll probably

196

go to jail for the rest of my life for something that wasn't even my fault."

"Were you hooking?" Tulie asked.

"Yes," Rebecca said with vehemence. "She was."

"Was this one of your tricks?"

"No," Elise said. "We were leaving, but the damned stupid Camaro wouldn't start. I asked this cowboy to give us a lift to a motel, and he took us to his house instead. He *kidnapped* us. And then he tried to rape me."

"Can't rape a whore," Niles said.

"Just shut up," she said. "He broke my wrist."

"And so you shot him," Tulie said.

"Yes."

"Where were you, Rebecca?" Tulie pressed. Tulie wanted to get to the bottom of this, but more important, she wanted the focus on Elise. Let the Songster be thinking about Elise for a while. Until the sun comes up anyway.

"Sleeping," Rebecca said with great innocence.

"Sleeping with Dennis," Elise said.

"Dennis? Who's Dennis?" Tulie asked.

Buck thought this was fabulous entertainment. Tulie really knew how to grill these girls to get all the information out of them. She, not Niles, should have been the Songster's prosecutor. Maybe then his bowels would be settled. Maybe then he would understand why everything seemed to be so crazy. Why did everybody act so crazy? Now here were these girls . . . and they were just as bug-fuck as everybody else. He'd never get it. He'd never understand people. He hoped that didn't mean that he would never understand himself.

"A guy," Rebecca said.

"Okay, okay," Tulie said. "Start from the beginning."

"I don't want to talk about it, Tulie," Rebecca said. "I just want to go."

"Go where?" Tulie asked.

"That's the problem," Elise said.

"You'll never go home again," the Songster said, his low voice taking everybody by surprise. The hair on Tulie's neck prickled at the sound of his voice. "If you go home, you will end up in prison. If you just leave, they won't find you."

"Sure. Run all my life."

"Run or sit in a cell," the Songster said.

"Listen to him," Niles said. "He's done both."

Elise blew her nose. "What are you running from?"

"Same thing," Niles said.

"You killed somebody?"

"You *killed* him?" Tulie gasped. "I thought you just shot him."

"Yeah," Rebecca said. "He was dead all right. Yeah, he was real dead."

"Could anybody identify you?" Tulie asked.

Rebecca and Elise both laughed, a bitter-sounding laugh. "Yeah," Elise said. "Yeah, I think we were pretty identifiable tonight."

No shit, Tulie thought. "What happened to this Dennis guy?"

"He was still sleeping when we left," Rebecca said.

"You sure he wasn't dead, too?" Tulie asked.

"Dead drunk maybe," Rebecca said. "But not dead."

"And you stole his truck." Tulie sounded exasperated. "You're pretty stupid, Elise."

"What would you have done?" Elise asked defensively.

"Well, first, I wouldn't have killed him," Tulie said. "I would have hurt him, and then I would have called the police. Right from there. When you run, you look guilty."

"Should I go back?"

"Go back and cover your tracks," the Songster said. "Get in your car, get out of town, and never come back."

"I can't do that."

"Why not?"

"Well, for one thing, there's that Dennis guy. And Rebecca. Rebecca wants to go to the police. And for another thing . . ." Her voice caught on a little sob. "I've got nowhere to go."

"Did you kill him in passion or cold blood?" Niles asked.

Elise thought about that for a minute. "I don't know," she said, and a chill ran through Buck. "Is there a difference?"

"Supposed to be," Niles said.

Elise shrugged. "He wanted to rape me," she said simply.

"Where's the gun?" Tulie asked.

"I have it."

"Gun?" the Songster said. He leaned forward and put his hand between Tulie and Elise. Tulie shrank away. She didn't want to touch him. "Let's see it."

"No!" Buck said, putting an elbow up over the back of the seat and pushing him back. "You just keep your damned gun in your damned . . . thing . . . keep it to yourself."

"Hey, c'mon," Niles whined. "I want to see it, too."

The Songster pulled back and hit Buck's arm. "Get your *fucking* hands off me," he said.

Tulie cringed, put her head down. She wanted to disappear.

Elise opened her purse and pulled out the revolver. She handed it back to Niles.

"Is the safety on?" Buck asked.

"There is no safety," Elise said.

"*No safety?*" Buck was beside himself. "Put the damned thing away before somebody else gets killed. I mean it now. Come on."

But the Songster reached over and snatched the gun out of Niles's hand. "Gimme that," he said.

"Let me out of here," Tulie said, feeling the hysteria rise. "Now."

Nobody moved. She was sandwiched in.

"What are you doing with a gun anyway?" Rebecca asked.

"My dad gave it to me. It's for protection. That's what it's for, and that's why I used it. Protection. To keep from being attacked. To keep from being raped."

"So," the Songster said, "you're going to want a jury to believe that it was in self-defense? After you'd been hooking and you went willingly with this guy to his house?"

You're askin' for it, Tulie's sister said.

"They'll never believe me," Elise said.

"You're right," Tulie said.

"I'm going to have to have somebody look at my wrist. It hurts like hell."

"Let's see it," Tulie said. Buck opened the door, and the yellow interior light went on. Tulie gasped. The wrist was swollen to the size of a beer can. It was blackish purple and the skin was stretched so tight it looked shiny. It made her a little bit sick to her stomach.

He closed the door.

Rebecca opened her car door, scooped a double handful of snow, and handed it to Tulie, who held it to Elise's wrist. She flinched with the pain of it and then, bravado evaporating, began to cry again.

Rebecca picked up a handful of snow and began to slurp it.

Someone's stomach growled loudly.

Niles laughed.

"Stop it! Stop laughing! *Help me*. This is serious. I'm in real trouble here, you guys. Can't somebody help me with this?"

"Hey," Tulie said, "this is your mess. I'd just as soon get out of here."

Elise moaned.

"It's up to you," the Songster said. "You tell us. Go back or go forward?"

"I don't know," she wailed.

The night quieted. Even Rebecca stopped shivering while Elise made her decision.

She thought about her family; she thought about her useless education. She thought about the wasted future that stretched before her like a thirsty road winding through the desert of trials, prison, and accusatory stares from her parents and her siblings. There was no hope on the horizon. No hope at all. Just a long road of misery that led to death. Why prolong it?

"Those Russians," she said, and her brief future clicked into place in her mind's eye like an intricate pattern of dominoes falling in spirals.

"What?" Tulie said. She was sick and tired of Elise.

"*Lizard wine!*" Elise said. "Lizard wine. Of course."

"What's she talking about?" Buck nudged Tulie. Tulie shrugged.

"It's what Ross said," Elise explained, "about people doing things they hate to do because they think it's good for them. It's like drinking lizard wine.

"The question is"—she went on after a pause—"going back to Bend and turning myself in, is that the right thing to do or is that drinking lizard wine? Or escaping and being on the run forever, never seeing my family again, is that the right thing for me to do, or is *that* drinking lizard wine? How do you know? How can you tell? Who knows what's the best thing to do? Who knows what's best?"

The car was silent.

"That's the point, I guess." She barked out a harsh laugh. "Nobody knows. Nobody knows if the wine helps you live longer because of the lizards or if you live longer because you *think* it helps you live longer." No one spoke. "And those Russians? They die anyway," she whispered. "It's nothing but a fucking joke. Life is just a fucking joke. Who wants more of it? *Why would they want to live longer?* I get it. *I get it.*"

Tulie wondered briefly if that was something worth thinking about later.

"Fuck," Elise said. "I'm going to die. I should die. I deserve to die. I *want* to die." She whipped around in the seat. Tulie's heart gave a lurch. "Give me the gun."

"*No*," Buck said, and tried to intercept, but the Songster merely handed the gun up to her.

"Here," he said. "Blow your brains out."

WHEN ELISE WAS BORN, HER MOTHER WAS A WAITRESS in a doughnut shop and her father a plumber's apprentice. Elise came into the world on Minnesota welfare money and slept in a dresser drawer that had been pulled out and laid on the floor next to the mattress that her parents slept on. Jessica, her mother, was nineteen; Paul, her father, was twenty-one.

Four days after Paul's twenty-second birthday he was working on a residential repair job with his boss, replacing some old and rusted pipe. As the job neared completion, Paul stood behind the plumbing truck taking inventory of the fittings they had used inside the house and tallying them up on his clipboard.

That same morning Walter Van Eyck, an elderly man, woke up feeling a little weak and shaky. Walter checked on his ailing wife, took two aspirin instead of his usual one, show-ered, shaved, put on his coat and hat, and headed for the drugstore. He had to refill a prescription for his wife, and she couldn't wait another day.

As Walter turned his Cadillac down the street, a series of blood vessels began to rupture in his brain.

It was a quiet neighborhood, a homey, tree-lined street, and Walter just softly fell asleep and died. As he did, the car slowed and swerved gently toward the curb. By the time Elise's dad heard it behind him and turned around, it was too late.

The Cadillac hit him going about five miles an hour, pinned him to the plumbing truck, and neatly pinched off both his legs just below the hips.

Two days after his amputation surgery, Paul was on the telephone. He knew a gold mine when he saw one. He and his lawyers cleaned the widow's clock as well as the coffers of her insurance company, his boss's insurance company, Social Se-curity, the plumbers' union, and everybody else he could think of.

He netted, after legal fees, a little over two and a half million dollars.

That was his big break, and he swore he would use it to great advantage for his family.

But it was almost six years before life settled down. Elise was seven by the time the settlements were finished, the money was banked, and the trials were over. By the time Paul had gone to as many physical therapists as his good nature would allow, by the time he had finally given up on prostheses and accepted the wheelchair, his baby girl was in second grade, and he'd missed it.

So had Jessica. She had been busy with lawyers, too, and with her invalid husband, his mood swings, and their tight budget.

When everything finally came back to normal, Elise hardly knew them, she'd spent so much time with baby-sitters.

Paul insisted on a large family, now that they had unlimited money to throw around. Jessica began popping out babies and hiring nannies to take care of them. She also hired gardeners and cleaning people to care for the new house and the lawn. Paul spent his entire day exercising and managing his money.

He was going to make life good for his family, oh, yes. This was his chance.

So he made money, and he provided everything he could for them. He bought them their every desire, and he doted on his babies. But Elise was left out. Elise had been part of those difficult years. She was just another thing to be dealt with, another situation to be handled, another inconvenience in an incredibly inconvenient life.

By the time they had time for her, she was already independent. It was a good thing, too, because her window of opportunity had slammed shut with the arrival of the first of her siblings.

"There's a difference between making money and earning money," Paul said a thousand times to each of the seven children. "When you work with your hands, with your back, with your sweat, you're earning money. But when you invest that money and it works for you—well, now, that's *making* money. And that's what makes happiness."

When Elise was in grade school, she had stars in her eyes about her daddy. She wanted to grow up and marry him. He was the biggest, handsomest man in the world. He was so smart and so rich he didn't even need to walk places; he could stay in his chair. Sometimes at night she would sneak into his rich-smelling office, with the bookshelves full of leather-bound books and the guns on the wall and the green-shaded lamp, and she'd listen to him on the telephone talking money to people in foreign countries. Now and then he would lean back and laugh with a booming laugh that warmed her heart. And sometimes he would find her, and she would crawl up into his chair and snuggle down under the pretty little blanket. There was plenty of room in the chair for her because his legs weren't hardly long at all.

One day he told her that she was too old to sit in his lap anymore, and Sonja, the next sister, took her place.

Paul began to travel, and Elise grew older and became busier with friends and school activities, and the whole family, it seemed, had individual things to accomplish until they hardly ever saw one another anymore.

The older she became, the more her mother looked like an old woman who tried to be young. Elise was ashamed of her. Whenever she saw her father, it felt as if he were only checking up on her progress. He'd kiss her cheek and say "Do you have everything you need, Elise?"

And she'd say, "Yes, Daddy," and he would say something like "You're such a good girl, Elise. Bring my briefcase in, then, would you please, darling?" And he would tuck some money into her hand, wheel to his den, and begin working.

In retrospect, Elise realized she had been on her own from the time she was small, but she hadn't known it at the time. She only knew that she had been replaced in her parents' affections by all the younger siblings and the rich lifestyle. She took a backseat to their new, moneyed friends, their shopping trips, their cruises, their romance of a dream too good to be true. In retrospect, she supposed she symbolized for them the bad times, the poor times, the times of creditors and hardship.

In retrospect, she suspected she had been an accident, an unwanted pregnancy. The rest of the children were planned, welcomed, because Jessica and Paul had plenty of money to welcome them with. But Elise was out of step. She had needed her parents the most when they had nothing to give her. Paul's tragedy, the surgery, the long and arduous rehabilitation, the lawsuits, the tears and heartbreak. Her parents had had enough to deal with just the two of them. She was an outsider, and they had nothing left for her.

In retrospect, Elise grew up by herself and became old enough to hate that glossy, jet-setty life her parents repre-sented. Beneath that veneer, Elise was certain, termites had eaten away all the substance. And Paul had packed it full of money to keep the whole thing from collapsing.

Money. Now there was something worthwhile.

Elise was smart. She inherited her father's crafty knack for sizing up a situation and boldly working the angles. She fig-ured out how to make their homelife work to her advantage. She understood the minimum requirements—in school, in family participation, in behavior—to get by invisibly. As long as those minimums were met, she was left alone to do as she pleased.

And what pleased her most was doing things her parents would hate if they knew.

At thirteen she discovered sex, drugs, and rock and roll. In these she thought she had found the keys to the universe. There was nothing better than to take a hit of acid, smoke some dope, drink some wine, and have slow, easy sex while listening to AC/DC on headphones. She took great pleasure in living her double life: the dutiful daughter, the average student versus the wild thing who was loyal to whoever had the best drugs and the biggest cock.

She went to school loaded, kept beer in her locker. No-body noticed. She took acid on Thanksgiving and sat down to dinner with the whole family. Nobody noticed.

For her sixteenth birthday Paul bought her a used Mustang,

and she went to work full-time, with a renewed sense of dedication. Her job, her career, was to get through school, and it was tough. There were so many other things to do with her time, her freedom, her mobility, and her money. School was her job, and she worked hard at passing all her classes. She wanted nothing to interfere with her good times and her free ride.

Graduation. Finally. The family came to see her wear her cap and gown and receive her diploma. She endured their hugs and congratulations and kissed them all. They wanted to have a party and cake and ice cream. She told them to go on ahead, she'd catch up with them.

She had other plans.

She stuffed the cap and gown in the trunk of her car and drove to Gene and Laura's house.

Gene and Laura were both nineteen, had been married for about a year, and had a baby. They lived in a one-bedroom apartment on the third floor of a run-down building. Gene worked on an assembly line; Laura got high. They sold drugs to fill in the financial gaps, and they always had really good drugs. Weekends at their place were usually full of action.

When Elise walked in, Gene and Laura were fighting. The baby was crying. Some kind of red sauce bubbled on the stove. When Elise knocked on the flimsy screen door, Laura looked at her with exasperation and pushed the hair out of her eyes. "C'mon in, Elise," she said, then began picking things up in the living room.

"Hey, if it's a bad time . . ." Elise said, but Gene interrupted her.

"Not a bad time at all. Come on in. Want a beer?"

Laura gave him a look, but Elise couldn't decipher it. She took the beer from Gene, stirred the pot—it looked like spaghetti sauce—and then sat down. Laura put the wet, screaming baby in Elise's lap, went into the bedroom, and slammed the door.

"How about some dinner, Elise?" Gene asked.

Elise put the baby on the floor. She didn't need to deal with that. It wasn't her kid.

"Yeah, sure. Hey, tonight was graduation."

"That's right! Hey, good for you. I imagine a few folks will stop by." He threw a small foil-wrapped ball at her. "Graduation present."

Elise opened it carefully. "What is it?"

"Opium. Ever smoked it before?"

"Never."

"We better eat first."

Gene changed the baby, put him in the high chair, and fed him spaghetti while Elise picked at a little and Gene ate two helpings. Elise liked Gene. Laura was almost like her sister, but even so, she flirted with Gene when Laura wasn't around. Gene liked it. He flirted back. Elise would sleep with him if the occasion presented itself. So far it hadn't, but she knew that Gene liked her. It was only a matter of time.

When they were finished eating, Elise was itchy and antsy to get on with the celebrating. She even tackled the sinkful of dirty dishes while Gene took a plateful of spaghetti into Laura. Laura came out shortly after, with her empty plate and a smile for Elise. Her eyes were puffy from crying. Elise hugged her, took her plate, and washed it. She was eager to get to the opium.

Opium! As with the taking of all drugs, there was a certain amount of ceremony to it. Laura put the baby down, while Elise watched Gene unwrap the foil, heat the black ball with a match, then pinch off a little corner of the tar. He rolled it into a tiny ball and dropped it into the little bowl of his hash pipe. He handed the pipe to Elise and said "Be careful." They waited for Laura, then passed the pipe quickly among the three of them so as not to waste any of the harsh smoke.

It was good. It was real good. By the second hit off Gene's little pipe, Elise thought she had found home. She lay back on the broken couch and fell into a half dream where she was mildly aware but uncaring about the things around her. More people arrived, toked on the pipe, and lay on the floor. Soft music began—or was it in her head? Someone began to tell a story. Was it her? The story spun out and then there was silence again. Every now and again she roused herself when the pipe passed by her. Each time it was as if she were waking up, although she didn't think she had ever really been asleep.

And then it was morning. Elise opened her eyes and sat up. She stumbled to the bathroom and barely made it before throwing up everything in her stomach. The bathroom was a mess; Laura never cleaned it. It smelled bad. Stale urine. She heaved some more, then made her way back to the living room.

Someone was sitting in the corner, the opium pipe in his hand. There was something wrong with him.

Elise went to the kitchen, found a loaf of bread, and ate a piece. She wasn't hungry, but her stomach needed something. It was too unsettled, too tender.

The guy in the corner hadn't moved. His face was gray. His lips were blue.

She touched him. He was cold. He was dead.

She backed away from him and went to Gene. He was sleeping on his back on the floor. She touched his shoulder, and he opened his eyes, instantly awake.

"Gene, there's a dead guy here."

Gene sat up. "Huh?"

Elise pointed.

"Eddie," Gene said, and rubbed his face.

"He's dead."

"Huh?"

"He's *dead*."

Gene looked, rubbed his face, looked again. "Jesus Christ," he said. He crawled on all fours over to Eddie, felt his hand, felt his face. He took the pipe out of his hand and put it on the coffee table. "Eddie, you fucker," he said.

"I better go," Elise said. She slipped the last of the opium into her pocket, got her purse and her keys, and left.

It was six o'clock in the morning. She didn't know where to go or what to do.

She turned off the radio and just drove around the quiet Saturday morning town, trying to understand the fact that somebody had just died. Probably from a drug overdose of some sort. Somebody that Gene knew, somebody that he probably sold drugs to.

Somebody died. Dead.

It could have been her.

But somehow it was unimportant. What was important was that she had been there when he died. Somebody could tell somebody that she had been there, and her parents could find out and fuck up her free ticket to four more years of subsidized freedom.

She went home and hoped the police wouldn't call. She lay on her flowered and frilly bedspread and hoped that Gene would handle the situation without involving her.

All she wanted was more opium. She took the foil out of her pocket and opened it up. There was only a small piece left. She got her pipe out of its hiding place in her closet and smoked up a tiny ball, then lay back and enjoyed the waking dreams that unreeled before her.

All weekend long she smoked and slept, smoked and threw up, smoked and stayed alone in her room.

When it was gone, she wanted more. She wanted more badly. She wanted more so badly that it scared her. She paced her room and tried to scheme out how to get more without going by to see Gene and Laura. She didn't want to see them. She didn't want to know how they had handled Eddie. She didn't want to feel as if she'd ditched out on them when they needed her.

Hell, they didn't need her.

She needed them. She needed their connections. She had no idea where she could get opium on her own.

After she spent a couple of days obsessing about how and where to get more, a new perspective dawned. If opium could become that important in one weekend, think how important it would become in a week of steady smoking. Or a month.

Maybe it was a good thing that Eddie guy died, because otherwise she might have gone off the deep end for a drug that made her feel so good.

Elise stayed away from Gene and Laura, and she stayed away from all drugs except beer, smoking a little dope now and then, and men. All summer long. She spent time with the family. She thought that the idea of leaving them for four years away at college would make her want to be closer to them.

But it didn't.

Paul bought her a pistol and took her out to the firing range to teach her how to use it. That afternoon was the first time Elise thought he had ever taken her seriously. Just as she was about to leave. Instead of making her feel loved, and wanted, and a member of the family, it just pissed her off. It was too late.

In August, she left Minneapolis and flew to Oregon to begin life as a coed at the university. A good-looking coed. A party coed. A popular coed.

Her first three years were busy ones. The fast-paced, devil-may-care attitude that most students had suited her. She partied with the hardiest, doing the very minimum she needed to do in order to slide by with acceptable grades.

After seducing a professor, after getting laid in Republican headquarters on election night, after hiking in the Sisters Wilderness on acid, she began to think she'd seen it all and done it all.

Then one night at a party a fresh-faced boy sat down on the couch next to her. "Say," he said, his face flushed with drink and his eyes bright, "you're beautiful."

Elise smiled condescendingly at him. *God*, she thought, *they get younger every year.* This kid looked like early high school.

"How would you like to do me a favor?"

Elise raised her eyebrows. It wasn't likely.

"See that guy over there?" He pointed at a boy in a green and blue rugby shirt with khaki shorts and hiking boots. He had one hand in a pocket, the other wrapped around a beer. His hair was short. He looked preppy. He looked athletic. He looked clean. He looked young and high school, just like the boy sitting next to her on the couch.

She nodded.

"He's a virgin," the kid said.

Elise frowned. "Poor baby," she said.

The boy laughed and slapped his knee. "That's what I say. He says there's nobody interesting, but I say he's just shy."

Elise wasn't making a connection. "So?"

"So he thinks you're interesting."

Elise stared this jerk right in the eye. She was offended and about ready to get up when he said, "And I've got fifty bucks."

She laughed out loud. The last thing she needed was money.

But then, it was a different kind of money, wasn't it?

She looked back at the kid across the room. The two friends made eye contact, and the one standing turned beet red. He turned and walked away. The one sitting next to her seemed agitated. "So? What do you say? Huh? C'mon."

"Okay," she said. "I'll go find a bedroom. You send him in."

He shook her hand and palmed her some folded-up bills. She stood up, smoothed out her skirt, and gave her best sashay as she walked out of the room.

She didn't even know whose house this was, but it was a house, and surely there were bedrooms.

There were. She found one, went in, and closed the door. She sat on the bed, waiting, wondering why she was doing this. It wasn't the money, she realized; it was the power. A virgin. He would remember her forever.

Soon the door opened a crack, and the boy she'd struck the deal with stuck his head in. "Hi," he said.

"Hi."

Then the door opened wider, and the other boy was shoved through and the door closed behind him.

He blushed, flustered, and tried to open the door, but somebody was holding it on the other side.

Elise got up and pushed the button, locking it.

The boy kept running his hand through his hair.

"I won't hurt you," she said.

He opened his wallet and pulled out a foil-wrapped condom. "Here," he said.

"That's for you," Elise said.

"Oh, yeah, of course," he said, his face turning redder than ever.

She took his hand and led him to the bed, then sat down and patted the edge. A virgin. What a treat. She'd never had a virgin before. She barely remembered being a virgin. She just knew she would try very hard to make this a nice experience for this kid.

She felt old, wise, in control. It felt good.

"What's your name?"

"Sean."

"I'm Elise." She began by scratching his back, ever so lightly. Then she pressed her breasts against his arm and blew softly on his neck. She had to pick up his hand and put it on her thigh, but as soon as she did that, he got into the spirit of it.

He kissed her; he kissed her good. His hands began moving of their own volition, and those hands knew how to get a girl out of her panties. This boy may be a virgin, Elise thought, but he knows his way around a woman.

Elise tried a few of the tricks she'd learned with teeth and tongue, tricks no high school girl knew. His little sounds of pleasure excited her, and soon Elise forgot she was working, she was just playing. She was playing and being played with, and she moved his hand and his mouth and showed him what she liked.

It was wonderful.

And when they were finished, they lay on the bed together and talked like lovers. She snuggled in the crook of his arm, her head on his chest. They talked about school and about parents and Sean drew his finger over her skin, playing with her goose bumps, curling her hair, toying with her nipple.

Then some clown started banging on the bedroom door.

"Oops," Sean said, and they both remembered, with a start, where they were.

They dressed and fixed the bed, and before they opened the door, Sean took her in his arms and gave her a wonderful hug. She felt more feminine than she had in a while. He was great. She gave him her phone number.

Then she let him leave first. She heard the shouts as he entered the living room and knew there would be some kind of celebration, but she didn't need any spotlight like that.

She fixed her makeup, then left out the back door.

And, like a fool, waited for him to call her.

As she waited, the realization growing that he wasn't going to call a hooker for a date—and that's what she had become, a hooker—she thought that perhaps she had discovered her calling. Calling.

She laid off the parties for a while and inspected the idea of this new lifestyle, this potential vocation. Fantasy thoughts of being a five-hundred-dollar call girl flowed through her mind. Fancy Fifth Avenue apartment, a closet filled with Paris originals, admirals and CEOs to entertain—it looked pretty good. It seemed powerful, having pillow talk with powerful men. But how does an aspiring call girl go about becoming one?

She could apply at an escort service. Lord knows, she was experienced enough in the sack.

But she was only experienced in gaining satisfaction, not giving it. If she applied for a job at an escort service, surely they would want to sample her wares.

She wasn't prepared for that. She had her own research to do first.

She discreetly began to offer her services, and she was surprised at how often her offer was accepted. The more experienced she got at sizing up a customer, the better her odds became.

She didn't need the money; she needed the sense of power it gave her. The power in her life had always been Paul. He bought and paid for her life, and the money she made from entertaining the men who wanted her was *her* money, and hers alone. The things she bought with it were *her* things.

She bought drugs with Paul's money. She bought sweaters and jewelry and silk blouses with her own money.

She skidded through the terms with average grades. She hated going home during the summers because Jessica and Paul and their children were in the house, cramping her style. From the moment she left her dorm for the summer, she lived for the day she'd be returning.

In the back of her mind was the fear of what she would do when she finished school, when she had her degree in psychology. Then what?

The party would be over, that's what.

Make hay while the sun shines, she told herself, and year by year, she partied harder and harder, the fears growing ever stronger. She felt as if graduation were following her around, reminding her that this wasn't her party at all; it was Paul's. Graduation followed her around, and so did Jessica and Paul, with their letters from home and their expectations for the daughter they said they wanted her to become. A lot of other things followed her around as well, things she cast off to drift in the wake of her pleasure and self-gratification. Broken hearts, broken marriages, broken promises, broken friendships.

By her senior year she had gone through most of the interesting men on campus. She'd blown her budget and at the last minute had to move back into the dorm, which Paul paid for. She had no friends, except her new freshman roomie, Rebecca, the silly twit.

Elise's fantasy of becoming a high-priced call girl began to fray at the edges when she noticed that she was beginning to look older than she should. She was throwing up after every meal now, trying to stay in her size two jeans. She couldn't party all night and still make classes in the mornings. She flunked a couple of classes, barely scraped by in others, was taking that stupid biology class for the third time. She wondered if Paul and Jessica would spring for another term if she didn't quite make it by June.

They wouldn't. She knew they wouldn't. Not if she was flunking.

But who needed a stupid psychology degree anyway? What good was it going to do her in the long run?

She knew she ought to be making some plans, getting her future together. But there just wasn't anything else she wanted to do. The idea of having a job, of working nine to five was ludicrous.

Her future was nebulous, totally up in the air. Elise didn't have a single idea where to begin with it.

Panic began to close in on her, and desperation followed her around like a puppy. She overreacted to almost everything, jumping at shadows, dodging memories, suspicious of everyone.

There weren't any men worth having—not full-time anyway—and she didn't even know where she wanted to live, in the West, in the Midwest, or in New England. And maybe, just maybe, one day, her past would start catching up to her. Maybe, just maybe, one of these days all those she'd fucked over, those she'd ripped off, those she'd stood up, those she'd cheated on would begin to line up outside the dorm and a policeman or some other authority figure (Paul!) would escort her down the row. Each one would calmly explain, in horrible, accusatory detail, what her offense had been, and at the very end of the line, the long, long line, would be a blue-gray dead guy named Eddie.

ELISE SHOULDERED OPEN THE DOOR AND JUMPED OUT OF the car into the snow, pistol in her right hand, her blackened wrist held tightly against her stomach.

Before Tulie could think about what Elise was doing, the back door opened, and Rebecca jumped out and took off after Elise, both of them running toward the lake, tripping and stumbling in the uncertain snow.

Tulie moved over and closed the car door, staying as far away from the Songster as she could get. "I know what they're doing," she said. "At least I know what Elise is doing. She's scheming. She's going to find out how to turn this bad situation around to her advantage. You watch. You watch. Somehow she'll make herself out to be the goddamned victim of this whole scene, and she'll just walk." She crossed her arms over her chest. "She'll skate. You watch. She'll skate."

Niles rolled down his window.

"Close the window," Tulie said. "It's cold."

"Wait," Buck said. He could hear their voices. He listened, but he couldn't make out the words. They sounded like two little cartoon mice screeching at each other in the distance. "Yeah, okay, roll it up."

Niles obliged. "Hey, where were we? Weren't we doing something when they came back?"

The Elise and Rebecca interruption disappeared. Tulie had just sentenced the Songster to death.

"Yeah," Buck said.

"The execution," Niles reminded him.

Tulie had her hand on the door handle, ready to jump out. She'd go sit in the truck. She could lock the doors and just stay in there until the sun came up.

They heard shouting outside, then Elise ran up and fumbled the truck door open. Rebecca chased after her, grabbed her by the coat collar, and pulled her away from the truck. Elise fell backward into the snow. Rebecca grabbed for the keys in Elise's hand, but Elise held on tight. Elise pushed her away, stood up, and they faced each other, the bright interior lights of the truck illuminating their faces, red with exertion and highly animated.

"Roll down the window," Buck said, but it was too late. Rebecca ran around the front of the truck. Elise jumped into the truck, slammed the truck door hard, and locked both doors.

A gunshot dropped snow from the tree branches and everybody in the car jumped.

Tulie's stomach lurched.

"Jesus Christ," Buck said.

"She shot one of the tires," Niles said.

Elise jumped out of the truck and, hatred pouring forth, stood next to the door. Her breath steamed out in gasping, infuriated, impotent fumes.

Rebecca walked over to the station wagon, the little silver gun dangling from one hand, and opened the front door. "It doesn't matter who has the keys, Elise. That truck isn't going anywhere. You get back in this car. Now, Elise. Get back in there now."

"Better do as she says, Elise," Buck said, leaning over Tulie's lap, "before she shoots out another tire. There's probably only one spare."

"Give me my gun," Elise demanded.

"I don't think so," Rebecca said, waving the pistol out of Elise's reach. "Now get back into the car."

Elise stomped over to the car, shouldered Rebecca out of the way, and squeezed in next to Tulie. She sat steaming, cradling her broken wrist. Rebecca gently closed her door, then opened the back door and got in behind her, next to Niles.

"I want my goddamned gun," Elise said.

"No," Rebecca said. "I'm not giving it to you. Are you *stupid*? Thanks to you, I lost my other contact lens out there. God, Elise, you're so stupid."

"I am not. Well, maybe I am."

"So," the Songster said, "what are you going to do?"

"Shoot myself."

"That's one option," the Songster said. "But not a very good one. Next idea?"

"Shoot you and then shoot myself."

"Getting warmer," Tulie said.

"What you need to decide," the Songster said, his low voice commanding attention, "is if you want to go to prison or not. If you do, your choices are simple. If you don't, then we'll all help you."

"We will?" Buck said.

"I won't," Rebecca said.

"You have the most to lose," Tulie said.

"It's Elise's decision," the Songster said.

"I don't know," Elise said. "Who said I was qualified to make this kind of decision?"

"That's what courts are for," Niles said. "Judges and juries and like that."

"I don't want to go to prison. And I don't want to spend all my family's money on legal fees either."

The silence in the car was a new type of silence. *At last,* Tulie thought, *we're not focused on the Songster and his sick ways anymore.*

Rebecca's teeth chattered.

Tulie turned in her seat and looked at her. The denim coat was wrapped around her, but her legs were naked. "You guys got a blanket or something back there?" Tulie asked. "Rebecca's freezing."

"Why you want to go out in the winter like that?" Niles asked. "You haven't got much more than underwear on."

"I didn't expect to be sitting in car in a campground all night," Rebecca said. "And running around in the snow chasing after some *stupid*—"

"Fuck off," Elise said.

Rebecca pouted silently. Niles rummaged around in the back of the station wagon and came up with a paint-encrusted dropcloth. He unfolded it and tented it over Rebecca's knees.

"I can't be on the run all my life," Elise whined. "I don't know what to do. I just don't know."

"You've got to go back," Rebecca said. "Go back and tell them it was self-defense and declare your devotion to the Lord."

Everybody booed.

"I mean it," she said, defensively, crossing her arms over her chest and letting the gun drop into her lap.

"Yeah, she was serving the Lord wearing that dress," Niles said.

"In a cowboy bar," Buck said.

"Turning tricks in the parking lot," Tulie said.

"Just like Mary Magdalene," Niles said, laughing at his own joke.

Rebecca brushed the little revolver from her lap to the seat between her and Niles. She didn't want to touch its cold metal anymore. It felt too smooth, too powerful. She tucked the stiff dropcloth closer around her and snuggled down into the seat. She'd said her piece, made her statement, and now she could be finished with the whole mess. It wasn't her mess. The thought floated around in her mind that she was a witness to most of Elise's intentions and actions. The idea that she might be called to testify against Elise made her feel a little nauseated. If she was called to testify, she'd have to make public her own intentions, manner of dress, and goings on in the bar and at that house, in front of her family and church. Maybe it would be better if Elise went ahead and shot herself.

As soon as the thought entered her mind, Rebecca was horrified. She pulled the paint cloth up over her face and began to pray.

"If we leave right now," the Songster said softly, "the snow will cover up all evidence that we were ever here. In the spring, when they open this park, they'll find that truck with a bullet hole in its tire, and that bullet hole will match the bullet hole in your friend. There's nobody else here, just the lake. They'll drag the lake for your bodies, they'll search the hills, they'll go talk to people at the university, and if you're not there, they'll give up. They'll stamp the case 'unsolved,' and go on about their business."

"They'll talk to our families," Elise said.

"*Our?*" Rebecca came to life. "*Our* families? Why would they talk to *my* family?"

"Because you were there," Tulie said.

"You've *got* to go back, Elise," Rebecca said, and then she began to cry. "My parents will die," she said. "My mother will hate me. They won't understand at all."

Her whimpering hit a soft spot inside Buck. What if this were Cecelia when she became older? He empathized. "Sure they will. They'll understand. Everybody's entitled to a mistake or two. Your parents love you. They'll forgive you."

"Not my mother," Rebecca said, shaking her head. "She'll call me a slut and say I'm turning out to be a bad seed, just like my birth mother."

"You were adopted?" Niles asked.

Rebecca choked out a yes, the dropcloth crinkling. She hiccuped and blew her nose on a corner of it.

"Well, you were along on a bad ride," the Songster said, "no doubt about it. But Elise is the one who's in real trouble."

Elise moaned and covered her face with her hands.

"Okay, Elise," the Songster said. "You can go back to Bend and turn yourself in, or you can go to Eugene and turn yourself in. Either way, you're going to jail."

"Even if she turns herself in?" Niles asked. "Doesn't that say she has nothing to hide?"

"If she had nothing to hide, she'd have called the police from that guy's house," Tulie said.

Elise sobbed.

"This is your other option," the Songster continued. "We can go back to the house, drop off the truck, and erase any evidence of your presence there."

"They saw us leave together," Rebecca said.

"Who?"

"Everybody at the bar. And Dennis."

"Yeah," the Songster said, and Buck heard an evil grin in his voice. "Dennis."

He said that in a way that made Buck's heart pump. Dennis sounded like a project for the Songster. He'd probably love to go up there and just take care of that Dennis guy, just to satisfy his killing lust, the fucking pervert.

"You could just disappear," Tulie said. "Go back to the dorm right now, get your stuff, and get out of town."

"I wouldn't know where to go or what to do."

"You learn," the Songster said softly. "You just learn. You get lost in a big city where nobody cares."

"Is that what you did, Songster?" Niles asked.

Silence.

"Yeah." Elise sniffed. "How do you know all this?"

"He killed three women," Niles said.

"Kill me," Elise said quietly, soberly, seriously.

The Songster snorted in disdain. Tulie's stomach turned over.

"I mean it," Elise said.

"Yeah, Songster," Buck said. "You can do it. You have a flair for that type of thing. A talent."

"Shut up," the Songster said.

"Knife or gun?" Niles asked.

"Gun," Elise said.

"Hey, Songster," Niles said, "know how to use a gun?"

"Shut the fuck up. This is her problem, not mine."

"What's a matter, Songster? Can't help a lady with a simple request?" Buck goaded. "No *balls*, Songster?"

A venomous silence poured forth from the Songster's corner of the backseat. Tulie was glad that there were six of them now, not just four. It wasn't just her against the Songster anymore, or Buck against the Songster; it was the five of them against the Songster. Maybe only four. Elise and the Songster seemed to have joined leagues. Or maybe it was just the Songster against life.

"This isn't funny," Rebecca said.

The back door opened behind Buck, and the light went on. Then the door slammed and Buck's door opened and the Songster jerked him out by the back of his shirt. Buck fell backward into the snow, his boot catching between the door and the floor.

Niles scooted over to where the Songster had been sitting and rolled down the window to see what was happening.

Elise looked into the backseat and saw the gun on the seat next to Rebecca. She pushed Tulie over, cried out at the wrenching of her wrist, lunged over the seat back, grabbed the gun, and, with an evil look of triumph, spun around, opened the car door, and got out, backing away, gun to her temple.

"No!" Rebecca said, and threw off the dropcloth. She had wished for Elise to kill herself, so now if she did, the sin would be on Rebecca's soul. "Elise, don't. Oh, God, please don't."

Elise ran back toward the lake, and Tulie watched Rebecca follow her, both of them tripping along in their stupid high heels with bare legs in a cartoon reenactment of fifteen minutes ago.

Buck didn't have time to recover from his backward dumping into the snow before the Songster had a knee on his chest, squashing the breath out of him.

"Get off me," he wheezed, feeling the pressure in his cheeks, hearing his blood rush in his ears, afraid his ankle, caught in the crack of the car door, was going to break.

The Songster's twisted face looked down at him, the angle and the light casting dangerous shadows.

"I ought to bust your fuckin' head," the Songster said, his hair wild and his eyes cold.

"Get *off* me," Buck said, and tried to buck him off, but he was stuck.

"Don't fuck with me anymore," the Songster said, his lips tight. *"Don't fuck with me."* He bounced his weight on Buck's chest, and Buck felt his ribs creak to the breaking point.

"Okay," Buck said. He knew when he'd been beaten. He couldn't fight the Songster, not at this great a disadvantage.

The Songster stood up, and Buck dislodged his foot, then

turned on his side and curled up, trying to breathe life into his bruised lungs. He felt the cold snow on his cheek; he felt it stuffed down the collar of his shirt.

The Songster had to be stopped. He was too full of himself, thought he had too much power. *Yes,* Buck thought, *the Songster has to be stopped. Here. Now.*

He rolled to his knees; then, with one hand on the car door, he pulled himself up. The Songster watched, his breath pluming out, his face red. "I mean it, Buck," the Songster said. "I'm finished with you."

Girlish squeals came from the lake, and as soon as the Songster turned to look, Buck put his head down and charged. He hit the Songster square in the solar plexus and heard a satisfying grunt and whoosh of air as the Songster went down under Buck's weight.

But even though Buck had been a varsity wrestler and had fooled around with boxing, the Songster was streetwise, and as soon as he hit the ground, the glint of sharpened steel glistened in his hand.

Buck sat on the Songster's chest and punched him in the nose so hard he felt the nose give way and heard his knuckles crack. Then he felt Gloria's main asset pressed against the crotch of his jeans.

"You move again"—the Songster sprayed blood from his broken nose—"and I'll cut you a twat."

Buck was hot. He wasn't afraid of the Songster. Not now. His eyes nailed the Songster's as he reached down with swelling fingers and picked up a handful of snow. He picked up another handful, slowly, deliberately, never taking his eyes off while the Songster coughed and spit blood, his nose bleeding and swelling blue. The Songster had no leverage for the knife, it was an empty threat.

Buck packed the snowball nice and tight, and then he

looked at the Songster with what felt like an expression to match the Songster's own evil. He felt horrible power. He felt cold fury. He felt as if he could kill. "Ready?" he said. Then he slammed the hard ball of ice into the Songster's face again.

The Songster bucked hard and threw Buck off onto his side. In a heartbeat the Songster was on his feet, and one boot kicked out and caught Buck in the back and rolled him over like a sack of beans. The next kick caught him squarely in the belly.

Buck curled up with the fiery pain. The Songster stood over him, drizzling blood to the snow right in front of him.

"I'll kill you, you son of a bitch," the Songster said, and pulled his foot back for a final kick at Buck's head.

Buck caught the boot and pulled the Songster over onto his back. He landed hard, and the knife flew out of his hand, twinkled end over end, and clattered to a rest on the Pontiac's roof.

Niles hovered over the fighting men like a little banty hen. He did everything but wring his hands. "Stop," he said. "Stop it!" He turned to Tulie, who leaned against the hood of the car. "Stop them," he pleaded.

Tulie watched in fascinated horror. Fights were nothing new to her. She never found them stimulating like some of the girls; they always seemed stupid to her. But this fight was different. It was all she could do to keep from finding a branch or something and bashing in the Songster's head. She had to keep her hands curled into fists, she had to keep her feet rooted to the spot, or she would get right in the middle of it. That would not be smart, but oh God, she prayed that Buck would kill that worthless jerk.

Buck had been concentrating all his power on the Songster's smashed face. He punched the Songster again in the nose, and Tulie saw the Songster slump, as if he had lost consciousness for a moment.

Tulie wanted Buck to kill him, but this wasn't a very pretty way to do it.

Buck pushed the Songster away from him, and just as he was ready to get up, the Songster grabbed him by the hair and elbowed him hard in the ear.

"Ow!" he screamed, and fingers went for the Songster's eyes.

She shook her head. "I'm not getting in the middle of that."

"You can't let the Songster just *kill* him," Niles said.

"Get the knife," Tulie said, nodding toward the roof of the car. "Songster can't kill him without the knife."

Niles picked up the knife, examined it with reverence.

Girlish screams came up from down by the lake. Tulie stood on tiptoes, trying to see what was going on down there.

And then everything went into slow motion.

A rough hand grabbed her around the waist. Before she could move or cry out, she was ripped off her feet and blood from the Songster's pummeled nose sprayed across her cheek.

Before she could catch her balance, he lifted her off her feet again and turned her around toward Buck, who was trying painfully to get to his feet. He was having a hard time. Tulie's long hair was caught in her eyelashes, but the Songster had both her arms at her sides, and he held her tightly. She felt his heavy breathing on her neck.

"Niles," he said.

Tulie could see Niles look up from his fascination with Gloria.

"Kill for me, Niles," the Songster said softly.

Niles's brow furrowed. "Me?" he asked.

Tulie struggled, but she was held fast by a strong man. She could barely get enough breath, he was squeezing her so tightly, and little black globes began to float lazily up in front of her eyes.

Niles walked around the car, fingering the blade, holding it first with its blade down, the way a slasher would, then holding it with its blade out as he would if he were to stab something. He took a couple of practice stabs, a couple of practice swishes. He smiled at the feeling.

"That's it, Niles," the Songster said.

Tulie found her voice. "Niles," she said, gasping, "listen—" and that voice was choked off with a squeeze from the Songster that made her last word end in a squeak.

Niles stood directly in front of them. "Songster?" he asked.

Tulie noticed that the night had receded and a gray dawn had sneaked up on them. Pine trees in the distance were beginning to take definition from the dark sky behind them. Tulie could see their tops awash in a sea of mist that covered the ground and the lake.

Sanity was supposed to come with daylight, she thought.

Then she saw Niles look beyond them, seeing something interesting.

Buck.

Niles cocked his head wonderingly, then cringed.

The Songster tried to twirl around, but Tulie's boots were in snow. A second later broken glass rained down on her as Buck smashed the empty tequila bottle across the Songster's head.

The Songster fell forward, his arms still around Tulie. She went facefirst into the snow, with his dead weight on top of her.

Crying, hiccuping, furious, she desperately tried to scrabble out from underneath him. His arms were still around her; his blood still dripped onto her face. She got her torso free, then turned over and onto her back, pulled her feet out from under, filling her boots with snow. "Oh, God," she said, "oh, God, oh, God." She wanted to hope he was dead, but he still breathed.

She wanted to get his knife and slit his damned throat with it.

Buck stood in front of her, the jagged remains of bottle dripping tequila in one broken-knuckled hand. His breath came as hard and as rough as hers.

She got to her feet, brushed tears and the Songster's blood from her face, and looked around.

The sky had lightened even more.

Everything looked cold and magic with the fresh snow.

Except where the men had wrestled. That snow was all bloody and mashed down.

And the Songster still breathed.

She put her hand to her head and felt glass. She bent her head over and shook her hair, and pieces of glass sparkled to the snow below.

Then a gunshot startled snow from the tree above them.

"Jesus Christ," Niles said.

"What?" Buck said. It was as if he had just come back to consciousness.

Tulie caught her breath. "Rebecca," she whispered.

Then a low moan wafted up over the hill, and they all knew there was big trouble.

WILLIE GURT WAS BORN TO A RUNAWAY TEEN—TURNED—
street-corner prostitute in Denver. Carol Gurt, sixteen, hated
the unexpected pregnancy. She unwillingly retired to her
room when she showed too much belly to find anyone willing
to pick her up, ate poorly, and took long, resentful walks when
urged to do so by the woman who ran the run-down boarding-
house for hookers.

During the pregnancy she was consumed with the big decision: keep the kid or give it up. She didn't want to keep it, but
she certainly didn't want to give up her parents' grandchild
before they knew about it or could meet it or bestow their
love and gifts of money on it. What had come between her
and her parents had nothing to do with a baby.

That was the deciding factor. She kept the baby for them,
although they would never know about him.

After the baby was born, she paid minimal attention to him,
keeping him in a box that she shoved under the bed whenever
she got a customer to come home with her. She named him
Willie, after the boy who had stolen her virginity in junior
high.

Willie slept with his mother in her double bed in that run-
down hotel as he was growing up, going out into the street or
sliding under the bed whenever she had a guest. Until he was

ten, he thought he was her brother because that's how she introduced him to strangers.

When he was eleven she included him in a hundred-dollar trick and tried not to listen to her heart or her gut while Willie cried under the weight of the man. But while she bravely withstood that first-time pimping of her young virgin son, she couldn't ignore what it did to him. She could barely live with the look that glinted from his eye from that moment on. It was a constant reminder. And it made her escape through drugs that much sweeter.

When Willie was thirteen, Carol began his heterosexual education. He still slept with her, and one night she seduced him. If they were going to be partners—and his uncommon young face could bring in a lot of money—she thought she'd better break him in right.

Willie quit school. They tripled their income, which wasn't much, but it bought decent clothes and decent food and paid the rent. Willie grew tall and handsome, his face wearing many edges. Carol continued his education, hardly admitting to herself that it was Willie's profile, Willie's physique, Willie's musky manhood that seriously stirred her juices for the very first time.

Willie complied with her scheme. He was a healthy, willing student, and he began to turn tricks on his own, along with the kinkier ones his mother dug up.

But he never laughed. Willie had stopped laughing when he was eleven.

He always had money in his jeans, looked and acted older than he was; that made it easy for him to fall in with a weedy crowd that enjoyed its violence. Only Stark, the leader of the pack, felt uncomfortable about Willie's age, and he told the boy to get lost.

Willie just stared at him, standing his ground, while the others came to his defense.

"He can't stay. He can't fight. He's too young. Young means unpredictable. He can't be trusted."

"I can be trusted," Willie simply said.

"Yeah, but can you fight?"

"Sure," he said, he who had never been in a fight before.

"Okay," Stark said. "You'll fight Greener. Just to first blood. You got a knife?"

Willie shook his head and looked down at his feet. Stark pulled a sleek eight-inch blade from a sheath under his jacket, kissed it, and handed it to Willie.

"Greener?"

Greener, a tall, skinny creep with long, stringy hair and a long scar down the length of his left biceps, came forward and pulled his knife from his sleeve. He laid the blade flat in his hand and began to circle.

"To first blood, you guys. Don't get carried away."

Willie, scared half to death, just threw the knife at Greener. It grazed his arm and stuck in a sheet of plywood behind him. Blood seeped out the slice in his shirt.

"Jesus," Greener said. Everybody else laughed.

Willie stood his ground, adrenaline pumping through him, his eyes wide and sweat running down his chest.

"First blood," Stark said. "The kid stays."

"Jesus," Greener said again, pulling at his torn sleeve.

Willie looked around him, unaccustomed to attention, and he shuffled his feet.

Stark pulled the knife from the board and inspected it, then came over to him. "You're a lucky kid," he said. He noticed all the others watching them, and he swiped around at them with the blade. "Get out," he said, and they dispersed, leaning against walls, lighting cigarettes, talking quietly among themselves.

"I think we'll get you a knife like this tonight," Stark said. "You need to know how to care for a beauty like this. She will save your life someday. You don't just throw her at somebody and run away."

Willie's face burned.

Stark walked away. Willie leaned against a wall and crossed his arms over his chest.

That night they robbed a pawnshop, Greener shimmying in through a rooftop vent. Upon Stark's orders, he brought back a beautiful knife with a hand-sewn scabbard and Stark gave it to Willie. Willie stuck the knife in his pocket. He couldn't wait to get home to inspect it.

He named her Gloria.

Within a month Stark was in prison, and Willie began practicing with Gloria in earnest. The other guys coached him. Nobody was as good with a knife as Stark, and Willie wanted to take his place. The other guys wanted him to. They all carried guns, but Stark never did. Willie didn't want to, either. He wanted to partner with Gloria.

Within a year Willie knew everything there was to know about Gloria, including her best tricks.

Then Harpo tattooed "Sharp is Silent" on Willie's chest.

All the time his skill was growing, all the time he was desperately trying to do something he could be proud of, there was an anger growing inside Willie. It was shame, pure and simple. Shame that his mother opened her legs for anybody with five bucks. Shame that he would bend over for or suck the cock of anybody with just about the same. The guys he hung out with knew what he did, but they never talked about it. It embarrassed them as much as it did him.

One night when Willie was fourteen, he came home about

midnight. He bumped into a john coming out of his room, a big fat, greasy guy who was tucking in his shirt and seemed to be in a hurry. Willie opened the door and saw his mother tied to the bed, her face bruised and torn, her clothes ripped to shreds, and scratches all over her belly. There were bite marks on her breasts.

She was drunk.

Willie wanted to puke. Instead he untied her, and she slapped him. Then she covered herself with the threadbare bedspread and began to cry.

He brought her a tissue and a cold washcloth, but he couldn't put it to her swollen face. He just paced. The anger came up to a simmer.

"I'm not going to do this anymore," he said.

"Don't be stupid. It's what we do."

"Not anymore. I'm not going to do it anymore, and I don't want you to do it anymore either."

"Willie," she said, "I'm not the Kmart checker kind of girl."

"You could be something else. You could be a lot of other things. What are you going to do in another ten years? You're almost thirty. You going to be one of those old whores doing BJs in the alley when you're fifty?"

"I'll meet a guy," she said, the standard fairy tale line she always used when talking about the future.

"Where? On the street? A pimp? A john? Maybe a short-order cook in a diner. Maybe a sick bartender. Good, Mom, good."

"Shut up. You got anything?"

Willie fished a joint from his pocket and threw it to her. She lit up and inhaled deeply. She offered it to him, but he shook it off. He kept pacing.

The anger was beginning to roil.

"I want us to move out of here."

"Hey, if you don't like it, *you* move out."

He looked at her in disbelief and then wondered why he was so shocked. She didn't care much for him; he was in the way, and always had been, unless he was making money for her. "You cold bitch," he said, and began throwing his stuff into a duffel bag.

She lay on the bed, watching him with swollen, slitted eyes, toking on the joint.

"Honey?"

Willie loved it when she called him that. He stopped but wouldn't look at her. "What?"

"C'mere." She patted the bed next to her.

He sat on the edge of the bed, the anger knotting his muscles. He needed to hear her out. He wanted to leave, he wanted to get out, but he didn't really have a place to go, and he was afraid she wouldn't survive without him. She began to scratch his back. It felt great. "I own your soul," she said.

Soon, with the smoothness of a professional, she had him on his back, had his jeans unzipped, and was working him. She flipped over onto her back and pulled him on top of her. He found her wet and ready, he drove in deeply, and he knew she was right. She did own his soul. She had stolen it clean away and left him an empty man.

And that's when she made her mistake.

She began that whore talk. Willie had heard that talk a million times before. He'd heard that talk from his box under the bed when he was but five weeks old. He heard her talk like that to a zillion other guys, but she'd never used it on him before. Never. It was the kind of talk that kept a john thinking he was really making her see stars while she was making her grocery list, counting ceiling tiles, and keeping an eye on the clock.

The anger boiled up to the top of the lid. He raised up and

looked down on her mangled face, saw that whore's grin on her, and hated her so much that he . . . that he . . .

"This is the best, baby," she said, and somehow Gloria was in his hand. He slid it between her ribs, feeling the meat part cleanly. She made a small noise, indistinguishable from her practiced whore sounds. He felt her heart beat around the end of his knife—the handle pumped up and down—until, with a flick of a wrist, he sliced it in half.

And then he came. He came hard.

Now he *really* knew all of Gloria's tricks. He wiped her off on the nasty bedspread, then wiped himself off on it, pulled up his jeans, grabbed his duffel bag, and left.

They both were better off.

On the street. Alone. He thought about Greener's place; he thought about the alley where they all hung out, but in light of what he'd just done, they seemed trivial. Inconsequential. All of them, Greener, Stark, Harpo, Wretch. All of them. And all of what they did. It was hollow, game playing. Willie was finished with games. He was ready for life.

Life wasn't exactly what Willie Gurt expected. Carol, minimalist mother that she had been, had still been a mother. She still bought the groceries and fed the two of them. Fending for himself was fine, it was necessary, but providing for himself in all areas overwhelmed him. For the most part he attacked life with a vengeance, but there were times, lonely times, when he was tired and beaten down and he just wanted to curl up and whimper.

He hitchhiked from Colorado to southern California, where he didn't need so many clothes, where the climate was not out to kill him. He fell in with some guys who were older, and he threw his duffel bag behind a couch and began sleeping there. He never asked to stay, and he was never invited, so he tried to make himself as inconspicuous as he could.

He got a job washing cars, and soon he was parking cars. His eighteenth birthday found him working construction and renting a house with four other guys, each with his own bedroom.

Willie liked his booze, he liked his reefer, and he liked his roommates' girlfriends.

Worse, they liked him back. Girls, all kinds of girls, flocked to Willie. They hung on him; they yearned for him; every one of them wanted to be known by at least one other person—preferably female—as Willie's Girl. But that never happened. He didn't care much for girls in general. He bedded them when he wanted and otherwise ignored them.

He had no girlfriends, and he had no male friends. Tension always sprouted between him and the men he came into contact with.

Willie was a loner, and that was just fine by him.

His physique filled out with the hard labor of construction work as he went silently about his business. Soon he was a carpenter's assistant—dependable, competent, and quiet. He never caused trouble.

From an outsider's point of view, it looked as though Willie glided effortlessly through life. Inside, though, Willie was so filled with hurt and guilt and confusion that his guts seethed like worms writhing and steaming, and nothing settled them.

In learning to care for himself, he learned how much his mother had done to care for him. Every little thing his young mind grappled with, he knew his mother had also wrestled with and conquered. One day he realized that when his mother was his age, she made a living, had a room of her own and a little boy to deal with as well. It floored him. And his guilt grew hotter and infected even more of his innards.

One day the boss's daughter came to the building site to deliver a message, took one look at Willie, and lost all her senses. She took to hanging around the gate at quitting time, trying to talk to him, but he ignored her. For a week. On Friday night he took her home, and on Monday morning his pink slip was with his final paycheck.

He decided to head north, where it was cooler. No more mothers, no more daughters. He'd pay for any woman he wanted from then on.

He hired on with a crew of Spanish-speaking fruit pickers and picked strawberries up into the Willamette Valley in Oregon. He smelled the fir trees, felt the earth with his hands, and recognized it as God's country. This was where he'd stay.

When everybody else migrated on to Washington, Willie got a room in a residence hotel in Portland and found a job loading freight in a warehouse on the river. He listened to the guys talk and found out where the girls were, then got cleaned up after a backaching day of work and went downtown. The girls were out, standing around in the late-summer daylight. He walked through them, then turned around and came back through another time. There was one pouty one who leaned against the wall, looking at her shoes. He ignored all the others who laid hands on him and made lewd remarks, and he went right for the quiet one. He stood beside her. She looked up. "Hi," she said uncertainly.

He just looked at her.

"Twenty-five dollars," she said.

He took her elbow and steered her back toward his place.

She was young, shy, and uncertain. Inexperienced. She came into his room and sat, shyly, on the corner of the bed. Willie closed and locked the door, then stood and looked at her.

This is what his mother must have looked like when she was sixteen, he thought. Turning tricks when she was pregnant.

"Most of my customers are old and ugly," she said, and she looked up at him. "You're really"—she looked down and picked at the bedspread—"something."

The worms in his guts writhed.

"Do you talk?"

"Yeah," he said, and sat on the bed next to her.

"You're kind of spooky."

"No, I'm not," he said, and he gently gathered up her hair, pulled it away from the nape of her neck, then leaned over and kissed it tenderly.

She stood up and pulled off her dingy cotton sweater.

Back to business, Willie thought, and disappointment hit him. Now and then he'd like a little romance. Now and then he'd like a little affection. Sometime he'd like to have a girl he cared for, one he could be tender with.

She started in with the whore talk as soon as he took his shirt off. "Ooh, baby, you look so good. I can't wait to see what else you've got for me." The mouth was sweet sixteen; the words were thirty-five, old and used up.

"Don't talk like that," he said.

"Like what?"

"Like a whore."

"Hey." She crossed her arms over her breasts, shy again.

"Who taught you to say those things?"

"Rose."

"Well, forget them. They're not you."

"What's me?"

He touched her back, and goose pimples rose up under his fingers. "Soft, tender, young, and sweet. Don't try to make yourself old yet. That'll come. But now, you're what, fifteen?"

She stiffened again.

"Relax," he said. "I'm no cop."

"Yeah," she said. "Fifteen."

"Good." He unbuttoned his jeans, and she slid out of her skirt, leaving her garter belt and black stockings. "Take those off, too," he said.

She frowned, then did as he asked. She handed him a condom, and he put it on. Then they slid up the bed together.

I could teach this girl a lot, Willie thought. *She's young. I could make money off her for a long time.*

As soon as that thought crossed his mind, his gut churned with memories of that life. Living in the night. Knowing only the scum. He never wanted to go back to that. He didn't want to pimp.

When they were finished, the girl pulled the sheet up over them both, and they lay there quietly, looking at the ceiling. Willie was glad. He wanted some company. And it was at rare moments like this that the guilt in his belly was silenced.

"Can I stay the night with you?"

"Why?"

"I don't want to go out there again. I'm afraid most of the time."

"Why do you do it?"

"What else?"

"Christ, a zillion things. Wait tables."

"Too young for a food handler's permit."

"Work in a library."

"I need a work permit. I'm too young to do anything legitimate. I *have* to hook."

"Go to school."

"Got to have a family and an address and money to do that."

Willie wanted this girl to go to school. He wanted it so badly he could barely see. He wanted her to move in with him. He'd support them; she could go to school every day and graduate from high school, something he'd never done. It was the craziest, most outrageous idea he'd ever had.

"What's your name?"

"Martha. Martha Douglas."

"I'm Willie." He looked over at her, such a child, with the sheet pulled up to her chin. "Go to sleep, Martha."

She smiled at him, then turned on her side, her back to him, and soon she was asleep.

Willie stayed awake, looking at the ceiling. He wanted someone to care for, but he was thinking more along the lines of a wife or a lover. Not a little girl.

Life was strange.

Martha moved in. They moved out of the residence hotel and into a little apartment. Willie registered her for school. He went to work in the mornings, and she went to school. He taught her to cook the things he knew how to cook, and she took to it. Soon there was a hot meal ready for him every night when he came home from work.

Willie insisted on separate beds.

And so it came to be. Willie, barely twenty, had adopted a fifteen-year-old prostitute and turned her into a normal teenage girl. Martha adjusted rapidly to high school, and Willie even got her to send a postcard home to her parents, telling them that she was all right. She didn't give them an address. That would take more time.

Their apartment became a home, where they could relax, be together, be alone, eat well, rest peacefully. It was bliss. Willie found Martha, with her bright eyes and ready wit, to be infinitely entertaining. The shyness vanished, and a poised, well-balanced young woman began to emerge.

Martha found Willie to be odd and distant, but not unpleasantly so. There were times she would sit on the couch and watch him watching television and try to figure out what made him so strikingly good-looking. There was nothing she could pin down. Individually his features were too sharp, too exaggerated. His nose was too long, his eyes weren't even, but there was something so extraordinary about the combination that it made women turn and stare as she and Willie walked down the street together.

He didn't even notice.

Over the months Martha lost all apprehension she ever felt toward Willie and began to love him.

But while he was brother/father/friend, and he offered her home/security/warmth, there was an element of excitement she'd grown accustomed to that was down on the street, not in the halls of high school and not in their cozy apartment. Now and then she'd go visit her friends down there, surprised at first at how ratty they looked. Gradually she went more often, and soon she began to look ratty herself.

Then she turned a trick for a little extra cash. And then another.

Willie suspected what she was doing and didn't know what to do about it. One day he drove down to the corner where he had first met her. There she was.

He pulled up. She saw him and turned away. He got out of the car, walked over to her, disappointment and hurt building into rage, and he asked her politely to get into the car with him. He dared not lay a hand on her.

She followed him into the car, and he screeched rubber all the way to the apartment. They got out and went upstairs, where he leaned against the door and said breathlessly, "Why?"

She shrugged her shoulders, and his rage broke through.

He grabbed her hair, pulled her, screaming and crying, into his bedroom. He ripped the buttons off her blouse, pulled her skirt up around her waist, and tore the panties right off her. "Is this what you miss?" he asked through clenched teeth as he forced his way into her. "I loved you," he said, "and you stole my soul." Gloria, hiding under his pillow, found his hand, and as he looked down and saw something that looked like triumph on Martha's face, Gloria slid inside and found that pumping place, that soft heart that made her handle jiggle in beats per minute.

"Mama!" Willie yelled as he came, and the knife snicked cleanly through her heart.

He sat for an hour with his head in his hands, knowing his life was over. Then he called the police.

Luckily news of a similar crime six years previously in Colorado had never reached the Oregon police. Extenuating circumstances were brought to light, and Willie Gurt ended up doing only ten years.

In prison he kept to himself. Sometimes a week would go by without his having uttered a word, earning him the nickname Songster. He did his time, and he got out. He got a job working construction in Salem, Oregon, and when he finished his parole time, his parole officer handed him a business card.

"This guy," the parole officer said, "will always give you a job."

The Songster carried that card with him as he bounced around in loneliness and solitude for the next few years. And when he needed a job, he hitchhiked to Eugene, Oregon, and looked the guy up.

The guy ran a painting crew. The Songster signed on, found a train of abandoned boxcars out in the country, in the middle of the wide-open spaces that he craved, made a friend out of a guy who had an old Pontiac wagon and a sidekick named Niles, and he dug in.

But the worms in his gut still churned.

TULIE AND NILES WERE RUNNING OVER THE HILL BEFORE Buck actually realized what had happened. He listened but heard nothing but the muffled silence of woods full of fresh snow, their running footfalls, and the Songster's juicy breathing through swollen tissue.

Then that moan again, deep, soul-laden, and Buck was sure it melted the lower layer of snow just as it melted the lower layer of his heart.

Buck threw the broken bottle into the weeds, left the unconscious Songster, and walked up over the hill. He saw Niles and two of the girls standing down by the water's edge, looking down at the other girl lying in the snow. He wanted to run away. He wanted no part of this. He wanted none of the responsibility, none of the blame; he didn't even want to know what had happened. And yet he felt responsible. He felt like the only adult. He began to run, his chest, his back, his hands aching with each jarring step.

Elise twitched on the ground, her throat an oozing red rose. Rebecca stood to the side, the gun loose in her fingers.

Elise's mouth moved; her eyes rolled; bubbles churned out of the wound.

"Holy shit," he said.

"We've got to get her to a hospital," Niles said, but Buck knew it was way too late for that.

Elise began to convulse as her chest heaved, trying to draw in untainted breath, but each time she inhaled, she sucked in another lungful of bright red blood.

Buck felt dirty, like a sick voyeur, as they all stood around and watched her spasm and gurgle her last breath. She looked so pitiful. Her broken wrist flopped in the snow, one fingernail with all its polish chipped off.

Buck closed his eyes. *Death is an intensely personal experience,* he thought. He would never forget seeing Ronnie's body in his little casket. He remembered being alone for days after that, just thinking and playing with his and Ronnie's things. *We should have given Elise the dignity to die by herself,* he thought, *the way Cara was alone for the death of our baby. The way Cara had the dignity to grieve by herself for the death of our baby. No. The way you walked out on Cara because you couldn't deal with the death of her baby. You were glad, you asshole. You were glad the baby died because you didn't want another, and if Cara had to grieve over it, well then, that was her problem. Her problem and nobody else's. You schmuck.*

Buck had a real desire to see Cara, not for the first time, but this time he wasn't afraid. He wanted to see her; he wanted to see Kaiser and Cecelia, his little angel. He ached right through his guts and into his bones to see them. He wasn't afraid, for some reason. He realized that he could die and Cara would never know. Cara could die—or Kaiser, for God's sake —and he would never know.

He had to get to a phone. He had to call her. He had to call her now. He wanted more of their life.

He wanted to go home.

It wouldn't be easy. Cara might be married. Kaiser might not even remember him. Cecelia wouldn't remember him at all. He'd have to start over, but he didn't want to miss the years he had left with them. Soon, before he knew it, they'd be twenty-one or twenty-two and maybe dead of a . . . a

. . . a mistake. He closed his eyes and made fists around his resolve.

He needed to call. He needed to call now, face the music, find out what had happened with his family. Throw that old Pontiac into gear and head for Chicago.

He opened his eyes and looked around.

Oh, yeah. There was this mess to deal with.

The silence, now that the gurgling had stopped, was like a soft prayer. Steam rose from Elise's blasted neck.

"Well," he said, "let's get this show on the road." It sounded so insensitive that he was ashamed of himself.

"What do we do?" Niles asked.

"She's so still," Tulie said, staring down at the body. "I've never seen a dead person before. I mean, she's so *quiet*." Tulie felt as if she were in the presence of greatness. Death was here. Death, the common denominator, the great equalizer, the other option. Death. Bigger than Tommy, bigger than Anna Marie, bigger than an education, bigger than life. More powerful than Elise, that was certain, and as Tulie watched Elise's skin darken under those fingernails with the chipped polish, life clicked into a perspective that she had somehow missed all these years. File your fingernails, yes, keep them nicely polished, but keep in mind that when life's fractions are reduced, perfect fingernails don't mean shit.

"Yeah," Niles said. "She's not breathing or nothing."

Buck tensed as he heard the Songster's footsteps behind him. Instead of rising to the bait and looking behind him, he watched the faces of those opposite him. Tulie gasped, wide-eyed, then her expression turned from one of alarm to one of narrow-eyed hate. She looked at Buck, and a silent message passed between them. They made a pact. Rebecca, still dim from watching Elise die, was slow to look up and slow to react. The Songster stood right next to Buck when she finally squinted up and saw him, and when she did, she caught her breath in horror and brought her hands up to her face. The forgotten revolver flew from her fingers gracefully, end over end, across Elise's body and made a deep hole in the snow right in front of the Songster, who bent over, picked it up, and pointed it at her.

With a soft sigh, Rebecca crumpled to the ground, her face as pale as Elise's. Tulie could barely breathe, certain that the Songster would edge that short barrel over a few inches and put a bullet right through her.

So what's important, she asked herself with zinging clarity. Looking good when she died or tending to Rebecca, who needed her? Tulie kept her eyes fixed on the Songster while she knelt, then turned her attention to Rebecca.

"Don't touch that gun," Niles said, way too late.

Buck couldn't believe it, but Niles had the Songster's knife in his hand and was waving it around.

The Songster calmly straightened up, with the revolver in his hand, and Buck could see what had made the girls jumpy. His face was a swollen, bloody wreck. One eye was cut and puffed closed, the other eye only a slit. Blood matted his hair and covered the front of his shirt. He looked as if he had just climbed from his grave.

"Drop the gun," Niles said with a true sense of the dramatic, and he stepped up next to Buck, the knife waving loosely in the air.

"Shut up, Niles," the Songster said between busted lips, and Buck felt queasy himself when he saw the bloody saliva between the Songster's teeth. The Songster spit a red gob into the snow.

"He was going to shoot you in the back, Buck," Niles said, the knife relaxed to half-mast. "Ain't right to shoot somebody in the back."

"Well, his back ain't to me now, is it?" the Songster said, and raised the revolver. He pointed it squarely between Buck's eyes.

"Stop it!" Tulie shouted, and her voice sounded simple and girlish, not at all with the commanding authority she'd heard in her mind before she said it. The mighty presence of death still held this group in the palm of his hand. Rebecca had been overcome by it, but Tulie was not about to be death's next chipped fingernail at the hands of the Songster.

It wasn't much of a barrel to look down, but Buck's brain went numb just as effectively as if he'd been looking down the double barrel of a shotgun. He didn't know what to do. He thought again of Cara.

"He's unarmed, Songster," Niles whined. "You can't shoot a man—"

"Fuck off," the Songster said, and as his grip tightened, a snowball from Tulie slammed through the air and into the gun. Fire spit from its short snout and the bullet knocked snow from the sapling it splintered.

Niles lunged at the Songster and Gloria slid between his ribs as smoothly as if her space there had been prearranged.

The gun went off again, pointed down at the ground, and Niles fell away, sat down on his butt in the snow, his face contorted with pain and confusion.

The gun went off again as the Songster staggered backward, his emotions unreadable in his beaten face. The empty gun clicked over and over again as the Songster continued to pull the trigger. He finally raised his arm again, pointing the gun at Buck's head, grinned, blood and saliva running out of the corner of his mouth. "Bang," he said, then fell backward into the snow and lay there, his uneven breathing marked by the short bursts of steam like puffs from a volcano.

Gloria's handle ticked with every heartbeat.

Tulie closed her eyes and took a deep breath. As she did, she felt an eerie satisfaction, as if death had been pleased to accept the Songster. The pall lifted as death left with another notch on the handle of his scythe, and Tulie felt desperate for time alone, to think this whole night through. A window had opened in her experience, and through it she glimpsed, for the first time, the truth. The truth was that she knew nothing. She knew nothing about people or their intricate, evolutionary relationships. She knew nothing about human nature or the things that motivated people. She realized she had never known her parents, her sisters, Anna Marie, she didn't know Tommy, and she had only just this past minute begun to know herself. It was a stunning revelation.

Niles began to cry, his face scrunched up like a five-year-old's. He looked like a little boy, too, sitting in the snow. "He was going to kill you, Buck," he said.

Buck touched him on the back, on the head. It had happened so fast Buck wasn't exactly sure what had happened or even *if* it had happened. "It's all right, Niles," he said. "You're right. He was going to shoot me." Buck looked over at Tulie, who was rubbing a small snowball on Rebecca's bloodless face. "Jesus Christ what a mess," he said.

He needed to take a leak.

When he came back, his hands swollen and frozen into painful, skinned claws, he saw that Rebecca was awake, leaning into Tulie, her bare legs cherry red as they sat on the frozen ground. Tulie had her arm around Rebecca and was whispering softly into her ear.

Elise's eyes were already glazed over with ice.

Niles stood over the Songster, whose breath no longer plumed.

Buck put his hand on Niles's shoulder.

"He's dead," Niles said. "I saw it. I saw him die."

Buck bent down and retrieved the empty revolver, clicked open the cylinder and ejected six spent casings. He walked to the lake's edge and threw them at the water, where they scattered in six tiny splashes. Then he leaned over and tried to skip the gun off the top of the water the way he and Ron used to skip stones. It didn't skip. It plopped once and was gone.

Morning had arrived, and while the sun had not yet come over the mountains to the east, its rays turned the hills on the opposite side of the lake bright gold. A beautiful, crisp morning. Filled with ugliness. Would it have been different if he had agreed to take the girls home right in the beginning? Could all this have been avoided or only postponed? Was it his fault that the Songster was dead? Was that a bad thing, or was it good that the Songster would never kill another woman? He felt a pressure in his soul; he felt like making a confession.

Niles crunched through the snow and stood next to him, looking off over the water. "*You* were supposed to be the executioner, Buck," he said, and his voice was cracked with pain.

"I know," Buck said. "But you're my partner. It's the same thing."

Niles silently contemplated that. "What are we going to do with him now, Buck?" he asked. "Should we sink him? Let the fish eat him?"

"I have a wife," Buck said, "and two kids. A family." He didn't have anything more to say.

"You're my family," Niles said.

That was too much of a responsibility for Buck, but he had no words to voice it. He just kept looking out over the lake at the sunrise.

Niles heard his silence. "Go home to your family, Buck," he said.

Buck nodded, his throat thick. He put his arm around

Niles's shoulders, and together they watched the morning become day.

When Rebecca felt she could stand, Tulie struggled to her feet with frozen legs and helped the girl up. Rebecca clung to Tulie with a child's desperation. Tulie felt old, wise, adult, in charge. They started up the hill, then Tulie remembered that Elise had the keys to the truck. She stopped and looked back. Buck and Niles were watching them. "Get the keys," she said.

Buck walked over to Elise's body. She looked cold. He squatted down and buttoned up her coat, then fished in the pocket for the keys. "C'mon, Niles," he said, and together they followed the girls back up the hill.

The heater in Ross's truck was far superior to the one in the drafty old Pontiac, so the four climbed in. Buck, with the keys, sat behind the steering wheel, then Tulie, Rebecca, and Niles all squeezed in and Niles closed the passenger door. Buck fired up the truck, revved it for a minute or two, then turned on the heater. Slowly warm air began to circulate. Slowly Rebecca stopped shivering.

"I didn't kill her," Rebecca said. "At least I don't think I did."

Nobody said anything.

"She was going to kill herself, and I tried to get the gun away. I don't know who pulled the trigger, but I don't think it was me."

"It's okay," Tulie said, and put her arm around the girl.

Buck's ear began to hurt. He touched it. It was hot and swollen.

"I'll take Elise to the police," Rebecca said.

"You'll have to take this truck," Buck said. "I'll change the tire."

"What about the Songster?" Tulie asked.

"I'll take care of him," Buck said, without having any idea of what he would do. His hands were damned near worthless; he was sure several knuckles on his right hand were broken. His chest hurt every time he breathed, and the pain in his back where the Songster had kicked him flared up whenever he moved. He couldn't take care of the Songster; he couldn't even change the truck tire. He wanted to go home. He wanted to go call Cara, and then, depending on what she said, he wanted either to make tracks for Chicago or to crawl in a cave somewhere and lick his wounds.

"You going to sink him?" Niles asked.

Buck shrugged. "Everybody warm?" he asked. He turned off the engine. "Let's finish this."

Niles opened the door, helped Rebecca down, then ran to the Pontiac and got the dropcloth. Tulie knew Buck's hands were in no condition to do any work, so she pulled the jack from behind the truck seat as Niles and Rebecca walked down the hill toward the lake.

"Wow," Niles said, surveying the two bodies. "It looks like there was a plane wreck or something here."

They spread the dropcloth on the snow next to Elise. Rebecca knelt on the ground next to her head. "We've got to close her eyes."

"Close her eyes?"

"Yeah. You do it."

Niles crouched down next to Rebecca and touched Elise's forehead. It was cold and lifeless. He pushed on her eyelids. They were hard, like bubble gum. "They don't want to close."

"They have to."

"You try."

Rebecca began to make little whining noises, but she gently took Elise's eyelids and forced them out and down over the glazed, frozen eyeballs. One didn't go down all the way but hung crookedly like a bad shade. Rebecca rocked back on her heels and then stood up, wiping the moisture from her nose and cheeks onto the sleeve of the jacket. "Okay," she said.

They muscled her shoulders onto the cloth, then Niles brought her feet over. Niles folded over the excess cloth at the head, and Rebecca folded it up at the feet, like a burrito, and they rolled Elise over twice. Just as Niles was ready to lift the body to his shoulder, to carry it to the truck, his eyes met Rebecca's, and all the strength left him. He sank down into the snow.

"Lisa?" he said.

Rebecca frowned at him. It was the first time she'd seen him face-to-face in the light and close enough so that she could see him without her contacts.

"Little Lisa?"

Rebecca scooted back away from him, falling over and sitting in the snow. He approached her on all fours. "Lisa?" he said again. He frightened her, but she was taken by some sadness in his face. She cringed while he examined her, like a little kid will stand still and cringe while a dog licks its face.

She sat, frozen and still in the snow, while he came closer. She felt tears come to her eyes again, and as he touched her cheek, touched her nose, the tears ran out and down her cheeks.

Niles couldn't believe it. The same teeth, crossed in the front. The same rich brownish auburn hair. The same thick black caterpillar eyebrows. The same dark, dark blue eyes with dark lashes. Lisa.

Lisa. She had his mother's nose. She had his chin. She had his build, tall and thin. Snow had begun falling again, and little flakes landed and stayed on her eyelashes. "September eighth?" he asked.

Rebecca's eyes opened. "Huh?"

"Your birthday. September eighth?"

"No," she whispered, then cleared her throat. "March twenty-seventh."

"Oh, Lisa, oh, my God, Lisa," Niles said, the date notwithstanding, and he crawled closer, to touch her hair and to touch her with both hands, but she sniffed and shook herself, scrambled away, and stood up and got away from him, kicking at him.

"I'm not Lisa," she said.

Niles seemed puzzled for a moment. Then he rubbed his cold hands over his face and looked at her again. No, no, it wasn't Lisa; it wasn't her at all. "No," he said. "Of course not." Could have been. Could have been. Could have been.

"I'm Rebecca."

"Yes, but I had a daughter—"

"*Rebecca!*" she shouted.

Niles stopped.

"Now," Rebecca said, her voice soft again. "Let's get Elise into the truck. Please."

Niles shouldered the corpse and walked up the hill. He could come upon Little Lisa or Big Lisa at any time. Is this how he wanted to meet them? Over some hooker's shot-up body? Niles had some thinking to do. He made an appointment with himself to do that very thinking as soon as he could.

Rebecca followed Niles up the hill and realized that her birth parents might not be the perfect shining examples of parenthood she had always fantasized that they were. They could be like this guy. They could be shiftless, stupid bums. What could she have been thinking? She would destroy that birth certificate as soon as she got back to her room. Tear it up, burn it up, and never, ever let her wonderful Christian parents know she had ever thought about replacing them. Her parents, the parents who would stand by her throughout this whole Elise ordeal. Her wonderful parents. Her wonderful, understanding parents.

Niles put Elise into the truck bed. "We had to close her eyes," he said confidentially to Buck, then shivered. "Yuck."

Rebecca frowned. "I don't want her rolling around back here."

Niles brought the flat tire around to the truck bed and wedged Elise in. Tulie let the truck down off the jack and gave the lug nuts a final tweak. Then she put the jack behind the driver's seat and washed the tire dirt off her hands with snow.

"You're ready to go," Buck said.

"I can't drive," Rebecca said, "I don't have my glasses."

"I'll drive," Niles said. He looked at the questioning faces. "It's what family would do."

Rebecca climbed into the passenger's seat and fastened her seat belt.

Tulie walked around the front of the truck to close her door. She felt like tucking Rebecca in. Instead, when Rebecca turned and looked at her, Tulie again had that overwhelming feeling of a great presence, only instead of death this time, it was life. Growth. Rebecca had changed, and just in the last half hour.

Tulie no longer saw Rebecca with jealousy or lust or pity but saw her as just another human, walking blindly through unseen, unanticipated obstacles, over uneven terrain.

Only not quite so blindly, after last night.

"I'll see you," Tulie said lamely.

Rebecca nodded, attempted a smile, pulled Dennis's jacket closer. "Thanks," she said.

Tulie closed the truck door, feeling she owed Rebecca something, but she didn't know what and she didn't know why.

Niles lit a cigarette, coughed with the first drag, then held out his hand for Buck to shake.

Buck held up his swollen paw, and Niles looked down in embarrassment. "Well then," he said, "guess I'll see ya."

"Yeah."

Niles got in, started the truck, and Buck and Tulie backed off while he backed out, turned around, and drove slowly out of the campground.

Buck's body began to ache again. He saw that the driver's door was still open on the Pontiac, the interior lights on, and he hoped it would still start. That would be the icing on the cake, he thought. He limped over, his ribs hurting more and more all the time. He slid into the driver's seat and closed the door behind him, laid his head back on the seat, and closed his eyes. What he needed was a toothbrush, a big plate of ham and eggs over easy with hash browns, and an ice-cold Heineken. A couple of aspirin.

He rested for a long moment, feeling the pain in his torso and his ear recede, feeling his hands ache even more. He opened his eyes and looked at them. They needed medical attention. He was glad Tulie could change a tire, and he hoped she could drive, too.

He looked around, but she wasn't in sight.

C'mon, old boy, he said to himself. *One chore left.*

He opened the door latch with his wrist and stumbled out.

With cold-reddened fingers, Tulie wiped the blood from the Songster's blue face with handfuls of snow. She scratched off the trails where it had dribbled and dried. When it was clean, she sat down next to him and looked at him: the ultimate bad boy.

So this is where they wind up. Where and how.

If he hadn't done that knife thing—

She heard Buck come down over the ridge and sat quietly

until he stood next to her. "There was a time when I could have loved him," she said, surprising herself.

"He would never have loved you back."

So there it was. The plain and simple truth in all its black-and-white and bloodred horror. The reason she had loved the bad boys. They were safe. They were dangerous, but they were safe. Consistent. Emotionally unavailable. They could rape you and kill you, but they would never love you. So attractive.

Maybe she could be satisfied with a little less passion.

"I'm going to go call my wife," Buck said. "Do you think she'll take me back?"

Tulie shrugged. "Maybe. Maybe not." She looked again at the mashed face of the dead man and wished she had kissed Rebecca good-bye. A small kiss, maybe on her forehead, at her hairline. Just an expression of emotion, of affection, of human-ness, of sisterhood, of acknowledgment . . . something. "What are we going to do with him—what's your name again? Buck, right?"

"My family calls me Don." He straightened up as he said it. He was ready to be Don again.

"That's a better name."

"I don't know what to do with him," Don said. He held up his battered hands.

"Yeah," she said. "No shit. Look at his face."

"I used to box."

Tulie nodded, still looking at the Songster's blackening face. "You're still the champ."

"Let's just drag him over—" Don gestured at the woods.

Tulie stood up and grabbed the back collar of the Songster's shirt and started pulling.

She dragged him away from the parking lot, along the trail that ringed the lake. With frequent stops so she could pant and mop the freezing perspiration from her forehead, she dragged him over rocks and roots and felt the back of his pants fill with snow and dirt and little stones. Then she left the trail, dragging him a short way into the woods.

When far enough from the campground, she wrestled him into a sitting position and propped him up against a big tree. She leaned against the tree and caught her breath.

Don tried to pull the knife out of the Songster's chest, but it was in there solid. It was too much for his hands.

Tulie put a foot on the Songster's chest, wrapped her coat sleeve around the hilt, and pulled it out. With her best pitching form, she threw it and it sailed out over the water, turning and winking gracefully end over end before splashing down.

They stood looking at the Songster for a long time, both of them wondering what had gone on in a mind like that, both of them knowing that no matter what their individual sins, they were nothing in comparison.

Don looked at the Songster's puffed dead face and understood for the first time in his life what people meant when they said that life was unfair. He'd always tried to do his tiny part to make things come out even, and while there was a certain symmetry to nature, life was not necessarily fair. Ron's death was not fair. Songster killing those three women was not fair.

"Should we close his eyes?" Tulie said.

Don shivered, remembering what Niles had said. "No," he said. "Let's let him look out over the lake. Let's let him look out over nothing but peace and tranquillity." He stooped and looked at the Songster's face. "He's only got one eye open anyway."

"Bye, Songster," she said. "Don't tell anybody we were here, okay?" She was feeling the effects of the night. Her neck ached where the Songster had pulled her backward over the car seat, her hands ached from pulling him through the woods, her knees were cold, and she was tired. Bone tired.

"He won't," Don said, and they walked back to the car in silence.

The Pontiac started right up, and Tulie backed it out, turned it around, and drove gently over the snowpacked road to the highway. Don replaced the chain across the entrance to the campground.

"To a phone, please," he said as he slammed the door behind him. "And then, I think, a doctor."

Tulie turned the big, skinny steering wheel, and the Pontiac obeyed her, chugging onto the highway toward Eugene. She turned on the headlights and the windshield wipers against the falling snow.

"Think Niles and Rebecca have the good sense not to mention the Songster? Or us?" she asked.

"Don't count on any kind of good sense coming from either one of those two," Don said. "Speaking of good, that was one hell of a well-placed snowball. I'd be dead if you hadn't hit that gun square."

"I used to pitch softball," she said.

"You're still the champ," he said.

She thought about the snow falling on the Songster's hair, not melting, just accumulating. In a startlingly female way she wished she had smoothed it down a little bit or something before leaving him.

He was the end of an era. She wished she had kissed him good-bye, too.